THE FIRST VICTORIAN

The First Victorian is set in the early years of Victoria's reign when the steam train vied with the horse, when agricultural labour was moving to the new industries in town and when women had yet to achieve the status of second-class citizens.

The story revolves around Celandine, an innocent young country girl destined to become a fallen woman, and the high and low-life Victorians she encounters in her fall: the sly priest the Rev. Mr. Blackstone; Puffing Billy the navvy; Jem Pickles the butler who made a fortune writing away on his master's crested paper; Miss Grigg, common enticer to the most extravagant bordello in London; William Miles Esq., the financial wizard, whom some believed to be a thief and a swindler.

These and many others give a fascinating and uninhibited glimpse of the Victorians. Told with a sensitive and gentle humour, it is not for the puritanical as Celandine sinks lower into the dark side of Victorian life and comes to surprising terms with the taboos and double moralities of our ancestors—many of which still linger and inhibit us today.

THE FIRST VICTORIAN

or

Sweet Celandine:

Being an Account of that
Young Woman's Tender Years
& the Part Played by Her Mother
Lucy Spencer. Telling How They Lost
the Battle to Preserve their Moral Recti-
tude & Sank to the Depths of Dishonourable
Degradation. With an Account of Those Good
& Upright Pillars of Society whom Celandine Heeded
Not, in Her Descent from Respectable Servant Girl to
Artist's Model & Eventual Lodgement in an Infamous
Saloon of Pleasure, & also Describing Those Unfortunates,
with Hidden Vices, Who Brought It to Pass. Including a
True Account of Crime & Low Life & Murder Most
Foul. Narrating also of Their Betters, who Practised Base
& Beastly Offences on Remote Estates. Disclosing Trivia
of Our Times, from Finance to Fustigation, Ignored
by Histories & Romances, being Destined for the
Private Cases of the British Museum. Finally,
Revealing the Surprising Consequences of
Such Swerving from Rectitude, &
Voluntary Embrace of Misery &
Death, which Might Well
Shock the Gentle Reader.

RON RICH

ROBERT HALE & COMPANY
63 Old Brompton Road, London S.W.7

© Ron Rich 1971
First published in Great Britain 1971

ISBN 0 7091 2168 7

Printed in Great Britain by
Clarke, Doble & Brendon Ltd.
Plymouth

CONTENTS

6 CONTENTS

1

THE MAKING OF A VICTORIAN

L u c y held her breath—a white mist hovering about her lips
from the cold air of the lean-to—as she felt Tom, her father,
stir next to her in the bed. She almost started at the touch
of his calloused hand on her shoulder, roughly stroking the bare
skin, but shrugged away with a moan, as though asleep. She
heard him sigh and climb from beneath the covers. What was
he about that he should show such consideration? This night
he had made poor simple-minded May sleep in the sacking
against the wall, where their five small brothers were wont to
sleep before the sickness had carried both them and her mother
off last winter. Tom had complained of May's fits disturbing
his sleep—yet she never had them at night. Why should he
carry on in this strange gate?

The pink behind her closed eyes told that the rushes were
still alight—another singular occurence. Lucy opened her eyelids just enough to spy on Tom. In the rushlight his white,
naked body was truncated curiously at the neck and wrists,
where his weather-blackened face and hands were lost amongst
the shadows of the wattle-and-daub roof. Tom shivered in the
icy air, pulled on his shirt and smock, and went out into the
autumn night.

Good riddance, thought Lucy. He must be away poaching.*
She could no more bear the touch of her father's rough, broken

---

* The labouring classes had been used to gathering their food and
fuel from the land until the Inclosures Acts began to take the common
land away from them. This, in combination with the severe game laws,
turned many of them into criminals.

fingers than the stale smell of beer and sweat that emanated from him. Will, her cousin, to whom she was promised, was of the same cast—clumsy and awkward. Mayhap H.M.S. *Rattlesnake* would be lost at sea and Will would never return to claim her.

Lucy returned to her dream of a man quite unlike her own menfolk. She had not seen him close until today. It was as though they had been waiting for her in the lane. His father, old Lord Furlingham, was drunk, port-red to purple in the face, his squat, thick figure swaying so precipitously in the saddle that he threatened to plunge into the mud before her at any moment. Lucy doubted that he was long for this world. Pretending that she had not seen them, the girl lifted her smock as high as she dared, picking her way amongst the puddles.

"Tall and graceful! By my oath, father, she's all you said and more."

"Lor' sir, you startled me," said Lucy, dropping them a curtsey. The young nobleman had a serious look to him, his face whiter than she had seen on a man. Furlingham swayed violently.

"Aye, Charles, there's good stock in these parts and not a man to say I've ever held back in my part o' it."

At this he convulsed so desperately, that he fell across the horse's neck and had to cling to the bridle for balance. From this recumbent position, Furlingham asked in hoarse dignity, marred only by a hiccough :

"Are you not aware, my dear, 'tis an offence to cause a disturbance on the highway?"

Lucy smiled up at him uncertainly.

"Indeed, sir, I cause no disturbance."

"As magistrate of this county, I say you do, you wanton baggage !" he shouted, "and nought but a kiss will cool it for me."

Lucy backed off warily as he lurched the bay nearer, but Charles manœuvred his nervously stepping mount between them and seizing the reins of his father's horse, whispered down :

"Cut it, my dear, sharp now"—and loudly to his father—"careful, sir, or you will have an accident."

Lucy hardly needed the encouragement as she lifted her smock and ran for a stile, set in the nearby hedge. She could not resist lifting her skirt high in impudence as she went over.

"By George, sir!" roared the Earl, "I think I've had me accident. Did you spy those twinkling buttocks?"

Even now half dreaming in the cold, damp hut, Lucy could imagine Charles' countenance. Irritably she threw one arm over her face when the latch rattled, determined not to leave her dream despite Tom's return. It was a moment before she realized that the covers had been lifted and that her chemise, riding around her waist, afforded scant protection either from the night air or her visitor. Lucy's hand was removed from between her legs and a voice said :

"That's man's work you are about, my dear."

Her dream had become reality and Charles' lips were upon hers. His skin was shaven and soft and smelt sweetly of clean linen and tobacco. He entered her easily, was this not what she had been longing for. How he had arrived here was un-important as he kissed her neck, her lips, and brought the girl to a pitch of passion. When at last he withdrew, Lucy heard herself scream :

"Sweet Jesus! Don't stop!"

She turned her head aside and sobbed with shame at her passion and blasphemy. He would think her a whore.

Then he was upon her again. She had not thought to be so instantly answered. This time the strokes were slower, his breathing heavy, even fetid : She turned to flinch back with horror from the bloated face and rouged lips of old Lord Furlingham.

Tom stood waiting in the shadows until the carriage should leave. It did no good to rage, he ruminated. As a young man he'd raged, when the gentry had used their sporting rights to his coppice and smashed down the crop around it, but it did no good. It were a little peddling thing to the lass, but the Earl could distrain for rent and Tom stood to lose his tools, the land, his whole investment. It was cold waiting. No matter how much a body was out in all weathers, he thought, you could never get used to the cold.

The first rays of day caught the tops of the hedgerows and sent long shadows across the fields of Chelsea. Strung across the lane from wild scrambling rose to thorn and woodbine stretched a fairlyland of dew-bejewelled cobwebs. Heedlessly, Lucy Spencer clutched her swollen belly and stumbled through the fresh webs, scarce noticing the small spats of dew amongst the beads of sweat on her face.

Lucy stopped to sway before a pothole. The contractions were coming faster now. Through a miasma of pain, the girl became sensible to the sound of fast horses and the dust trembling at her feet. She watched the black cloud swirl nearer over the hedgerows until a team of horses broke into sight. Uncertainly, she stood her ground as they thundered down, until she could see the yellow flashing teeth and the foam at their mouths. Then the lead horse was rearing around the pothole and Lucy was falling backwards as the carriage rocked by. She glimpsed armorial bearings on the side of the conveyance, the indifferent gaze of one of the travellers—and they were gone.

Lucy lay back painfully in the ditch under the hedge and waited for the baby to come. The dust slowly settled and the smell of hay came to her. She was staring at the tiny yellow-flowered celandine tumbling down the bank—when that dreadful and unspeakable agony which effects the delivery came upon her.

The carriage rattled up the hill to the palace in Kensington, past the huge elms to the ivy covered walls, where the standard drooped in the still summer dawn.

His Grace of Canterbury and my Lord Conyngham stretched their feet in the straw with relief and got down, stamping their feet, glad to breathe in the sweet smell of honeysuckle after the stale air of the coach. The doorbell rang unexpectedly loud in the sleeping palace, through to the gardens, waking a laggard cock to crow, and fluttering the rooks above their nests to caw black against the morning.

The day was Tuesday, June the 20th, 1837 and a young girl of eighteen, Alexandrina Victoria, was to be woken and told that she was Queen of England.

Some few miles away on the King's Road, a baby girl, Celandine, took her first reluctant breath of a new age.

2

BILLY MILES THE TOMMY-SHOP KEEPER

B L O W I N G a shattering burst of triumph, wholly unwarranted considering it was overtaking no more than pauper women on the road, the Royal Mail passed. The four in hand, the Imperial Arms on a chocolate ground and the guard at the back with his blunderbuss, were soon gone into the drizzle, leaving the straggle of workhouse women heading for the fields to regroup on the road.

Lucy Spencer prayed that her letter was aboard, bound for her father in Sussex. The bellman had taken the letter readily enough, but it seemed a great distance for a penny and a red mark to carry a letter.* Cart-ropes would not have dragged her back to Tom but for the pitiful condition of Celandine.

* The penny post was introduced in 1840 by Rowland Hill, when a red mark denoted a pre-paid letter until the use of postage stamps became universal. Before the invention of the pillar-box in 1855, letters were placed in a portable letter-box carried by the bellman.

A lone horseman rode unnecessarily close, forcing the file of women to the ditch and spattering them with mud. Already soaked to the skin, this further indignity could not rouse them from their apathy. Only the fear that the utter degradation inflicted on Celandine might well be repeated separated Lucy from the other women, and the hope that once away from this dreadful place Celandine might recover and perhaps learn to speak again.

Burn my body, thought Billy Miles, as he rode by. I'd love to tail the tall one with the big bubbies. Grimacing at the uncomfortable stirrings that the thought provoked and the peculiar aptness of the oath, Billy shifted in the saddle. He had been prescribed the blackwash externally and mercury internally, for he had brought back not only a foul temper from London, but a dose of the clap as well.

The old man had his varmin well enough trained, Billy admitted grudgingly to himself—for the women were from the workhouse where his father was Master. He doubted that they would have occasioned any trouble in the recent disturbances. Not that he cared a fig for the Master, the inmates could hang him from the poorhouse gates for all he cared. It was this spreading unease that had brought him back.

Word had gone about in London that an insurrection of Chartists was about to break out in the Metropolis itself, the signal for a general uprising being a simultaneous firing of different parts of the city.

When news came in that 30,000 colliery workers armed with axes were marching on Preston, and that police and military had been called out against an immense mob who had partially destroyed a cotton factory at Bamberbridge, Billy thought it was time he returned to protect his investment. Billy Miles held the concession to run the tommy-shop at Rochester Mill.

Trucking—the business of paying the workers in paper instead of real money—was illegal, but the Trucking Act was seldom enforced. Billy Miles had an arrangement with the manager at the mills, and those who would not accept paper soon discovered they were out of collar. The tickets could only be exchanged at his tommy-shop, and the workers must accede to his terms or starve. First he took a commission for the right to use his notes—so that the paper was not even to the value of the wages due—then by dint of short weight and long prices for cheap tainted goods, Billy had begun to amass himself a small fortune.

The dull, sodden sound of hooves changed to a more confident ring as Billy turned onto the turnpike. Now he could see across the drenched hedges to the mill and the smoke pouring from its stack. Still standing, and the men at work, he thought with relief. But rebellion was in the air, with things as they were he would take his fortune to London. He preferred the protection of the much reviled New Police in the Metropolis to that of the local constabulary.

Billy Miles rode through the mill gates only to become immediately occupied with the control of his mount, shying violently from the confrontation of a carriage-and-five. Biting off a curse, Billy slid to the ground as he recognized the crest on the carriage and on the canary yellow coats of the servants, as that of the new fifth Earl of Furlingham. Cautiously, he led his horse forward past the coach, but its owner was nowhere to be seen. What the devil was Furlingham doing here when he had never yet set foot on this part of his property?

Holding the horses' heads, the grooms watched Billy's mud-splashed figure squelch by. Their wigs had gathered a fine coat of drizzle, producing a hoary effect quite outdoing the powder that lay beneath them. The drenching rain had been less effective in improving the grandeur of their sky-blue waistcoats, silver buckles and silk stockings, howsomever, they deemed themselves sufficiently fine to treat of Billy with the disdainful silence that they reserved for members of the lower classes not in livery.

The leading groom spat after the retreating figure : Damn the new Earl, who planned to take their livery away from them. He would dress them in plain black and stand them with unpowdered heads. As plain dressed as that same working class in whom he took such an unnatural interest. Furlingham was the hardest of beggars—forever visiting factories and mills on his estates and not a thought for the likes and comforts of his servants. The old devil was the one, thought the groom, a sudden call for the carriage and you could be off for two gin sodden nights in an expensive whore-house, and he always left word to look after 't'lads'. Else he'd take it into his head to dash through the countryside and roister a week away in some great country house. You looked after yourself there with the minxes below stairs. The rain gathered in a droplet at the end of the groom's long nose, as he recalled a particularly lively second chambermaid.

Billy rounded the corner of the mill and stopped short to see that his tommy shop had been reduced to a smoking rubble. The walls and stock had vanished, even the high stout counter that his assistants had sheltered behind had gone. Only the smoke blackened iron rails of his counting house still stood and the charred high seat whence he had commanded a view of the shop.

Two men standing at the edge of the burnt circle turned towards the newcomer. One was Grimston, the mill manager— dodging nervously from one foot to the other as though he had contained his water overlong—the other, tall and soberly dressed, could be none other than Lord Furlingham.

Billy Miles adjusted his travel-stained beaver hat and advanced towards them, with a look of grave concern masking his furious deliberations. If the safe had been emptied then he was a ruined man—yet if such a vast sum of money was uncovered some explanation might well be called for. There were various loan schemes he was engaged in, and certain arrangements with the foreman, that even Grimston had been unaware of.

He cast back in his mind. Despite old Furlingham's profligate waste of the famly fortune, the new Earl had inherited one of the richest estates in England along with the title. He was one of twenty noblemen who possessed more than 150,000 acres in the United Kingdom. What could be his concern with a burnt out tommy-shop?

"My Lord, may I present Mr. Miles who runs the shop."

"Good day, sir. Can you account for these wretched people burning you out?"

"I am not fully informed on it, my lord, having but just returned from London. I would hazard some rabble-rouser has been at work here. They play the devil with the poor starving people; they take advantage by saying they have a charter to achieve here or a law to repeal there and promise to turn their tattered rags into flags of rebellion."

Billy was anxiously moving round to see into the burnt-out shell of the counting house.

"Dammit, will you keep still," shouted Lord Furlingham, "it seems you both have the devil's itch."

"Indeed, my lord," said Grimston, "you must forgive our concern. There never were such contented workers until the Chartists came here." What the devil was he blabbing about, thought Billy, a man like Furlingham would be more concerned with profit than the condition of the workers. "A young fellow called Owen Bookbinder is behind it," continued Grimston, "always spouting Chartism and addressing the Working Men's Union. He called a meeting the very night of the burning."

Billy could now see into his broken safe, empty but for the ashes of his account books.

"By God! I'll be even with Bookbinder," raged Billy, "and I'll pay back the varmints who did this thing."

"Perhaps we could discuss this more calmly," squeaked Grimston in an agitated voice. Miles could see Grimston waving his hands and shaking a white face behind Furlingham's back.

"The pox on you, Grimston, you're too soft on the workers. Give 'em over to me Lord Furlingham and I'll make 'em pay for their depredations twice over. They can starve for a week until they get their paper."

"Be quiet, sir!" roared Lord Furlingham, "I abhor both your blasphemy and lack of principle. I think there is no further reason for your presence here." He turned to the manager as though Billy Miles had ceased to exist. "Grimston, I am not convinced entire of your lack of complicity in this matter. I shall be sending an Inspector of Factories here and also a minister. I expect you to devote your energies to seeing that the workers have decent working conditions, full bellies and are taught the way of the Lord."

Billy Miles stared at him with his jaw hanging open. Who would have thought that the degenerate fourth Earl would have spawned a gospel grinding social philanthropist.

"What of my investment?" he demanded angrily.

Furlingham did not look at him.

"If this person is not off my land in ten minutes, Grimston, have him beaten by the servants and put off. Then institute proceedings against him for engaging in traffic contrary to the Truck Act."

Billy Miles returned to his mare. He was not foolish enough to continue remonstrance with so powerful an opponent. But he vowed that if he should ever pull himself up to such a height, he would do Furlingham what injury he could. There was one, however, more easily accessible. Miles' animal-like yellow eyes looked out vengefully towards London—where no doubt Owen Bookbinder was heading.

3

THE CHARTIST

TEARS of joy ran down Owen Bookbinder's face in the red flickering torchlight. Nor was this the only singularity to be observed in his countenance amongst the crowd. The thousands of young London artisans, who because of the nature of their long hours had been unable to return home before the procession, were dirty and sweat begrimed where Owen was clean. The only colour in their pallid complexions came from the glow of the torches and the same light that lit Owen's strong healthy features travelled uneasily over that peculiar flatness of feature of the majority, caused by the want of a proper quantity of adipose substances to cushion out the cheeks.

Tears and joy were both commodities to be eked out sparingly amongst this assembly.

From where Owen stood on Ludgate Hill, the thousands of torches pinpointed into the distance down the thoroughfares, as though he were at the axis of a wheel and they were the spokes. All London must be wending its way towards him, each citizen bearing his personal torch of freedom. It was here that he belonged amongst these people. It was for this he had given up his middle-class life. There was a spirit of freedom in the air. It was impossible that the establishment could stand up to the people and oppress them longer.

They were a good-humoured crowd, the shouts and cheers as they passed the house of one of their idols changing to boos and cat-calls at a newspaper office that did not favour their cause. There was menace too, as evidenced in the occasional pistol shot and in the numbers of red caps of liberty—symbols of the French revolutionaries—that adorned the tops of the banners. Owen read their messages as they came by: 'For children and wife we'll war to the knife', 'He that shall not work neither shall he eat', and the terrible warning, 'Tyrants believe and tremble'.

A sudden sobering thought dissipated Owen's excitement in the scene: there was scarce a grey head amongst them. They were an army of undernourished children—few exceeding the height of five foot six inches—marching on bowed legs to their salvation.*

Shivering, Owen Bookbinder pulled himself away from the torchlight procession. It was a goodish walk to Bethnal Green and he was already late for his meeting. The way was lit by the torches down to Bishopsgate, past the homes of the labouring classes, where the day-time unemployed had left their scruff marks at boot level and grease at shoulder height. Soon he turned off into a hideous stew of courts and alleys leaving the red glow of the torches far behind.

A yellow wisp of fog slunk ahead of him like some whipped animal: picking its way over piles of filth of all kinds, sniffing around the effluvia coming from the bloated carcase of a dog floating in a stagnant pool, and rearing suddenly as it reached the lighted area of an isolated gas lamp fed from the noxious fumes of a sewer deep underground—reaching out frantic febrile fingers as Owen strode into another darkened stretch.

The more material threat of loungers and loafers was there too, shrouded in the mist, but Owen knew these stews of London. He was young, strong, carried a heavy stick and didn't look as though the pickings would be worth a broken limb, still he kept his eyes well-skinned for a sudden rush from the shadows. His main concern was with adjusting again to the vile stench of the alleys after the sweet air of Kent.

Heralded by a blaze of light, music and shrieks of laughter, half muffled by the fog, Owen came to an oasis of life at the

* Chadwick's Report on the Sanitary Condition, 1842, gave 16 as the average age of death of a mechanic and his family in Bethnal Green.

outskirts of Bethnal Green. As he approached the string of shops and night houses, the harsh light of two naked gas jets outside the penny gaff illuminated the thoroughfare from beyond, turning the figures there into grotesque characters from a shadow-play. He discerned in sharp relief: a concertinaed stove-pipe hat; a woman seated on the cobbles, open jawed and vacant, her baby's head hanging carelessly in the gutter; the quivering pointed nose of a greyhound surveying the scene from inside its owner's ragged jacket. Then he was amongst the costermongers awaiting the next performance at the penny gaff. Seemingly mesmerized by the effects of the music coming from the German band of a fiddle, a cornet and two flutes, playing in the open-fronted ground floor of the place—the costers thrust forward a sea of pennies towards the money taker. The harshly-lit posters and crudely-drawn paintings of the favourite comic singers, frozen in their most humorous poses, serving only to whet appetites further for the entertainment which lay within.

Owen knew full well that the uproarious sounds coming from the upstairs room was no evidence of the jewels of wit coming from the performers, yet it was some colour in lives that were starved of gaiety. And their masters would forbid Sunday entertainment and close down such places entirely if they could.

Couples danced in the road as Owen threaded his way past. The girls, bedizened in cheap finery and broken feathers, egged on to further exertions by their young companions, smoking pipes and clinking coins in time to the music. One mechanic,* clapping his hands, had an enormous polka dotted cravat, shaped like a kipper, that hung almost to his knees. The whole effect being somewhat spoiled by the large areas of unwashed skin showing through his tattered shirt. The smell from the dancers was stupendous.

* Mechanic—term used in Victorian times for those who engaged in manual skill or labour.

Generally, Owen had observed, the costermongers were much better dressed than those in other occupations. Especially on a Sunday when only dire necessity would drive them to work. They were very fond of silken neckerchiefs, both boys and girls, which the men wore tied at the neck with the two ends hanging down over their waistcoats. They were particular that their trousers should be tight at the knees, belling out at the bottoms to nearly cover their boots, in which also they were very particular, and sometimes tastily ornamented at the caps. The women took care to wear their petticoats sufficiently short that they could display the much admired boot.

Nearly all of the costermongers were Chartists, ruminated Owen, their leaders attending meetings and being very adept at stirring up discontent—perhaps too inclined towards violence. Yet Owen doubted that most of their followers who proclaimed themselves ardent Chartists, understood the six points.

He had left the lights and music behind him, when a child stepped from the shadows. She was a pretty girl of about thirteen, wearing a cheap, velvet cotton cape edged with tinsel, over a stained cotton dress. A feather straggled from her bonnet down over her dark hair.

"Are you good natured, Charlie? Wanna tannersworth?"

Owen stopped, horrified by the contradiction between her childish appearance and the words she spoke.

Taking his disquiet to be consideration, she said quickly:

"I'm clean, sir, I ain't nivver done it afore, honest!" And with that she stooped swiftly, to pull the hem of her dress up to her chin, displaying a smoothly perfect body, looking in the pale light as though carved from Carrara marble, elegantly turned, down to the smallest dimple. Only the tiny nipples trembling in the night air broke the effect, reminding Owen disconcertingly of the quivering pink nose of the greyhound he had observed.

Embarrassed by the quickening of his own desire, Owen blurted out:

"No, my dear, pray pull down your clothes."

But the girl merely shifted her weight to one hip and cocked her pretty face to one side.

"Go on, sir, a joey, the werry lowest terms, tu'punce each for me and my chap to sit the front seats of the gaff this night."

She nodded her head back to the doorway she had come from, and Owen saw the shadow of her protector.

Owen thrust his hand in his pocket for sixpence, looking steadfastly at the girl's feet. Her slim, naked ankles—disappearing into enormous, broken highlow boots—he found to his acute discomfort, to be even more arousing. Thrusting the money at the girl Owen strode red-faced away.*

Furious with himself and those that could ignore such conditions on their doorsteps, yet occupy themselves with the Society for the Propagation of the Gospel to Foreign Parts— Owen pounded down North Street oblivious to his surroundings. Which was particularly fortunate since he was in a long narrow street where the houses were mostly owned by pig-dealers, the central sunken gutter of which was allowed to accumulate quantities of putrefying animal and vegetable matter, the filth produced from the pigs seldom or never being removed or cleaned away, resulting in a stench that was peculiarly dreadful.

Turning into Abbey Street, Owen Bookbinder made his way to the Trades Hall. The name posted over the gas-lit entrance barely concealed the swirling coloured glass design beneath, reading 'Chinese Salon'. So full was Owen's head of his dream of people freed from want and ignorance, where all had the right to human dignity, that he paid no heed to the burly figures standing in the shadows.

* Sexual intercourse (criminal connection in Victorian terminology) with a girl under the age of twelve was a criminal offence in 1840, although only a misdemeanor if she was over ten. Despite fierce opposition, the age of consent was raised to thirteen in 1875, and ten years later to sixteen.

There were some five hundred inside the hall, already aroused by the singing of the Chartist hymn and the oratory of the speakers. Owen swelled with pride to be one of the leaders of the movement, which, with the people solidly behind them, would make a bloodless revolution in England.

"Put your trust in God and keep your powder dry," said the speaker proposing the first resolution. A comparatively peaceful sentiment with which Owen could concur but that met with some disagreement from certain physical-force Chartists in the hall. Their opportunity for action, however, arose rather more quickly than they had anticipated. The doors burst open with a tremendous noise and Superintendent Pearce* appeared, a naked cutlass in his hand, followed by a considerable body of inspectors and constables.

For a moment it seemed that the extremists might make a fight for it, but their verbal courage melted away before the menace of the long staves and cutlasses that the police had been issued with—of a sudden there was a rush for the exits.

Amazed at the speed with which events moved, and making no attempt to escape, Owen was very quickly taken and held to the front of the hall. Why had he allowed himself to be so preoccupied with romantic notions? he asked himself. He recalled now that he had observed groups of men outside, and should have properly warned the assembly.

Wryly, Owen considered he at least had an opportunity to study police methods at close hand. Glancing about him he noted how many of those detained were the ring-leaders of the movement. It was very strange that the police should have done so by hazard. At last his mind was beginning to

---

* Nicholas Pearce, a previous Bow Street patrolman, became one of the most famous detectives of the 1840's. Long before a detective office was formed, Pearce, often teamed with Sergeant Thornton, was given scope as a roving investigator in matters of serious crime in the Metropolis. The investigation at the Trades Hall was probably the first in an office which eventually became the modern C.I.D.

work. He searched out Superintendent Pearce's figure at the back of the hall conversing with a Chartist known as Gould. Pearce broke away from the man and hurried over to the prisoners held before the speaker's platform.

Owen studied the policeman, confident and energetic, a professional amongst these amateur revolutionaries. He paid scant attention to his prisoners.

"Sergeant Thornton, have a search made beneath this platform."

"Right away, sir."

Now, Superintendent Pearce turned to the Chartist leaders he had detained, hardly glancing at the quantities of knives, daggers, bullets and percussion caps that his constables unearthed. Without emotion he told them :

"You will be immediately conveyed to Bow Street Police Station where certain charges will be made against you. It will be to all our advantage gentlemen if you would decide to come peaceably."

Owen Bookbinder watched him as he walked away. It would be transportation—or Newgate at least. Sooner or later he would be free, he had learnt his lesson and the Movement must learn it too if they were to ultimately succeed. They must become professional revolutionaries.

4

THOSE THINGS CAUTIOUSLY HIDDEN
FROM THE GENTLE SEX

DREAMILY enjoying the unexpected taste of freedom, Celandine paused in the steep climb up the bridleway to listen for Dick. The only sound was that of the drone of insects hovering over the wild flowers in the warm, still air. Dick had gone from sight up the dappled green tunnel made by the ash trees meeting over the path that stretched above her.

Of a sudden she felt quite alone, the only sign of humanity being the stumps of hazel rods by the path, cut to make fences or wattles to fold the sheep.

"Dick, wait for me," she called nervously. Her voice stilled the wild life and the countryside held its breath. A nuthatch broke from a hawthorn bush startling her. Gradually the murmur of the insects resumed.

Stifling her panic, Celandine continued the climb in a more determined fashion.

It was quite unlike the Rev. Mr. Blackstone to release her lightly from her tasks, but this day he had insisted that she should accompany his son Dick on a message to the nearby village of Ridlington. 'Big Dick', as the village lads called him, was thirteen years of age, four years her senior, and was of an enquiring turn of mind. He was convinced that his father wished to be rid of them to entertain a visitor, and for this reason had hurried Celandine to Ridlington and halfway back at breakneck speed, in order to return to the house. For Celandine's part she would have been as happy to spend an idle summer afternoon, as ferret out the minister's business.

Celandine came out of the tunnel to a ridge on top of the hill and found Dick, standing stock still by the side of the bridlepath. He was peering intently through a gap in the hedge to the fields below and did not look up as the girl came next to him to see for herself.

"I've heard tell of it," he whispered, "but never thought to observe it myself."

The wheat stubble far below was almost covered with a pulsating brown mass.

"What is it?"

"It's an acre of hares gathered and acting in a very heathen fashion. Find me a stone will you?"

"You'll not throw that far," said Celandine, searching the path.

Dick selected a stone from her, the size of a walnut, his face strangely flushed.

"Watch close and see."

The stone flew out true over the field and fell like a thunderbolt amongst the hares. For a moment they ran every which way, climbing over each other's bodies, huddling together in small groups and coming all together again like sheep in a flock for protection—and then the stone forgotten, were copulating once more.

Dick laughed and glanced at Celandine, "There's no stopping them." He took her hand and led her over the last of the crest of the hill, seeming no longer in such a hurry.

A golden sea of uncut barley rolled away from them down the hill to a wide ditch, beyond which was a lean-to where Celandine's grandfather had once lived and now housed one of his labourers. Tom's tenant farmland continued on from this to the new cottage he shared with Lucy and Celandine. Despite his improved condition Tom's living was still little better than one of his workers. Shimmering through the heat haze in the distance Dick and Celandine could see the minister's house, just outside the small village of a mill, an alehouse, six cottages and a church.

Their white smock frocks—commonly worn by girls and boys in Sussex—dropped beneath the level of the barley as Dick led the way, treading between the furrows in order not to break down the crop. Both children had been thoughtful and silent since they had seen the hares.

"Dick?"

"Yes."

"I want to ask you something."

Dick stopped and plucked a head of barley. "What would you ask me?"

"Mayn't we rest, you have hurried me so?"

"If you want."

Dick pulled at the stalk between his teeth, and watched Celandine settle back in the corn with a sigh and close her eyes.

"Do people do that, Dick? I mean like the hares. Do they carry on in that fashion?"

"I suppose they do," said Dick guardedly.

"How very strange, why do you imagine they would do such a thing?"

"Why, to have babies, why else?"

"People as well as rabbits?" asked Celandine opening her eyes quite shocked.

"Where else do you think babies come from?"

"I didn't think on it till now—folk's babies I mean. I asked Mamma about Aunt May's baby boy once, where it came from, and she boxed my ears until my head rung." Celandine was silent for a moment frowning. "Boys are made quite different from girls aren't they Dick?"

"Father says that such things are best kept hidden."

"Is it so very wicked then?"

"It weakens a man just to think of it."

"Goodness! I wonder that God allows it. How very terrible to be a man."

Dick looked carefully about him : there was nought but the waving barley. He sat next to Celandine with sudden decision.

"It is the night that is the worst for a man. If one's thoughts are wicked in the day, vital energy can be drained away at night."

Celandine sat up to listen, her eyes wide.

"How drained away?"

"A fluid from the backbone escapes that contains all the vital energies. Such emissions can reduce a strong-built man to blindness, madness and the strait-jacket. It is known as spermatorrhaea."

"How learned you are Dick."

"My father has lectured me much on the subject. It seems there are some who actually encourage the emissions in secret vice, but they are soon spotted. The pale complexion, the emaciated frame, the glassy eye, the clammy palm, the averted gaze—all indicate the frigger."

A passing fair description of the Rev. Mr. Blackstone himself, thought Celandine.

"At least you are not a victim, Dick, for you are so well set up and healthful."

Dick shook his head. "It is a battle, were it not for the device my father had made for me, I fear I would be less healthful. It is a metal ring worn at night, with teeth that cut into one as soon as a certain degree of erection occurs—warning of an impending emission. It is then necessary to jump from the bed and sponge down with cold water. It is a great saving on the life fluid, but I fear of late, a terrible wastage of my sleep."

"I cannot quite follow you, Dick. This life fluid that comes from a man, of what use is it?"

"Why its proper use is in marriage, in moderation, to bring about a family."

"It would seem a fearful danger for a man to have children. How then is the affair managed?"

"The husband places himself in the round hole of his wife and the thing is done."

Celandine shook her head firmly.

"That cannot be. Mamma would never consent to such an undertaking. Of that I am certain. Besides there is no such round hole as you speak of. It is quite a different shape. I took you to be informed on the subject."

"It is of no consequence," said Dick angrily, "nor a fit subject for discussion between us. For if I am to be a priest I must renounce the temptations of the flesh and seek salvation through the blood of Christ."

"You need feel no shame Dick, that you have never seen a woman, for I too am as ignorant and not seen a grown man." Dick frowned, Celandine was uncannily accurate in her interpretation of his anger. Spy as he would on the servants and his mother when they were undressing, he had seen nought but a dark hair at the bottom of their bellies, and had built a picture in his mind from books he had procured and furtive discussions with his male cousins on the fashion in which ladies were made.

"Dick, I'd show you mine if you would but show me yours."

The boy stared at her and said nothing. No such sexual notions or feelings should enter into a well brought up child's head or affect its body. Perfect freedom from, and indeed, total ignorance of any sexual affection was always the rule. Yet increasingly he found himself torn between his curiosity, excited on these subjects, and his father's teachings.

Celandine sighed: "But then I suppose you never will be a real man now."

"What do you mean, I shall never be a real man," said Dick, jumping to his feet.

"Why Granpapa says priests are only half men, for all their ranting and carrying on," said Celandine innocently.

"I'll show you then if I am a real man or not," shouted Dick—and furiously pulled his smock over his head, to the intense interest of Celandine.

"I was but teasing, Dick," she said softly, "pray don't be so vexed."

Dick laughed, embarrassed, and sat next to her. Whether from the heat of the sun on his naked body or the evil indulgent thoughts that were crowding his mind—Dick felt himself becoming aroused.

Celandine studied him with awe.

"A great thing like that would surely split a lady asunder. There can be little pleasure in this business for either party." She lay back in the barley and closed her eyes. "I for one shall submit to no such thing. Doesn't the sun make one sleepy, Dick?"

Neither spoke for a while and Dick observed the girl, who appeared to have fallen asleep, doubtfully.

Celandine felt him lift her smock and turned her head in modesty. It was curious she thought, that the wicked indulgences they were allowing themselves should promote such a strange excitement. She flinched as Dick pursued his enquiries further, yet still she did not move. She would endure much to hold his affection, for there was little to be had in the strict religious confines of her home.

Dick's head swam and his loins ached. It hardly seemed possible to effect an entry. A picture spun before his eyes from when he was a little boy. He heard again Eliza Cowan's shout: "What does that boy do there", as they hoisted the great Staffordshire bull by chains into position for mating.

Celandine screamed as Dick turned her over and wrestled with her.

"No! Richard, no!"

"Let's try, Celandine, please let's try," he sobbed. The girl rolled away from him and with one frightened backward glance, jumped to her feet and was away down the hill.

Dick sat amongst the barley and discovered to his mortification that he had spent. With dismay he wondered how much of his valuable vital force he had expended in wandering from the chosen path of purity. Already it seemed that his eyes were affected as the barley field swam before him. When his rapidly beating heart slowed and his eyes began to focus again, Dick realized that a more pressing concern was whether Celandine would blab to her mother. He shuddered to think what course his father would take if it should come to his ears. Pulling on his smock, Dick stumbled down the hill after the girl.

Mamma was very wise not to marry again, thought the girl as she jogged down the hill. No wonder married people were so morose, there seemed more pain than pleasure in men and women coming together. It was a puzzle that Dick had been so prepared to harm her and reduce himself in that fashion. There was nought there that interested her she considered.

Her feet chased a cabbage butterfly about to alight on a poppy growing between the furrows. It fluttered whitely from side to side, always a few feet ahead of her, down the hill. Celandine leapt the ditch at the bottom and watched the butterfly flutter back into the field. Pausing for a while to remove the irritant husks that stuck to her skin beneath her clothes, she set off back to the minister's house.

Hot and breathless, Dick, who had come across the fields at a furious pace, watched from the hedge at the end of the lane and marvelled at Celandine's composure. Ribbon freshly tied, smock brushed down, for all the world as though nothing untoward had occurred—the girl turned into the gate of his home.

The visitor smiled broadly as the front door closed behind him. So gratified was he with his recent transactions, that with uncustomary benevolence he pressed a sovereign into the hand of the country child who held the gate, mistaking her fear for timidity. Without a glance at the coin which she clutched, Celandine stared after the man trembling. She could not recall having seen the gentleman before, yet those flat yellow eyes had reduced her to weakness and terror.

Billy Miles swung his cane with satisfaction and headed for the 'Horseshoe and Magpie' and his supper.

5

THE MILLING COVE

FOR want of bacon, Billy Miles ordered bread, cheese and ale from the landlord at the bar. It seemed a poor sort of place but the ale was a good local brew and Billy was not averse to simple food on occasion. He had eaten in the cheapest of slapbangs in London before he finally sat on Sir Edward Locke's banking stool and started to mend his fortune. He knew he was in luck when the chief accountant didn't come in one fine Monday morning and Sir Edward sent for him confiding of all things, 'That he had no head for figures'. Billy Miles did have a head for figures and had already discovered that the bank was in some difficulties. By judicious balancing, some of which could have been determined fraud, Billy presented a balance sheet that would continue confidence on Sir Edward Locke's Bank acceptances in the market.

It was not long before Billy Miles had stepped from chief accountant to manager. The other directors were not villains, but proud stubborn old men who had lent recklessly to merchant accounts that were friends of the board.

The failing accounts began to recover, Billy curbed the speculative investment that they had embarked on in French railways and Australian land—and the ageing Sir Edward, trusting him implicitly, signed anything that Billy placed under his nose.

It wasn't until Sir Edward had a stroke in his office and his sight impaired that Billy began to include papers amongst the documents to be signed, that made over some of Sir Edward's personal bonds, resting in the bank's vaults, to himself—not sufficient to arouse Sir Edward's heirs' suspicions when another stroke carried the old man off, but quite enough to finance an enterprise for which Billy had long required capital.

There was none more reverent than Billy in his shiny silk top hat walking behind the cortège: nor more gratified to learn at the reading of the will that he had been remembered to the tune of £2,000. God helps those who help themselves reflected Billy.

Hand-coloured prints of Tom Cribb and other favourite

milling coves adorned the walls of the parlour and from the look of the battered face and brawny fore-arms of the man behind the bar, he too must have been a pugilist.

"Will you have a glass of something to drink with me, landlord?"

"I don't object to a drain, thank you, sir."

As the landlord walked behind the long bar-counter to draw himself ale from the taproom, the daughter arrived with the victuals for Billy Miles.

She was a big, healthy, foxy-maned girl of about seventeen—with a certain abandoned swing of hip and buttock that he had admired early that morning in the country girls, wending their way through the dust to the city. Despite large hands and feet, they carried their pottle baskets of strawberries with an easy, sensual grace, that straightway sent his imaginings to the juicy pivot of such rhythmic actions.

"That's a splendid sight for any man, Polly," said Billy loudly, looking directly at the curves of her big breasts beneath the simple blouse.

Polly pretended not to understand but her eyes sparkled as she put the tray in front of him.

"Lor' sir, I don't suppose it's the quality you're used to in Lunnon, but it's good country fare."

"And have you picked out a room for me?" The girl had taken his bags when he arrived that morning.

"Aye, sir, it's the best we 'ave, over the taproom."

"Where do you sleep, my dear," said Billy more quietly. putting an arm around Polly and bringing her close.

"Downstairs with my family, of course."

"Oh!" said Billy disappointed.

"'cept like now, when we've only one guest."

"And now?"

"Why, in the small room next to your'n," she whispered pushing his hand down as her father returned.

"Good health, sir!"

"Good luck to you!" said Billy, raising his quart tankard to the landlord. Polly had not moved away and from where her father stood behind the bar, he could not see Billy's hand resting lightly around the girl's thigh.

"Your trade seems quiet enough here, landlord." His free hand moved slowly up the back of the girl's leg until he was feeling her through the skirt, pressing the cloth between her firm buttocks. Polly betrayed no sign that anything was amiss.

"Too quiet, sir, 'tis the damn steam pots taking away the business. We seldom get gentlemen in the parlour these days apart from the squire or the minister. 'Course the taproom gets filled about sundown, but fourpunny beer won't keep me. I depends on the carriage trade."

Billy Miles doubted that even before the new railway line, the inn could have been much more than an occasional stop for coaches.

"So you know the Reverend Mr. Blackstone, perhaps you could be of service to me."

The landlord eyed Billy doubtfully. His customer didn't look a mealy-mouthed humbug to be an acquaintance of the preacher—more likely to be in league with the devil with those slanted black eyebrows and queer coloured eyes. He was his own man but he could ill afford to fall foul of the preacher. Nonetheless, he smelt money in this.

Encouraged by Polly's acquiescence Billy had slipped his hand beneath her skirt, only to be baulked of reaching his final destination on discovering that there was no ingress between the top of those sturdy thighs.

Billy had always considered such thickening at the top of a woman's legs to be an undesirable feature. He had given much thought to the leg question and had invented for his personal amusement the Miles Limb Meter. This consisted of four sovereigns, three of which he would persuade the lady of his choice to place between her slim ankles, the swell of her calf and her knees, proving, if they could be held firmly, the excellent straightness and proportion of her legs. The fourth he placed horizontally at the juncture, lightly kissing as it were the young Queen's head. If this final coin could be held steady without discomfort—then indeed were the legs of the first quality.

Few ladies were able to resist their curiosity regarding such a test of physical excellence—or the close proximity to so much gold. In truth, the findings of the Miles Limb Meter became purely academic at the completion of the test.

Fondling the girl with one hand, he took a draught of ale, reflecting that it would be a black day should these new-fangled drawers he had heard of in London ever become common.*

"Hook it!" shouted the ex-bruiser, gesturing with his thumb.

Billy's eyes narrowed and he put down the tankard carefully when the landlord continued, "and get those floors swept down."

Polly sulked off without a backward glance.

"Now sir, what is it you have in mind?"

Billy counted out five sovereigns on to the table, put his purse away and started to eat.

"I'll be honest with you, I'm in way of doing business with Mr. Blackstone and others of his colour in these parts and as the natural enemies of your livelihood I doubt there's any more suited than you to appreciate what wily rogues they are, or to know their characters and keep me informed from time to time of their doings."

The landlord slapped the bar a resounding thump with his huge hand.

"I thought I had you pegged right, sir, an' I reckon you'll need all the help you can get to keep top-side of them varmin, or my name's not Joe Salt."

* Drawers became accepted by the middle classes in the 1860's perhaps because of the wired crinoline which could become suddenly revealing. They were expensive and were not worn by the lower classes until the 1880's.

Billy smiled to himself and between bites, as the landlord talked on, added notes to the already impressive list of worthies he held in his black book. He had little doubt of his ability to outwit these pious gentlemen. Their laudable desire to build healthy dwellings for skilled artisans and their families —no doubt prompted by the excellent rewards to be reaped from real estate—had already provided him with a reputable group of fellow directors for his limited company entitled 'Buildings Trust'. But William Miles, Esq. liked to hedge his bets and the black book was insurance.

He could see Polly through the open door of the parlour, on her knees washing down the floor of the taproom—her skirts bunched and plump thighs showing.

"What do you know of the parson over at Ridlington, Mr. Salt?"

Billy was impressed with Joe Salt's further observations. If they proved to be accurate, a man of his strength and perspicacity was wasted in this country ale-house. He drained his tankard and got to his feet.

"I'm much indebted to you, Mr. Salt. We must talk again. I may have further business to put your way." He poured the gold on to the bar top.

"Obliged to you, sir," said Joe Salt showing his gums, "I'm half inclined to give that sort of service for the pleasure in it." But his gnarled hand had already pocketed the money.

"Would you provide a horse for the morrow I must ride over to Ridlington," Billy affected a yawn, "for the moment I'm plaguey tired. I shall have a lie-down in my room if you'd send up the girl with a bottle of brandy."

He heard the landlord bellowing for his daughter as he went up the stairs.

Billy was stretched out on the bed when Polly flounced in sulkily and put down a bottle of brandy and a tumbler.

"Will you give me a kiss, Polly?" Seizing the hem of her skirt he pulled her to him. He scarce had a glimpse of a flaming red bush that matched her hair when she pushed down her clothes furiously. "Addun sir, if I'm not back in five minutes, my pa'll no doubt come and dash your teeth from your jaw," she said, making no move to leave the room.

Billy Miles gave her a look that made the girl doubt that he would come off second best to any woman—or man for that matter.

"Then we mustn't waste time, my dear," growled Billy.

Her thighs are really too big for comfort he thought breathlessly, but then, that very night, after he had written his new prospectus he had every intention of reducing her with further violent exercise.

6

WILLIAM MILES ESQUIRE

THE building that Billy Miles raised in Warren Street—of stone, red and blue brick, ornamental ironwork and notched tiles—was as multifarious in its Gothic forms as in its symbolism.

To the passer-by, already proudly calling himself a 'Victorian', it was a further sign of the progress and great changes taking place all around him.

To any of the thousands of small shareholders, who had been circularized through the Nonconformist and temperance channels that Billy had carefully built up, it spelt security for their savings. If there were apparent anachronisms in the building they could be justified too. What could be more imaginative, yet eminently more sensible, than the soaring medieval turrets with their big sash windows?

The ecclesiastical cast of the imposing entrance was a comfort to the ministers and temperance leaders who had worked with such will to push the shares. If their consciences should prick them at the large unholy commissions they had received and the fact that there was still no sign of development in the dubious property that the Society owned in Westminster and Spitalfields—surely this structure indicated their clear intention to create model dwellings for clerks, shopkeepers and the rank and file of the commercial world.

To Billy's fellow directors, the building stood testimony to the personal energy and perspicacity of their manager William Miles Esq. Such was their belief in his ability to make them a fat profit, that they were quite prepared to overlook the doubtful nobility of the giant white letters above the striped stonework, spelling out BEACON PERMANENT BUILDING SOCIETY. In their high-minded sanctity they even condoned Billy's audacious experiment in using some female typewriters* amongst the clerks working in the broken light that the gaps between the lettering afforded.

The experiment with female labour, originally carnal in intent, proved surprisingly that women were more efficient at this sort of labour.

To Billy, standing at the window in the boardroom, just above the 'P' of PERMANENT, the façade below him symbolized merely a device to promote confidence in his use of the funds, in which a society of the new 'permanent' type allowed him considerable freedom—thus being allowed that arbitrary and free action and absence of control, that were essential to the ultimate development of his plans.† He had been prepared for a year or more against the day when that confidence might be lacking, by persuading Joe Salt to join his household as a bodyguard. With a close eye and a practised hand he

---

* Several machines had been produced by 1848 but they failed to capture public interest and few details have survived. The first practical model, called the 'Sholes and Glidden' typewriter, was manufactured by Messrs. Remington in 1873 and received public acceptance by 1882.

† Societies were not required to make strict returns on advances and interest on mortgages until 1894.

weighed the value of his reputation against the latitude he could take.

But the events of this Monday the 10th of April 1848, were beyond the power of Billy Miles to control, and before it was over his schemes could collapse as easily as the thrones that were toppling in Europe. Blood was flowing in Paris, Berlin and Vienna, as the workers rose against their governments. In England the upper classes waited with alarm for the great Chartist National Convention to hold their procession and meeting in defiance of the law.

Dr. Sugdon, the Presbyterian Divine, backed nervously away from the leaded windows as a child ran screaming the length of the boarded, deserted street far beneath them.

"They're on their way I think."

In the sudden hush of the boardroom, the assembled directors could distinctly hear the murmur of distant voices and tramp of thousands of boots.

"Such foolish men," said Lady Clara Vere, "if they were fitted for the vote God would have given it to them. It would serve them better to return to their labours, and trust in Our Lord and the wisdom of their betters."

"Well spoken Lady Vere, if they knew but half the strain of public service, they would not be so eager to take it upon themselves," said Mrs. Brigstock.

The Earl's daughter winced : The Brigstock woman must know that she was habitually styled Lady Clara Vere, yet she persisted in calling her Lady Vere for all the world as though she were a peer or baronet's wife instead of a 'lady in her own right'.

Her prominent adam's apple trembled against the Honiton lace tight at her throat, preparatory to making a tart reply when she saw Major Burton at the table. He had taken one of a pair of pistols from a duelling case and was proceeding to prime it.

"Lor' sir ! What are you at ?"

"The masses are our natural enemies, Madame. I've had these by me for fifteen years, ready at any year or any day to fight for my property or the honour of my daughters."

"Dear, oh dear!" panicked Lady Clara Vere, clinging to the more stolid Mrs. Brigstock. "Surely they'd not wreak vengeance on the fair sex."

"Don't be alarmed ladies," said Billy Miles. It was his opinion that any Chartist who had the pluck to rape this rattle-bag of old bones deserved the franchise. He was less sure of Mrs. Brigstock, a gleam had come into her dark eyes that tokened a revolutionary might well give her best.

"We shall be safe enough here and the Duke of Wellington himself has taken command."

"Ah! yes, the dear Duke." Her Ladyship suddenly became aware of her close proximity to the stout woman, and straightening back in her own chair, took a perfumed handkerchief from her *portemonnaie* and sniffed it delicately. It was very definitely a lady's duty to ameliorate the lot of the poor—to give them respectability in this life and the hope of happiness in another. It was one thing, howsomever, for Mrs. Brigstock to visit the navigators building the railways and quite another to come back smelling like one.

"Don't vex yourself," panted the Major, his bald head shining with the effort of accommodating his great girth to the table so that he could work on the pistols. "Would that I had the chance to use these on the rabble, but I doubt that I shall. I hear that the Enrolled Pensioners that I used to command in before I was retired for the second time, have been mustered by warrant of the Home Secretary. Some 1,300 officers and men with 7,000 military are sharing the duty of guarding the bridges over the Thames, garrisoning the Bank, the Mint and the Tower—many more are to hand in the provinces and can be speedily brought to the metropolis by the railways. In short, for the first time, the upper classes and the government are working in concert and have made the most unparalleled preparations to finally crush this rebellious movement."

"Indeed," joined in Dr. Sugdon, "I do hear that the exiled Napoleon III, now living in King Street, is to serve as a special constable."

"Such a comfort," murmured Lady Clara Vere vaguely.

There was some activity from the National Land Company office opposite and Billy watched them bring out five bales of signatures to the petition. The head of the procession was in sight now, two cars pulled by six horses apiece. Billy's dark complexion paled somewhat as he saw the grim and determined workers marching eight abreast behind. The suffering wage-earners had grown fierce and mad with bitter discontent. If all the rumours were true of hawkers vending secondhand weapons to the working class and of blacksmiths grinding pikes for their use: there wasn't a force in England to stay them.

Except perhaps their own fool of a leader, thought Billy—Feargus O'Connor, occupying a centre seat in the first car amongst the Chartist executive committee. The man who had devised the Chartist Co-operative Land Society, a hare-brained scheme to do away with the machine and return to the land. They stood as much chance of realizing that Arcadian dream world as his own directors did of witnessing their model dwellings fit for artisans and their families.

The bundles of signatures were loaded and as the procession started off again, Billy examined the men in the second car, the inflammatory orators and rabble rousers who were the heart of the movement. With a start Billy pressed forward against the leaded panes. Amongst them sat a man whom he still owed a grudge, Owen Bookbinder. The tommy-shop still rankled with him, although he had made good its loss many times since, it was one of the few occasions he had been bettered. Many years ago he had taken the trouble to have Bookbinder tracked down, only to find him safe from his revenge in Newgate Prison—not such a desperate situation as it sounded, since the Unions were supporting him in comparative comfort.

Billy swore that if Owen Bookbinder should escape with his hide this day, he would seek him out once more.

7

KENNINGTON COMMON AND THE SWELL MOBSMAN

"Have you passed many of these instruments around?" asked Owen Bookbinder thoughtfully.

"Not as many as I would like, but keep those, I have others."

Johnson tried to keep the anxiety out of his voice as Bookbinder examined the caltrops. They were made of cork, spiked and weighted with lead and intended for use against the cavalry horses. They were worth seven years deportation to Bookbinder if he was apprehended with them on his person and £25 to Johnson, the informer, if he achieved that apprehension.

"I hope you'll not deliberately stir up violence this day, it can only bring misery to the people."

Somewhat unnerved at these words Johnson relaxed as Bookbinder put the caltrops away. What a catch Bookbinder would be. He was not a fiery orator, inflaming immediate passions, but the true enemy, an idealist and intellectual, putting thoughts into men's minds that stayed there. People listened to what Bookbinder had to say.

"Did you say 'misery'?" asked a fiery young man with flapping epaulettes, turning around from the next seat in the car, "there's nowt more in the way o' misery to endure lest it be the treadmill or the stocks. This time it shall be war t' the knife."

Owen judged he was from the North and stood for the unemployed handloom weavers, whose choice was to send their children to the mills or see their families split up in the work-house. Their plight was worse than any other in the British Isles—but for the Welsh workers, beneath the iron-masters still persisting in the degrading trucking system.

Each faction was anxious to right his own particular wrong and only the majority of London artisans, not so sorely oppressed were less bent on blood-letting and could see that the franchise would solve all their problems.

Johnson, Owen believed, was from Cripplegate, and was slightly odd in his sanguine cast of mind.

"He who lives by the sword shall die by the sword," said Thomas Wragg, a bearded lay preacher from the Wat Tyler brigade of Chartists at Greenwich, "and it would profit not the way of the Lord to have the myrmidons of power cut off the head of Chartism and leave its poor leaderless body to its own devices."

Owen was glad of some support against the physical-force Chartists—even if it came from a preacher.

The argument raged on as the procession proceeded past locked shops, with the white faces of their middle class owners peering from the upper windows, thankful when they saw the ragged hordes, that their stock had been removed to places of safety.

They passed down the Kennington Road, the police offering no obstruction, and reached the common as a light drizzle began to fall.

Owen Bookbinder looked around him bitterly at the gathering and turned to the preacher, Wragg.

"Where are the 360,000 we were promised, there can be but a quarter of that number?"

"I fear as in the matter of the 5,600,000 signatures to the

petition, it had been necessary to practise a little deception
to keep high the hearts of men."

"Are there not so many signatures, then?"

"The signatures, yes, but not nearly that number of souls
that appended them."

When will the movement realize, thought Owen, that the
only weapons they needed were the truth and their own burning sense of wrong.

Johnson was deep in whispered conversation with the fiery
young man.

"Even with this number it could be effected easily on a
chosen night. An informant at the Chelsea Hospital told me
that when the enrolled Pensioners are not mustered, their arms
are stored almost unprotected in jails, court-houses and lock-
up houses all over the country."

Owen climbed from the car and went to a group that had
gathered around Feargus O'Connor.

"What is the confusion?" he asked a mechanic.

"Mr. Mayne, one of the Commissioners of Police has sent
a message to O'Connor, to desist in the procession or accept
responsibility for the consequences."

"Damn the police," roared Johnson who had followed,
"they'll not stop us now." But his voice was lost in the cheer
that went up as O'Connor rose to his feet.

He was a good speaker, very animated, and soon had the
crowd with him—but Owen unmoved by hysteria detected an
unbalanced note running through the oration. O'Connor
sobbed that he was their father, pleaded that they should
abjure from violence and go to their homes—since the bridges
were guarded and he wished not to make any widows that
day—and promised that the executive committee would present the petition for them. He then collapsed sobbing on to the
shoulder of a friend.

Almost at once the meeting began to break up. The light
rain discouraging many from joining the groups of arguing

men that formed. Owen wandered amongst them in the sea of flattened grass and mud that the men's boots had made of the common.

He spotted two acquaintances of his, Holman Hunt and Millais, both artists who were attempting something of a revolution themselves in paint. He was too dispirited other than to nod and pass on. So this was how the great protest for the people's charter was to end. The way of the physical-force Chartists seemed almost preferable to this miserable, whimpering defeat.

Johnson had already marked out several of the ring-leaders to the plain-clothes police and two of them were following Bookbinder, stopping apparently to listen to the speakers when he stopped, and moving on when he did. It would not be safe to take him until he was clear of the crowd.

Tiredly, Owen found the group he was looking for and pushed his way through to the fierce young man with the flapping epaulettes.

"Johnson's an approver, his men are amongst the crowd."

One part of Owen's mind was always alert for the signs: guile from someone who should have nothing to hide, an over-fed or too clean mechanic, men who held themselves differently because they were afraid or not at home in their environs. The movement pattern of a watcher at a meeting was different to the watched.

By the time the burly men had pushed through the crowd that gathered around them impeding their progress: Owen Bookbinder had gone.

Dyson came up quietly behind the old night watchman, as he stood gaping at the hole in the warehouse wall. Seizing fast hold of his nose, Dyson pushed it quite flat towards the mouth, so almost as to break the gristle of the nose, taking away the man's senses nearly. He let the watchman reel away from him and slipped the life-preserver, a small leaden ball secured around his wrist by a piece of gut, comfortably into the palm of his hand. With an unnecessary force, borne of the morning's frustrating labour, he struck the man senseless.

Spider had put up the job and Dyson swore once again never to embark on a burglary without he set it up himself. They had ascertained that the silk warehouse was to be closed for fear of depredations by the Chartist's rabble and with the connivance of the foreman from the leather warehouse next door—had effected an entry through eight feet of brickwork. They had observed the night watchman depart and had commenced the moment that the Camden Town traffic outside was sufficiently noiseful to cover the sounds of the auger and chisel, only to discover four hours later that their information had been inaccurate and instead of emerging inside the counting house, they were only in the silk warehouse, still separated from the safe by the locked doors of the counting house.

It was at this inopportune moment that the watchman had chosen to return.

"You've done for 'im," said Spider.

"He's still breathing," growled Dyson, making a ball from a piece of lint that had wrapped his tools, and thrusting it into the watchman's mouth as a gag. With his knife he cut a length of cord from his pocket and tied it around the man's head to secure the gag. "I thought the watchman was not to return till the night."

"That's what I was led to understand, Dyson," whined Spider.

Dyson raised his fist with the life-preserver in it and hissed, "Don't call me by name, have you never been out before?"

The only person who could have overheard the conversation, however, was the watchman, who, between his shattered nasal organ and the gag, was slowly expiring for want of breath.

"And I suppose," continued Dyson, "you'd 'ad it on good authority that we'd burrow out in the counting 'ouse. It's a wonder we didn't come out in Camden 'igh Street. Pass me them tools an' let's get on with it."

He selected a cutter from his tools, an instrument with a centre bit stock and two knives, to cut the lock away from the counting house door. There were two locks but in less than twenty minutes, the door swung open. It was an old type of safe in the counting house and would be quite amenable, Dyson believed, to the petter-cutter, which screwed into the keyhole and drilled a hole above it, sufficiently large to get to the wards of the lock. He was considering this when a policeman sprang his rattle outside of the warehouse. Dyson cursed himself, that's what came of working with joskins.* He should have remembered that the watchman would have unpadlocked the iron bar fastened across the patent lock outside and left it hanging. The policeman on his rounds had seen it.

Spider panicked and ran for the entrance; straight into the constable with his truncheon at the ready. Capital, thought Dyson, easing back through the tunnel they had made, that would hold the blighters for a while. He climbed to the roof of the leather warehouse, up a ladder and through a trap that he had previously made note of and—keeping low to avoid being seen from the street—made his way speedily over the rooftops. There was one bad moment when he had to leap a gap to an adjoining house, with the cobbles of an alley far below, but desperation spurred him on. When he found a roof with good cover that seemed to offer several escape routes, Dyson settled down and made himself comfortable. A light rain began to fall but he was not to be discouraged. He had the patience and no desire to be lagged again and did not intend to move until it was dark.

For the first hour or so there was some commotion in the street below and then shouting on the roofs a distance away. But no one approached his roof. That large gap would have

* Country bumpkins.

looked impassable in cold blood to a peeler, thought Dyson. He had entertained doubts himself at the time.

Although, as the long afternoon wore on, there were no further unusual sounds, Dyson was not tempted to leave his hideaway. He knew that down there, somewhere, at least two inconspicuous private clothes policemen were waiting for just such a move. It might be the time, he ruminated, to slip the country, to take that trip to America he had promised himself. There were said to be good pickings on the liners. Spider would be sure to blab and the police would be hot after him.

Dyson, who had once been a clerk in the traffic superintendant's office, amused himself identifying the sounds coming from the extensive buildings of the London & North Western station of Camden; the giant rumble from the Round House where the mighty locomotives were swung on the turn-table, the shriek of the engines blowing off steam before they dropped their fire; and the multifarious sounds from the goods department closer at hand, of the continuous rattle of wagons on rails, the steam cranes hard at work and the lusty cries of the porters.

Before it became quite dark, Dyson cautiously went to the edge of the roof and planned his descent to the ground. He memorized the route—it would be less easy to find when the light had gone. But it suited him well for it would leave him on railway property and he was quite confident of slipping through the receiving sheds undetected at their busiest hours.

At thirty minutes past seven o'clock, Dyson slid over the edge of the roof, down a pipe, across a lower roof, along a wall and dropped to the ground. To any one but an ex-railway man, the furious activities in the goods department would have been completely confusing. The pattern was familiar however to Dyson's eye, there being four streams of goods arriving and being despatched from the two general receiving sheds of the competitive handling agents of Messrs. Pickford and of Messrs. Chaplin and Horne, the labelling of the former being in black the latter in red. Dyson stepped through the maze of criss-crossing lines and turntables with apparent confidence. In this fashion and with an air of urgent business about him, he would not be discovered unless it were by direct confrontation with the railway police. He passed the loaded luggage vans being drawn by horse from the weighbridge to make up the trains—the dumb beasts showing surprising intelligence by leaping from the path of their own thundering load at the last moment before it collided with the stationary van it approached. On to the receiving shed and the great elevated platform lighted by gas, where the clerks sat before their desks with their wheeling porters beneath them. Then to the 'going out' side, which was of more interest to Dyson, where the agent's spring wagons and carts were being loaded. Dyson strode resolutely between the ranks until he reached a spring wagon, its load cleared and about to leave the station. Merging into the shadow behind the wagon, he climbed the back to hide behind the tarpaulin and was straightway rolled through the gates and out to the safety of the badly-lit streets.

8

THE PURSUIT OF PLEASURE

CELANDINE wriggled her small bottom guiltily in Tom Spencer's lap. She could normally get her way with her grandfather when she did that—on those occasions when her mother was not present. For Lucy would never tolerate such indulgent behaviour. A trifling intimacy was a wedge leading to serious vices. The good Christian considered all allowed and wilful sins, whatever be their magnitude, as an offence against her Maker.

"But you must remember when I was born, Grandpa?"

"Ah, I remember it well enough. It were a great nut year, that year."

"They say in the village that 'a great nut year is a great year for bastards', Grandpa."

"Well don' you let your ma 'ear you say that."

"But I had a father, didn't I? You knew him Grandpa. Tell me of him?"

"You ask yer ma, precious, 'baht that."

"Then I'll get down."

"Then get down."

"No, Grandpa," she said, stroking the grey bristle on his chin, making it rasp, "please tell."

"Pray what are you two at?" Lucy Spencer stood in the doorway, her face as hard and stern as an avenging angel. She was dressed in plain black, plain shawl and plainer leghorn bonnet. As she rested her basket of washing, Celandine scrambled down guiltily.

"Mother, please!"

It affrighted Lucy when she observed what a natural inclination the child had to amativeness. A desire to love and be loved, to caress, kiss and fondle. How could she help the child beat down the terrible temptations of a worldly and fleshly existence. Lucy rounded on Tom :

"I'll not have you maul the child about, Father. If you've set the men in the fields their chores—the cabbages yonder need the sight of a hoe."

"Hold your jaw, woman."

"I know what manner of man you are Tom Spencer," whispered Lucy, "be about your business."

Tom reddened and went from the cottage grumbling.

"I'm sorry Mother, please forgive me," sobbed Celandine.

"The Lord only knows how wicked you really are," said Lucy harshly, "only He can forgive you. You must pray for forgiveness to Him. Let us kneel now and pray."

Dutifully Celandine knelt and closed her eyes.

"'O Lord God, deliver us from our sins and let not the day pass without self-denial. Help us in our weakness, for unless we are fighting with ourselves, we are not followers of those, who, through many tribulations shall enter into the Kingdom of God.' Now dry your eyes and brush your hair, you must be at the Rev. Mr. Blackstone's an hour earlier for your lesson this evening. What is it Celandine?" The girl was looking at her strangely.

"I don't care about God, it's your love I seek."

Lucy seized her by the shoulders, but Celandine wrenched away.

"I hate your God, he's too unkind," she screamed as she fled the cottage.

Lord have mercy on me, prayed Celandine, walking along drying her eyes, Please forgive me, you know everything, so you know I didn't mean it. She continued so, virtuously, until she came to the ditch and feeling rather foolish looked up to the heavens. No thunderbolt descended and a low sun smiled down from a clear sky.

God seemed to have forgiven her, she hoped His forgiveness included the falsehood she had told to her mother. She didn't really have to be early to the Rev. Mr. Blackstone.

Whenever Dick was on holiday from the neighbouring Great School, they met in the same spot where he had tried to have his way with her four years ago. He had sworn a fearful oath, however, that he would never try to get her belly up, although on occasion she had almost overcome her fear enough to allow Dick to break his pledge.

She leapt the ditch into the field. They had barley in once more, which should provide a more comfortable trysting place than last season's Swedish turnips.

He was already there waiting.

"Oh, Dick, you look splendid, quite the gentleman."

He had on a pair of dark wool trousers the jacket to which he had folded carefully inside out and laid aside, revealing a brocade waistcoat the colours of which rivalled the ripe golden heads of barley.

Celandine felt abashed. Dick had become a man just since Christmas, while she had only grown upwards and not outwards. She was suddenly ashamed of the patched smock that barely covered her lucifer-stick legs, and the spots that were continually breaking out spoiling her complexion.

Dick swallowed.

"You've grown, Celandine." He went to kiss her lips but she turned her cheek to him, humiliated. She had seen his face, as he looked her up and down, in desperation to find a compliment to turn. She sat down quickly.

As ever, mere contact with Celandine was enough to arouse Dick, and when she tucked her long brown legs beneath her so carelessly that she showed her white belly, he quite thought the front of his new trousers would burst asunder.

Lord help me and enable me resist and overcome this temptation, he prayed silently, and sat down as quickly as she. He made to put his arm around her, but Celandine moved away.

"No, Dick." She sat with her chin on her knees, her huge eyes fixed on him accusingly.

"I wonder that you care to meet me still. You must know many fine ladies now that you have such beautiful clothes."

"That's all flam, Celandine, and you know it. I just wanted you to see me done up like a swell. Father says the waistcoat would suit more a member of the sporting fraternity than a minister's son. I had the deuce of a job persuading him that all monitors must wear such togs—that Dr. Skinner's son had just such a one in red. As for the fine ladies, they keep too tight a rein on us I fear for that, so much so, that many of the older fellows resort to coupling with their fags."

Celandine leaned forward with awakened curiosity, crossing

her legs cobbler fashion. Sometimes Dick wondered if she deliberately set out to tempt him from his chosen path.

"You don't do it with them, do you, Dick?"

"I must say it's not to my fancy, but no more is violent exercise and a cold bath.

"In my first year, the housemaster, Dr. Cornwall, would make the whole dormitory take exercise before lights out, then strip off and rub down briskly with a hard towel. It was quite a sight I can tell you, two rows of white wriggling little boys, agitating themselves furiously while 'Corny' strode betwixt 'em, abjuring them to put away evil thoughts and strive to honour and glorify God.

"To my mind, the only one it calmed down was old 'Corny', by the time lights went out everyone was thoroughly excited. Being green then, I said as much to my father who drove into a furious rage, and in short, wrote straightway to the Board doubting the medical and moral wisdom of such activities.

"'Corny' cut it out next term and we all suffered for it. He never has been quite so good tempered since."

Celandine had blushed furiously at the beginning of this recital and seemed lost in thought when he had finished. Dick was too disconcerted by the manner in which she was rocking to and fro tugging at her toes, to notice her discomfiture.

"What are the papers, Dick, lying on your coat?" she asked, changing the subject.

"Some tracts by a man called Jeremy Bentham that are so full of logical good sense that, I must confess, they could turn my whole world topsy-turvy." He looked doubtfully at Celandine, "But you'll not want to hear of that."

"Yes, please go on Dick," she said absently. She needed time to digest what he had just told her of his father.

Lucy Spencer was bent on educating both her daughter and herself. It was the one flaw that the Rev. Mr. Blackstone could see in an otherwise hard working, God fearing woman. The only talents a gentlewoman required, he considered, were

in reading an improving novel or perhaps to paint a little
watercolour. For a widowed woman of Lucy Spencer's class,
an ability to scrub, wash, cook and sew with suitable humility
were sufficient.

Nevertheless, in return for one day a week's unremitting
labour in his house from Lucy and her unpaid help at bible
classes—she was one of the few village women who could read
and write—he was prepared to give her daughter extra tuition
apart from that she received during the day from the 'School
for Providing a Bible Education to the Children of the Poor'.

Celandine had noticed a change in the Rev. Mr. Blackstone
at these lessons. His manner had softened towards her, and on
occasion he would look at her in a very curious fashion. Of
late when she had arrived flushed from running, he had mentioned several times the very subject Dick had been talking of,
how beneficial a brisk rub down could be after exertion. He
had always returned quickly to the lesson when his wife or the
servant had entered the study. The minister had completely
changed his mind about the treatment it would seem.

Despite her preoccupation she tried to follow what Dick
was saying.

". . . Jeremy Bentham believes that pleasure ought to be
pursued and pain avoided, and his principle of utility means
that principle which approves or disapproves of every action
whatsoever, according to the tendency which it appears to
have to augment or diminish the happiness of the party whose
interest is in question . . . if that party be the community
in general, then the happiness of the community."

The girl looked at him blankly.

"Well, it really means if we are all governed by self interest,
seeking pleasure and avoiding pain, it will be much the best
for everyone."

Celandine suddenly remembered that she had seen Mrs.
Blackstone earlier that morning, leaving for market with her
servant in the dog-cart. They would not be back until sundown.

She got to her feet and kissed Dick quickly.

"I shall be late."

"But Celandine I must speak to you. . . ."

"Shall I see you next week?"

"If you will, but. . . ."

"Until then Dick."

With a wave she was gone through the barley.

Seeking pleasure and avoiding pain, thought Celandine. She had not fully understood all Dick had spoken of, but that was clear enough. Benthamism seemed an admirable philosophy, yet her mother and the church considered all the nice things to be sinful. Could Grandpa be right, that preachers were a hypocritical canting lot? She broke into a run down the hill.

What a damn fool! Dick upbraided himself, he'd bored the girl insufferably showing off to her. No wonder she had run away before he had a chance to ask her to marry him. She was young but he doubted that her mother would have any objection to her marrying someone so much above their station. His father might well have apoplexy and leave away from him what property he could, but at the worst he could not quite cut him off without a shilling. The thing to do was to go down and have it out with him now.

A large pot filled with fresh marsh marigolds stood on the wide window sill, masking Dick from the view of his father inside the cottage. The Rev. Mr. Blackstone sat in a wing-back chair, looking over the top of his fingers pressed together to make a steeple. Between him and the branches of sweet-briar in the fireplace stood the slim boyish figure of Celandine; quite naked but for the towel she was rubbing herself down with.

Face flushed, eyes half closed, Celandine dreamily gave herself to the pleasure of the complete attention and approval of the church in the shape of the Rev. Mr. Blackstone.

Dick turned away trembling from the window, resisting the

impulse to throw the big stone pot into the room. It was quite plain that his father was gratifying his own beastly whims. His father, who had pressed on him with fearful warnings that electric alarum contraption as a protection against spermatorrhea, and even blistered him with red iodine of mercury until he was so lame he could scarce walk. It was not in his heart to blame Celandine but she must be protected. He resolved to clear his mind before taking any positive action. With a logic that was to hold him in such good stead in later years, that seemed to stand aside from the turmoil of his brain, he went quietly for his saddlebags, still unpacked in his room.

One thing was certain, he was not destined for the church or to share the roof of his father.

Without malice and only sadness, Dick first rode over to see Lucy Spencer. With this unpleasant duty completed he went on to the 'George' at Wickham where he could take the train to London. It wasn't until he was comfortably ensconced alone in a first class railway carriage with his saddlebags next to him, that he allowed the tears to roll down his face. Despite the pain in his heart his mind was quite resolved.

He would seek an audience with Superintendant Pearce— who was so much in the papers—at Scotland Yard, and try to enrol in the New Police. Dick found that he hated his father and all that he stood for with an undying hatred; but that he was still desperately in love with Celandine.

9

PUFFING BILLY

THE clouds gathered at the edge of the sea in the autumn afternoon, hanging down in judges' wigs, heavy with the intent

of serious business. Slowly the perky livery of the little train—
yellow ochre tinged with orange chrome in contrast to bruns-
wick green—muted in the fading light and a last ray of sunshine flashed from the highly polished Etruscan brass funnel.
Shrieking with protest, irritably dropping fire from its box,
impatiently grinding sparks from its black iron wheels—the
'Sharpie' locomotive pulled up the gradient, and sent smoke
and cinders racing back over the carriages.

The navvy, sharing the open-sided carriage with Celandine,
looked out at the first gusts of rain—his blackened, down-
turned clay pipe thrusting into the wind roared, sizzled and
belched out smoke and streaks of orange, in unconscious emulation of the fiery little engine.

It was the first opportunity that Celandine had of studying
the man since she had boarded the train at Lancing and her
mother had placed her in care of the tongue-clacking apple-
cheeked country woman and her brood of five. Celandine's
senses had been fully occupied with the tugging children—
screaming from the eldest boy's spiteful pinches—and the
over-riding chatter of their mother, who, without a pause to
rest her tongue, boxed a small ear soundly whenever one came
within range. The blow invariably landed on an injured party
only serving to redouble the tumult.

The family had got down at Holland Road Halt, the far-
mer's wife shouting advice long after they were out of earshot, and left Celandine alone with the big man. He was
built like an oak, and despite his obvious strength and out-
landish dress there was something reassuring about him. He
wore a white upturned felt hat, and a square-cut velveteen
coat over a red plush waistcoat. Moleskin trousers covered his
stout legs, on the end of which were the largest pair of ankle-
jacks with hobnails Celandine had ever seen—one black and
one brown. By his side was a bundle wrapped in red- and
white-spotted silk, and a gallon stone bottle of gin.

Slowly the clay pipe, set in the black moustache, turned

out of the wind, and Celandine fancied she could see distant
horizons in his clear grey eyes. He took the pipe from his
mouth, showing even white teeth.

"They calls me, Puffing Billy, ma'am."

"For a reason not hard to look for I'll be bound," laughed
Celandine. "I'm Celandine Spencer."

"That's a pretty enough name that suits you well, ma'am."
He puffed at his pipe and nodded seriously for a moment.
"But beggin' yer pardon, ma'am, I ain't just called so for the
obvious reason. There ain't many of us 'navveys' as goes by
our proper handles, there's men called by their origins like
Yorkey Tom, Brummagen Dick and Yankee Harry; or by the
shape of their persons such as Punch, Peggy or Wingy; and
some like Swaddling* Jim, named quite contrary, since he never
could stand preachers or the Irish; and others as earns their
nicknames. The latter's how I came by 'Puffing Billy', but it's
a story as I could 'ardly recount to a young lady like yerself."

Celandine was at once flattered that he should call her
ma'am and treat her like a grown-up, and disappointed that
he would not finish the tale for her. She resolved to try and
appear more worldly.

"Is it spiritous liquor that you have handy in that bottle, Mr.
Puffing Billy?" she asked casually—as though fully acquainted
with the demon drink.

"Indeed it is, ma'am. There's more liquor passed through
this bottle than ever came out of the Woodhead tunnel. She's
more constant than any wife, sticking by me and giving solace
on many a tramp for work. If I ever needs reproach her for
running dry after a long randy, why then, next pay-day is
soon around and I seize her pretty neck and she presents her
wet lips to me once more."

Concealing her disquiet at the unexpected turn the conversation had taken, Celandine wondered that for such a
terrible sinner he was so singularly unashamed.

* Swaddler: an itinerant Irish preacher.

"Might I take a small sip? I find it can be quite efficacious against the cold on a long journey like this," she lied—having only ever been allowed a glass of porter when she was unwell or with her meal on Sunday.

There were no seats in the carriage and Puffing Billy needed just such an excuse to stumble across the rocking boards and join Celandine where she squatted in a corner.

"Well, if that ain't downright hard of me to taunt you so and not offer you a little."

One great arm came around her thin shoulders and the other with the heavy bottle hefted across it, proffered her the drink.

Celandine took a deep draught. "Sweet Jesus," she choked out. Tears came to her eyes, her throat burned as though she had been poisoned. "I needed that," she gasped.

"Well taken, my dear," laughed Puffing Billy. "It'll do you no harm to lay in some stock." He patted her back gently, and her head snapped forward violently with each pat until Celandine was considerably relieved when he lifted the bottle for himself. She now knew about the demon drink; it was a thousand fiery devils clawing through one's entrails. It did, she observed after a moment, prove wonderfully resistant to the wind and rain beating in through the open sides of the carriage. Nevertheless, it seemed prudent, considering this huge fellow who had passed so easily from 'ma'am' to 'my dear', to tuck her long skirts around her new boots.

Celandine had never thought to possess so many fine clothes. Due to the providence of her mother, her box on the roof of the carriage contained one print dress, one black dress, caps, a white and grey apron, underclothes and a spare pair of boots.

The Rev. Mr. Blackstone was not yet aware that his indulgence with Celandine had been observed, nor that his son leaving home and Celandine being sent into service were not only connected but were a direct result of that indulgence. His horror, had he known to the extent to which he had undermined Lucy's faith in the will of God, would only have been exceeded by the knowledge of what Lucy had in mind for him in the future. But Lucy had confided in no one, only telling Celandine that it was time she had her morals attended to, and to that end, was being sent a considerable distance to the home of the Honourable Mr. Joseph Arkwright, where she would take up the post of under housemaid at ten pounds the year—providing her own tea.

Puffing Billy had the fullest intention of attending to Celandine's morals but not in the manner that her mother had in mind. Celandine squealed as he lifted her on to his lap, quite unable to resist him or the gin that was put to her lips.

Breathlessly she wiped her mouth. What encouragement, she wondered, had she given, to make him treat her so. It wasn't that she didn't like him, for she did, but he was very familiar on such a slight acquaintance.

"Kindly put me down, sir," she protested, "I would return to my place."

"It ain't in my way to see a young lady drown, and if you'll look for yerself you'll see a mess of water where you were sitting."

There's a deal of truth in what he said, thought Celandine. The holes bored in the floor of the carriage serving to always keep cool the feet of the travellers, were not always so effective in their role of draining away the rain, and a large puddle had been forming beneath her. It was becoming increasingly difficult to gather her thoughts, but it seemed to her that she had been unduly harsh with him when he had only been thinking of her comfort.

"So why not stay for the nonce, and take another drain of gin."

It would have been heartless to refuse.

"That's right, my dear, what you need is your little boiler stoked up. Why! you feel as cold as a tally keeper's heart."

Celandine's head had fallen back on Puffing Billy's shoulder, her bonnet all awry. A most unusual occurrence was taking place. She was staring at the end of Puffing Billy's pipe, which would unaccountably become two pipes and then revert back to one. The puffs of smoke, or occasionally two puffs, increased in tempo exactly coinciding with the rhythm of Puffing Billy's big hand restoring her circulation. It was really a very soothing sensation. How good it was to find someone who cared enough to show such kindness to her, and how unentitled she had been to doubt his motives. If he was a sinner it could only be his circumstances that had made him so. A jolting began to run through the carriages, breaking up the spell-binding rhythm. Of a sudden she became aware that she was being soothed beneath her clothes, the clay pipe came sharply into focus, and with a frightening intuition Celandine deduced why Puffing Billy was so called.

As the train juddered to a halt, the carriage gave one final terrific jolt, throwing her off her perch on to the wet boards. They had arrived at Brighton Station.

The big navvy picked her up philosophically.

"They do say, ma'am, that the joy is in the travelling and not in the arrivin' and I wouldn't be one to argue wiv that."

Despite his blurred vision, 'Old Jones' the coachman picked out Celandine easily enough from the travellers. The gentlefolk from the first and second class carriages had already passed through the booking hall, he wasn't looking for her there. They were followed by persons of an inferior type from the third class, all men—farmers and a sprinkling of clerks. The fourth class were still straggling down the promenade; a seed seller with two trays, cakes, sweetmeats and fruit in one tray and seeds in the other; an old 'Christ-killer' shuffling along with his head down and then the bit of a girl he had been sent for. He who had once been crack dragsman to the Marquis of Sligo, with his Lordship up on the box forever taking the reins from him. Now he was reduced to this young madam, ladying it along with some great fancyman of a navvy carrying her box on his shoulder. Mrs. Saward would need teach this young limb her place.

"Spencer?"

"Yes, sir."

What could be seen of his leathery face, between the low crowned hat and the high collar of his multiple caped ulster, looked down at her with contempt.

"Follow me, girl." Ignoring Puffing Billy, and tracing an erratic course, rather as though from so much coaching he had never completely acquired the use of his land-legs, he led the way into the hall.

"Oy! Flat 'at," shouted Billy after him through a furious cloud of smoke, "I 'opes you can lay a straighter track in your conveyance than you're takin' nah."

"Hush!" whispered Celandine, whose gait was just as un-steady as Old Jones. She was completely overawed by David Mocatta's Italianate palace of steam that seemed to float hazily around her—peopled with bewhiskered gentlemen in tall silk hats and elegant bonnetted ladies, busked tightly in the middle between their formidable bosoms and many layered skirts. There was nothing like this to compare in the country.

"Mark my words, ma'am, 'e's a mean 'ound of a man, the sort t'cock his leg at you one tick and cringe down t'lick the boots of his master the next."

"Do be quiet, Mr. Puffing Billy, you'll cost me my position."

"That might well be a good riddance, it's no way t'live as a slave to another, you'd do better to join me on the tramp and share my shanty. You ain't never gonna be 'appy, toadying to the likes of 'im."

It was true, thought Celandine, that she certainly felt very much out of place. She wasn't used to skirts around her ankles and her boots squeaked. One day she promised herself she would have clothes like these fine ladies.

They pushed out into the pelting rain on to the uncovered

court, between the waiting carriages, broughams and hansom cabs—their drivers cursing and jockeying fiercely for position.

An 'ound was he, thought Old Jones, slave was he, he'd show 'em in a trice that they'd underestimated his capabilities as much as they 'ad 'is 'earing.

A humble wagonette stood at the edge of the court, dangerously close to a wall dropping sheerly down to the town. Old Jones climbed to the seat without a word.

Puffing Billy lifted the box into the back and turned to the girl: "If yer should change your mind, I might give up a navvying and settle down wiv a shop or public house."

After a brief moment of panic when she realized that she would have no friend at all when he was gone, Celandine took his hand and shook her head.

"Thank you, Mr. Puffing Billy. It was well meant, but I shall be all right now. Good-bye." He lifted her up next to the driver who straightway whipped up the horses and they were off, nearly catching Puffing Billy beneath the wheels and almost pitching Celandine on to the horses. Old Jones pulled viciously on the reins as they skeltered through the gates, slewing the wagonette around in a half circle. Celandine held on for dear life and caught her breath, glimpsing, for a moment, Brighton spread beneath them pierced with church spires and in the watery distance a post-mill—then they were plunging down the hill in a sea of mud.

10

IN MRS. ARKWRIGHT'S SERVICE

THE sun was respectfully glancing off the gleaming windows, burnishing the polished doorknobs and drying the whitened steps of the pleasant Regency Crescent—when Celandine was dropped as unceremoniously on the wet pavements as a sack of coal.

The net curtains behind the windows quivered in irritated sympathy down the crescent and a worried face, topped by a bobbinet cap with long flowing ribbons, appeared behind the area railings. Like an unsightly pile of coals, Celandine was to be shovelled swiftly out of sight.

"Quick, come down 'ere."

The girl who helped Celandine pull her box down the area steps was smallish and pretty enough, with brown eyes as bright as two buttons, that flashed hither and thither down the crescent to see who was about. Celandine judged her to be around sixteen years of age.

At last they stood with her box in a large flagged kitchen smelling damply of mould, the walls as wet as the pavement outside, despite the big roaring range.

"You're Spencer, ain't you? I'm Maudie Bates, the housemaid so you'll be helping me." She perked her dark head on one side as cockily as any sparrow. "Oh my, ain't you a sight."

Celandine's bonnet that had looked so smart that morning, hung wet and bedraggled around her head, dripping clean streaks down her travel-grimed cheeks. Her print dress, stained and smutted from the railway carriage, dripped in its turn on to the kitchen floor. Celandine giggled, she felt half drunk.

"What pray is this wretched creature doing in my kitchen?" The cook, standing in the doorway, spoke in a very creditable imitation of her mistress. With her short arms folded over a prodigious bosom, her pale blue eyes glinting behind steel spectacles—she presented a frightening aspect, only relieved by the round red nose that the spectacles rested upon.

"It's Spencer come, Mrs. Saward."

"Send her away, I'll not have filthy vagrants in the house, she's more than likely the bearer of all manner of putrid contagions."

The thought of being cast on to the streets of a strange town terrified Celandine.

"I hold a letter from Mrs. Arkwright, if it please you, ma'am."

"Mrs. Arkwright," pronounced the cook, seemingly progressing into a furious rage which had its due effect on her diction, "knows as 'ow I'm used to certain standards in the 'ouseholds where I'm employed. In her absence I'm not prepared to engage no dirty infested brats, so be off with you."

"That's Mrs. Arkwright's sentiments exactly, Spencer," said Maudie, "she'd see at a glance that you'd never make no servant girl."

Celandine looked reproachfully at Maudie. She hadn't expected attack from that quarter, for a while she had thought that they were going to become friends. Surprisingly the girl winked back at her.

"Sometimes," said Mrs. Saward, thoughtfully, "I think Mrs. Arkwright is too 'asty. Let's 'ave a look at'cher." She came closer in examination and her small red nose wrinkled up. "You smell, girl, you've got a nasty smell."

Celandine was close to tears.

"I'm truly sorry, Mrs. Saward, but the motion of the wagonette was so violent that I had an attack of nausea."

What approached the most pleasant expression Celandine had yet seen, passed across the woman's face.

"You had an attack of nausea?"

"Yes, ma'am."

"In Old Jones' wagonette."

"Yes, ma'am."

"Ho!" said Mrs. Saward. Celandine detected a small advantage here.

"I vomited down Mr. Jones, ma'am."

"Ho! Ho! Ho!" said Mrs. Saward. "Ho! Ho! Ha! Ha! Ho! Hooooooh!"

Her good humour ended in a scream of pain and she

clutched a hand to one fat cheek. "Oh Lor', Oh quick, the whisky!"

Maudie ran to one of the cupboards and searched at the back. "It's that old tooth again is it Mrs. Saward?" She found the bottle and passed it to the cook who took two big swigs.

Mrs. Saward breathed heavily and put down the bottle, looking with fury at Celandine as the cause of her discomfort.

"We'll make a respectable servant out of you, Spencer. But until you're a fitting person for my kitchen you'll sleep and eat in the wash house with the boot-boy. Is that understood?"

"Yes, ma'am." Celandine only knew with her head spinning, that she had a reprieve.

"But first we'll scrape that lice and vomit from you. Take her out to the wash house, Bates!"

They trooped out to the back door with Mrs. Saward bringing up the rear, stowing the bottle away in an apron pocket.

The boot-boy had fallen asleep on the work bench, his spiky red head on a half-cleaned meat cover, the snot running into the corner of his open mouth and down one freckled cheek. Despite the surprising forbearance of the gentle cuff with which the cook awoke him—he immediately burst into tears.

"Stop snivelling boy!" she said shortly, "and bring me water from the copper."

Frowning, Maudie helped the girl off with her wet soiled clothes. Celandine climbed obediently up on the table and into the tub of hot suds. Mrs. Saward's strong, plump hand pushed the girl under water roughly and dragged her out again by the hairs of her head.

"All respectable servants," she gritted, "must develop 'abits of cleanliness."

Her eyes red from the coarse soap, Celandine accepted the penance that she must endure, and her rising guilt matched her anguish, as the cook pulled her cruelly to her feet.

c

Maudie winced as the woman soaped a scrubbing brush and scraped it harshly across Celandine's thin back. Why did not the girl cry out? Maudie was horrified at the sore red weals appearing on the white skin. It was as though she were witnessing some theatrical representation in which she took no part and could not prevent.

The boy, unwittingly caught in the concerted gaze of the two protagonists, had stopped crying. Despite the distant shocked horror on Celandine's face and the feat of challenging Mrs. Saward's steely glare that shrivelled blindly at him, his eye fastened involuntarily on Celandine's immature sex. The boy's sole preoccupation—apart from sleeping—being to position himself advantageously in the area as ladies descended their carriages; or beneath steps or stairs where the female servants were at work, in order to observe how nice and curious they were made beneath their clothes.

Celandine saw only the flat yellow eyes from her nightmares and welcomed with a fierce joy the birch on her small buttocks and the tearing of skin and the suds of blood that poured down her trembling legs washing away the guilt.

"Stop!" screamed Maudie. She had to pull the large woman away before she could break up the awful tableau.

Mrs. Saward looked uncomprehendingly at the bloodied brush for a moment. "Whatsoever thy hand findeth to do, do it with all thy might," she muttered, shaking her head as if to clear it.

"Just see that you stay clean and respectable."

The boy, his jaw hanging open, looked after her and wiped his nose with the back of his hand.

When Mrs. Arkwright returned from town to her residence in Brighton, with her family, a galvanic shock ran through the house, which made itself felt to its farthest extremities, namely the wash house where Celandine and the boy were scouring into brightness the big iron kitchen untensils.

The girl had been up since five. She had rekindled the range, opened the shutters, taken hot water to the cook's bedroom, taken up coals to the empty bedrooms and laid and lit fires all over the house in preparation for the family's return. Then she had helped Maudie cook the breakfast for the servants and taken her own and the boy's breakfast out to the wash house to eat. After that she had helped with the washing-up, swept, dusted and polished in the hall and washed down the outside steps while Maudie was engaged in the sitting- and dining-rooms. Together they had taken fresh linen from before the fire, where they had been airing, up to the bedrooms, first turning the mattresses before they made the beds, and after, laying warming pans between the sheets.

At eleven o'clock when the carriage drew up outside and Maudie tidied herself for the homecoming, Celandine was banished to the wash house. She was fit to clean the house; but not to sully it with her presence when its owners were about.

In many households an insignificant under-maid might have escaped notice, but not in the home of Mrs. Amy Arkwright. She was singular amongst her contemporaries in that she was concerned for the welfare of her servants as well as for the manner in which her home was run.

Nanny had taken the children up to the nursery straightway and Mr. Arkwright, muttering of duties he must attend to, went to the library. The servants had but five minutes repose, whilst Mrs. Arkwright caught her breath in the dining-room—sipping a glass of port, her eagle critical eye running over the brasses and looking for a fault in the sparkling dome on the wax fruit—when the call went out that 'Mistress would see the new gal'.

Mrs. Arkwright was a plain shapeless woman with a large nose and teeth that projected. Perhaps it was her lack of good looks that had encouraged her to develop the many other qualities that she undoubtedly had.

Her father, a baronet with most of his land in Canada, had a large family of boys and one daughter in Amy. She had almost despaired of marriage when their fortunes improved with the sale of large tracts of their Canadian lands for Railways. Coincident with the airing abroad of the rumour, that there was now money in the family, came the handsome Dundreary whiskers of the youngest son of Viscount Scraye, the Honourable Joseph Arkwright. She was considerably older than he, and had—as he admitted to himself—a face very much like a horse. But his legacy was squandered as a young man, largely on women, and he was reduced to £500 per annum. He got £1,000 per annum by her, and had never been let forget it.

Amy was soon disabused of his silky moustache, and after the birth of their son Montague seven years ago, had been quite content to reign alone in the big matrimonial bed whilst her husband, when he was home, used the dressing-room. Their daughter, Melissa, five years old, had been an unfortunate mishap when Arkwright had arrived home so well lushed one night that he had been under the misapprehension that Amy was Florrie, a gay woman of his acquaintance, from the Argyll Rooms. After her initial disappointment that love had not returned to their marriage, Amy locked her bedroom door at night and put renewed energy into running her home, or as cook put it, 'interferin' in the 'ouse'. To the outside world, however, they preserved the impregnable respectable front of a happy marriage.

Celandine took a quick look in the hall mirror before she approached the dining-room. She had taken particular care with her appearance that morning, brushing her rather dull fair hair until it shone, and with Maudie's help, pulled it back tightly from a central parting into a neat bun, beneath a clean cap. She had on her best print dress and had left her grey working apron in the wash house. Even the red spots that she was continually afflicted with, seemed less virulent on her scrubbed face, she considered. Celandine plucked up her courage and knocked on the door.

"And who are you, pray?" asked Mrs. Arkwright not unkindly.

"I'm Spencer, ma'am."

Mrs. Arkwright was favourably impressed with what she saw. The girl seemed clean and suitably humble, slim enough that she wouldn't eat her out of house and home, and yet not so slight that she couldn't handle a mattress. In any event she always preferred a plain girl for hard work and not to get into mischief.

"I hope you realize child, that this is a very fine opening. You must work hard, resist temptation, and not waste the time that belongs to another."

"Yes, ma'am."

"God's good work can be done as well in the kitchen as in church. Do you say your prayers, Spencer?"

"Indeed I do, ma'am."

"Well I hope you know the proper way, which is kneeling by your bed last thing at night, and not like some, lying in comfort under the covers. Where have they put you, child?"

"In the wash house, ma'am."

"In the wash house!" boomed Mrs. Arkwright, rising from her seat so ominously that Celandine backed away.

"Alone with that odious boy?"

Celandine nodded, panic stricken.

"Fetch me Mrs. Saward, this very instant."

The girl fled the room and returned some minutes later following the equally irate cook.

"I was hinterruped Mum, in making the dinner, which I do expect is now all cinders." Her hair stood frizzed out from her head as though it had come fresh from the oven, and the sweat rolled in great rivulets on either side of her button nose—meriting an attention for its glowing colour, quite disproportionate to its size.

"Mrs. Saward," said Mrs. Arkwright icily, "I did expect you to be engaged in that task. This is, however, a matter that will not wait. What, in Heaven's name could have prompted you to put Spencer to sleep with the boy in the wash house?"

"She's dirty," said the cook, wiping her spectacles—that away from the heat of the kitchen had misted up—and looking blankly at Celandine's neat appearance, added, "She's got dirty 'abits."

Mrs. Arkwright twitched her large nostrils and sniffed the air that was becoming increasingly laden with the fumes of whisky.

"She appears perfectly clean to me, and her habits shall be my responsibility, as," she added darkly, "are those of the whole household. Spencer, you shall be moved into the house. Now leave us. Mrs. Saward and I would speak alone."

Celandine closed the door behind her and was about to bend to the keyhole to hear what was passing between the two women, when the door to the library opened and Mr. Arkwright came into the hall.

He was of medium height, with black silky hair and whiskers. Quite handsome in a tired sort of way, judged Celandine, for an old man of thirty or so. He came straight to her.

"What's your name, my dear?" His eyes were a startlingly brilliant blue. She curtseyed:

"Celandine . . . I mean Spencer, sir," and felt herself blushing. Gently he took her chin between his thumb and forefinger, tilting her face up to him.

"Well, Spencer, would you like to . . ." he hesitated for a moment, "open the door for me?"

The girl flew to the front door, and taking his cane from the stand, Mr. Arkwright walked by her without another word.

Celandine waited in the kitchen for the end of the interview, with mixed feelings. She hardly knew what to make of Mr. Arkwright though he seemed a nice gentleman. She felt that

Mrs. Arkwright quite liked her, but was sure that the cook would be in a fury when she returned. But when she did so, Mrs. Saward acted almost as though they were confidants.

"As if I'd take a drink, except in a medicinal way. Me what reads the scriptures and 'as signed the pledge. Made me old tooth ache more than ever she 'as."

Recognizing the cue, Celandine rummaged in the cupboard until she found the whisky bottle. She was almost sure it was tears running down the cook's face and not perspiration from the heat.

"You're not a bad girl," said the Cook. "Not a vain little body like that Maudie." Now the tears were plainly running over Mrs. Saward's fat cheeks, thick and fast. "Ain't it the truth though, 'appiness is only compatible wiv goodness."

Bertram Brown, the footman, renamed more suitably Thomas by Mrs. Arkwright, took a draught of beer and sighed with satisfaction.

"For all their fancy ways in London, Mrs. Saward, they haven't the way of preparing victuals like that."

"Thank the Lord," muttered Lottie Simpkins the pasty-faced, dumpy nursemaid.

"Undoubtedly the best thing out," he concluded.

"Better out than in," whispered Lottie. Maudie stifled a giggle and Thomas frowned at the girls. Mrs. Saward, however, at the far end of the kitchen table, accepted the flattery smugly.

"I must say it brings out the best in me—to cook for a real man again."

This last was a slur at Old Jones, his head buried in his food, who had not been away with the family.

"Indeed, just so." murmured the footman. They smiled at each other with mutual satisfaction. Thomas flicked an imaginary speck of dust from his sky blue waistcoat. He knew that he was a considerable asset to the household. There was not another footman in the crescent who could match his extensive calves, and but for being a few inches short of six foot, would have held a vastly superior position with a Duke at least, and in fact had done so until the unfortunate matter of the Duchess of Scraye's chamber maid.

Thomas started as Lottie, uncannily, seemed to pick up somewhat of his thoughts, and said, as innocent as pie:

"Don't you miss her ladyship's maid, Mr. Brown? I fancied she was quite stuck on you."

How much did the jade know? For the nonce, Thomas was stuck for words. But not Mrs. Saward.

"Either eat with your charges, or mind your manners, Simpkins. In my kitchen, lower servants will speak when spoken to." She rose, as grandly as her bulk would allow, to her feet. "Come, Mr. Brown, we shall repair to my room. Spencer shall bring us the pudding there."

Celandine hurriedly cleared the table and set out the plates for the pudding. The family had eaten long ago; the waxed fruit was back in the centre of the dining-room table and a noise like a temporarily quiescent volcano trembled from Mrs. Arkwright's capacious nostrils as she reclined asleep on the horsehair sofa. When the girl had finished serving the servants, she would be free to feed the boy and Charlie the simpleminded fellow who helped in the garden and stables—and to eat for herself.

"Mind your manners," mimicked Lottie when Mrs. Saward had gone. "I'll swing for her one day, the hoity-toity old faggot. Don't stand looking at me so stupid, Spencer. Hurry along with the pudding. I must look to my charges."

"Such an unselfish concern for the welfare of the children, goes beyond the beyonds," said Maudie, quite straight-faced. "Tell me? How fare the sweet souls?"

"The little dears were quite worn out from their early rising and exhausting journey, so I put them to bed."

"Ah! I thought you might have."

"Sleep is very good for them."

"Oh! Indeed."

"And, incapacitating."

"Quite!"

"In truth, I think I shall join my little sweethearts in the land of Nod, if Spencer ever sees her way to serving the pudding."

At this, both girls broke down helplessly into laughter, holding on to each other for support.

Celandine thought that they were very rude to Mrs. Saward behind her back, who, despite her somewhat erratic temper, brought about by her nagging tooth, was a good Christian and had her duty to do in checking the servants. For the life of her Celandine could see nothing so humorous in the fact that the children were asleep.

11

MOTHER'S BLESSING

THE weeks sped swiftly by for Celandine, and although Thomas now helped with the heavy coals, there was very much more work for her with the family at home, than heretofore. When Mrs. Arkwright's day started, reading the family bible to her sleepy children and the servants before breakfast, Mr. Arkwright was just sipping his morning chocolate between the pillows—and Celandine had already been at work for three hours. But the girl was energetic and anxious to improve herself, readily learning the ways of the household. She learnt to take away the slops early in the morning, discreetly, although on one occasion she was so startled to find Mr. Arkwright's bleary eye fixed on her from beneath the bed-clothes that she had nearly dropped the chamber pot. She learnt to remove her working apron, tidy her hair and take the smudges from her cheeks on the way to answering the front door and to scrub, clean and polish, yet still keep her finger nails in condition to serve at table. And there was no opportunity of flagging if she had so desired—not with Mrs. Arkwright and her clanking basket of keys, bustling everywhere about the house anxious to inculcate habits of industry and frugality. Directing her in the best way to make blacking, that it was heresy to lay soap in a wet dish, that it was considered indelicate to mention the bugs one disposed of when turning the mattresses. So fully occupied were all her waking hours that she had no time to be unhappy. Before she fell asleep at night, alone in the attic room above the master bedroom, she followed Mrs. Arkwright's final instructions for the day : kneeling on the cold oil-cloth, she thanked God for the food in her belly and a roof over her head, and she was troubled no more by bad dreams.

After six weeks, she had been but once outside the house, when she had accompanied the family to church in place of Maudie, who had been given a special dispensation to visit her sick aunt at Rottingdean. She had felt quite the lady in her black straw bonnet and the black cloak that Mrs. Arkwright had supplied for the occasion—until she had seen the ladies in their fine clothes taking their places in the family pews.

This afternoon, it was a Saturday, she was to be allowed to accompany Maudie to visit her aunt, who was still poorly. Mrs. Arkwright was out on a visit and would not be back till late and whether it was a reward for her industry—the mistress had complimented her on her attention to her duties and even Mrs. Saward had conceded that she was a 'fair worker' —or the fact that the cook had finally had her tooth drawn, Celandine did not know, but she was to have the afternoon off. The mid-day meal was over and her last task was to carry hot water upstairs to Lottie, who had called for it in the nursery.

Both the nursemaid and the little boy were red in the face when Celandine entered the room. The one from fury and the other from crying.

"The little bleeder won't sleep," whispered Lottie, "but he must and will. I thought a warm bath might soothe him." A tub with cold water stood on the nursery floor.

Celandine had gathered from Maudie that the nursemaid was infected with 'scarlet fever', and though Lottie might be bound for an appointment with one of her soldier lovers, one could scarce blame the child for not wishing to sleep at three o'clock of the day.

"See how peaceful your sister is, Monty, and you make yourself a bother and won't take the draught."

"I'll not take it! Lottie, I'll not! I'll not! It makes me so dizzy and tired."

"Come then little goose, Lottie will make you feel more comfortable," said the nursemaid trying new tactics.

Celandine poured the kettles of boiling water into the tub whilst Lottie took Monty from the bed and lifted his long flannel petticoat over his head.

"There," she cooed, "isn't that better?" She sat him in the warm water. "Look I'll play with little Willy Winkie, you like that don't you?"

Indeed he appeared to, thought Celandine, a smile spread across his tear-stained face but still he shook his head from side to side.

"Now you'll drink your draught for Lottie, won't you?"

The little boy grinned still shaking his head.

"You shall," cried Lottie viciously—and the child roared, "or I'll pull it clean off. Quick! the tumbler there, Spencer."

Celandine wondered that the nursemaid could hold on to the little slippery thing in the threshing water. Reluctantly she held the tumbler and Monty, between sobs and gasps, drank it down. Only then did Lottie release him. Half drying the boy roughly with a towel, she pulled his petticoat on and put him back in bed next to the sleeping Melissa. Monty held himself and sobbed:

"I shall tell Papa."

"You squeak to the Master, and I'll tell him how you're always playing with yourself. How would you like that?"

The boy said no more.

Celandine was shocked to see a little boy treated so. It seemed very terrible.

"What was in the medicine?"

"I know not," answered the nursemaid carelessly, "some poppy-juice or other I imagine, a druggist gentleman friend makes it for me. It costs but a few pence but is most efficacious in giving me peace from the wretches."

"It is you that is a wretch, Lottie," said Celandine heatedly, "the vilest creatures to misuse them so. How can you be so savage?"

Lottie was taken aback, she had not seen this spirit in the girl before. "'Tis none of your affair, Celandine Spencer, nor are you run ragged by the young limbs, so you've no cause to go on this gate."

"I care not whose affair it is, you'll cease to dose the children or the mistress shall hear of it."

The nursemaid laughed. "And do you think the Missus cares, so long as she is not troubled."

"We shall see," said Celandine, picking up her kettles and sweeping out. The girl went thoughtfully to the kitchen and removed her apron. Surely Mrs. Arkwright was not aware of how her children were treated. Celandine remembered overhearing her instruct Lottie that until Montgomery was moved from the nursery, she was on no account to let the children see each other unclothed or expose themselves in any natural function. She could not know that Monty was so abused—should she be aware of the sleeping draught.

Celandine would not have the courage to face Mrs. Arkwright, but something must be done. She shuddered, supposing the children didn't wake up one fine morning? Perhaps if she dropped a hint to Mrs. Saward, she might frighten Lottie into better ways. Celandine hesitated outside the cook's parlour. She was ready to leave now and should have been gone but for this. It would be difficult to bring up the subject with the cook, who seemed to be so unworldly, intent only on the scriptures and her kitchen. The girl resolved to tell Mrs. Saward that she was about to leave and mention that Mrs. Arkwright's draught had worked a treat with the children. Gently Celandine knocked on the door.

There was no reply. The cook could be asleep after her lunch, if so she would not disturb her. Quietly Celandine turned the knob and looked around the door. The girl was so astounded by what she saw, that for a moment she could not comprehend it, and when she had done so—could hardly believe it.

Between the bows of Madras muslin decently swathing its curved legs, and the all enveloping bulk of Mrs. Saward— the ottoman on which the latter lay was almost lost from view. Mrs. Saward's own limbs were less modestly concealed : her stockings hanging down from mountainous legs set firmly on either side of the sofa. Mrs. Saward's petticoats and dress were thrown over her face while the boot boy's spiky red head was buried in the enormous flesh overflowing from the whale bone plateau of her corset, his thin buttocks working with an industry between her huge thighs, with which Celandine would not have credited him.

Softly she closed the door. It seemed hardly the moment to consult Mrs. Saward on a matter of household deportment. In truth she had good reason to doubt the cook's judgement in such matters henceforth. There seemed no end to disillusion and falseness. Grown up people speechified in one direction and then acted in a totally different manner that was very puzzling. Celandine decided to seek Maudie's advice as soon as they had a moment alone together during the visit to the sick aunt at Rottingdean.

12

THESE MODERN TIMES

WHEN the group of companies that Billy Miles had built up burst one after another like so many bubbles, thousands of small investors lost their life savings, whole families were thrown on the street, many wretches committed suicide rather than accept the reduced state of life the loss of their fortunes had brought them to, some started life anew, determined to repay their debts, others fled the country and snubbed their noses at their creditors.

Billy Miles survived it all with his huge fortune intact, and it was very generally said in the city about this time, that if only his advice had been called upon, the companies could have survived the storm.

There were just a few—whose voices were never raised—believing the man to be a thief and a swindler. But what accusations could be brought against the financier, when the books showed that at the time of his resignation as manager a few years before, all of his companies had been in good order?

The original Buildings Trust and Beacon Permanent Building Society had developed under Billy's tutelage to a dozen or so companies and two Joint-stock banks. He had invented inter-company finance. It was true that huge interest-free loans had been floated to companies outside of the group of which Billy was now manager, but the loans had long since been repaid. Certain holdings had been transferred at what could be considered nominal sums; yet it was manifestly clear that overtrading on baseless credit and false proclamations of prosperity supported by deceitful reports, had only occurred since he had resigned from the companies.

Many of the nobility sought his advice on extricating themselves from their difficulties in this crisis. Such countenance was given to him by society, that there was talk of him being taken up as a Member of Parliament—or even that he should be elevated to the peerage. At a time when the prerequisites for the latter honour were said to be £10,000 a year and a country estate—William Miles Esq. was eminently suitable.

One fine afternoon, Billy Miles sat in Lord Musgrave the Marquis of Marlow's pleasant house in Regent's Park, outlining a plan to alleviate the distress into which the crisis had plunged that representative of an ancient lineage.

"The family is nigh on ruin," interrupted young Freddy, hotly, "yet you suggest we make everything straight by inviting all London down to Marlow Hall. I ain't no financier, sir, but I fear you have taken leave of your senses."

"It'd save a deal of trouble if you'd allow me to finish, my Lord," said Billy to the Marquis' eldest son.

"Keep a still tongue in yer head, Freddy," snarled the old Marquis, "or you can leave the room. You ain't into your property yet."

It was an empty threat if that was intended, hampered as he was by entail, the Marquis could not but leave the estate to Freddy. Already, as Lord Musgrave, Earl of Swayneflete, Freddy had come into a fortune, which, unlike that of his father, had not yet been eaten away by reckless investment in vain attempts to keep up failing estates. Rather than be denied all knowledge of what he considered the mishandling of his future property—Freddy fell silent.

"Thank you, sir," said Billy dryly. "If I might indulge in some plain speaking I'll give you my opinion of the situation.

Your income hardly balances the demands made upon it by
the estate. In the long term you must have this managed on
a proper footing, but immediately, you need ready 'tin'. Short
of selling property—which I understand your son is not prepared to sign to——" at this Freddy shook his head furiously,
"your only remaining asset is the high regard in which your
noble family is held. All London would fall over themselves,
and pay good money, to be at any social function you held.
This is how I suggest you capitalize on that asset: put on a
tournament by the river at Marlow House, as was held some
years ago at Eglington, and make all fashionable London pay
through the nose for the privilege of being there."

"Dammit, sir," burst out Freddy, "D'yer mean ter say we
should turn the family into a peep-show and charge admission?"

The old Marquis scowled at his son and turned to Billy:
"Pray go on, sir."

"I think it can be managed a little better than that," smiled
Billy. "If as a friend of the family—with some reputation for
organization—you should leave the arrangements with me:
tickets would be sent to the most desirable of guests amongst
royalty and the nobility, and my agents would let it be known
about, that, for a personal consideration, tickets could be
acquired. Your profit in the matter need never become public
knowledge."

Through the french windows Billy could see Freddy's sister,
Lady Honoria, walking amongst the flowers in the garden.

"Do you not feel, father," said Freddy tightly, "that the
family's honour should not be lightly placed in another's
hands."

"I do concur, dear boy," grinned the Marquis, "unless of
course that person's honour is also involved in the profit accru-
ing from such a venture—the possibility of which, I am sure
Mr. William Miles has not overlooked."

Billy got to his feet and bowed. He had already assessed the commission to be derived from the lodgement of such a large body at inns about the countryside, for they could not all put up at Marlow Hall, and had considered the possibility of arranging a sumptuously appointed special train to convey the guests there, which could be managed quite profitably through the Railway company of which he was a director.

"If you will permit me, I shall join Lady Honoria in the garden, my lords, whilst you determine your purpose in the matter."

"The fellow's a terrible villain, sir, and not to be trusted," said Freddy, as Billy stepped into the garden.

"Mayhap that is so, my boy, but if he can be bent towards Honoria and an agreeable settlement arrived at, I should welcome him as a son-in-law."

"Marry my sister, sir, never! Why the fellow's a commoner. What do we know of his background? Could be a furriner with that swarthy cast to his countenance, even Jewish."

"Be proud as you will outside the family," snarled the old man, "but never forget how the line began in the bogs of Ireland."

The Earl of Swayneflete was silent. All foreign nobles, including Irish peers, were only reckoned Esquires in England.

"Lady Honoria Musgrave," said Billy, bending over her hand.

"How pleasant to see you, Mr. Miles."

'Pleasant' was too vapid an expression to describe his own sensations, thought Billy. One glance from those enormous violet eyes set in that sweet slender face, one movement from that well-bred figure and he was as randified as the devil.

"I am delighted to find you by yourself, Honoria, let us walk a little into the garden, there is something I would ask you."

Honoria looked about her with hesitation, and blushed.

"Would you not wait for Mamma's companion, Mr. Miles.

She has but gone to the house for a shawl. I should not wish to be compromised."

Billy felt a moment of vexation, but then, she was just seventeen and fresh from finishing school. He laughed.

"It is you I would converse with, my dear, not your mother's companion. As you so rightly say she will return instantly and your father and brother are within earshot, meanwhile, I think your honour is safe enough." Firmly he took her arm and led her deeper into the garden.

"We are well enough acquainted, Honoria, for you to call me William."

"I should be very pleased to do so, William."

"Thank you, my dear, then may I tell you what is uppermost in my mind. With your permission, I shall seek your father's agreement to call on you regularly."

"If Papa is agreeable William, I shall be very happy to receive you," said the girl, her long lashes masking her eyes.

They were out of sight of the house and Billy, seeking to break through the reserve of the girl in the manner he had always found to be most effective, seized her round her tiny waist and kissed her. With a small cry, she fell into his arms. Not quite expecting such immediate response, Billy's hands were, nevertheless, immediately at her bosom—when her head fell back lifelessly, her bonnet falling to the ground. She had quite fainted away.

The companion came hurrying to them as Honoria recovered somewhat and re-adjusted her bonnet—breathlessly she leant on the servant's arm.

"I am sorry to be so foolish, William, it must be the closeness of the day. I hope I shall be in a better way when next you call."

Billy was somewhat at a loss. He had never affected any distinction in his pursuit of females, whether they were gay, half gay, or ladies—women only being women and the horizontal role a great social leveller. But then he had never before flown quite so high as Lady Honoria Musgrave.

"What do you think of Mr. William Miles, Mamma?" asked Honoria, as she sat sewing in her mother's drawing room.

"I'm sure if your father considers him a suitable match, he is so, my dear. He is certainly very rich; an establishment in the metropolis and two estates in the country. Indeed it is more than we can keep up. Pappa is already talking of not finishing the season in town."

Lady Musgrave might have viewed the situation less equably, had she known of Billy Miles' other establishments— particularly the tavern in Shoreditch, where Polly, Joe Salt's daughter, lived with her husband and three children, the eldest of which was growing up to look exceedingly like Billy.

"All London knows he is very rich, Mamma, but what is your opinion of him?"

"He's a commoner of course and nothing can undo that, if he was to be knighted tomorrow. But then we must try and change with these modern times. They say his servants wear powder in the country, even when he is not in residence. I'm sure your father knows what he's at," said Lady Musgrave doubtfully. Her own impeccable lineage could be traced back to the conquest.

"He seems awfully *vigorous*, Mamma," said Honoria.

Freddy conferred with his younger brother, Lord Musgrave, Bishop of Easington.

"Not a shilling will I put to the affair, we shall be the laughing stock of the County."

"I don't know," demurred Bishop Musgrave, "whilst Church money could not be diverted to promote such a festival, Chivalry is, after all, the child of the church, and the church might well enhance the occasion with its presence." He could already picture himself, robed and mitred, followed by his train—treading the meads of Marlow. "The Bishop of Henley keeps a very good table, I believe."

Freddy glowered at his brother. Sometimes he considered that he was less than fortunate as first-born. His brother's meteoric rise in the church—due to the intercession of their uncle in the cabinet—had brought him at last to the Bishopric of Easington and an income of £25,000 a year, a castle, a palace, three houses, and countless preferments to distribute amongst the favoured. Whilst at Easington he was by far from being in the front rank of princes of the church, he was probably one of the richest, and could well afford the proxy he paid to carry out his cathedral duties.

"Perhaps I'll not go abroad as I had planned, just yet awhile," murmured the Bishop.

Lady Partridge made a point of being up and in the dining-room, dressed in her prettiest silk *peignoir*, when her young husband, Sir Anthony Partridge, Bart., stomped home for his breakfast. Anxiously she viewed his countenance for how well the gaming had gone, but was reassured in an instant.

"Morning, me dear, what a night I've had of it," he chortled, "never had such a lucky streak, would've taken 'em for every blessed penny, if they hadn't chucked it in. Damnable cowards."

"How splendid for you, my dear." So exhilarated was Sir Anthony with drink and success, that he perceived nothing remarkable in his wife's presence at breakfast, nor unusual in the absence of censure in her tone after his night spent at the tables.

"Fellows were so drunk, they were actually paying up in cash."

Lady Partridge could not prevent a small exclamation of horror, as he emptied his pockets of gold and soiled notes on to the dazzling white table-linen. Sir Anthony swayed over the pile and picked out a money order.

"Must get to the bank with this before old 'Ossie' comes to, and remembers what he's done."

It was very doubtful that the Hon. Michael Osserington would be out of his drunken stupor before Lady Partridge had seen that the matter was attended to.

"Darling, the Goodchildes are going."

"Going? Going where, dammit? There ain't no racing on."

"Why to the tournament at Marlow Hall, and the De Veres and the Uckridges and even that common Mrs. Hemmings, they've all had their invitations."

"S'pose the tickets have been delayed," said Sir Anthony pouring himself a brandy.

"All the invitations have gone out," said Lady Partridge, wildly, "and all London will be there but us. There are tickets to be had, Anthony, no one would know that we had purchased them."

"How much would these tickets be, m'dear?"

"Why fifty guineas, Anthony."

"Fifty guineas!"

His wife's eyes filled with tears. "But the Goodchildes are to be there."

"Oh very well, me dear, if your heart is set on it—but Lord knows it seems a strange way to treat horse-flesh to me."

Yawning, Sir Anthony kissed his pretty wife on the forehead and took himself unsteadily to bed.

"Fifty guineas for each ticket," whispered Lady Partridge after the departing figure.

"One hundred guineas!" said Daniel B. Monroe, to his friend and adviser Lord Clothfield. "Why if that is my entrance to society and my opportunity to become on terms with this wizard William Miles, I would pay double the amount."

"That does not include of admission to the dinners," Lord Clothfield told the American quickly.

The curate gazed at his egg with dismay. But it was not the sound country egg that disturbed him—he was still reeling from the tirade he had just received from his wife. They had been the constant accompaniment to his meals of late and were beginning to impair his digestion.

"Poor Withers is not quite dead in his grave, my dear," he gently chided his wife Mary. "Would not seeking out preferment before the event seem somewhat premature. In any vent, the outlay of such a sum as twenty guineas, when there are so many needy parishioners is hardly the act of a decent Christian."

"Then if you'll not do it I'll take myself to the Bishop. He's not so averse to a pretty woman, I've heard tell."

"Mary! What are you saying?"

"I mean it, I'll not carry on further this way." With that, the curate's wife swept out, leaving him alone with his egg.

Goodness me, the reverend gentleman thought, I really believe she would. There was no hiding behind his books and writings any longer. Ten guineas a ticket and the expense involved in the journey to Marlow Hall would make a large hole in their savings. But the living of St. Eggleton's was worth at least £600 a year, a great deal more than the £30 a year he presently received. The Rev. Mr. Withers could not last much longer. Poor old Withers, thought the curate.

It was generally agreed by all, that the decision to charge the lower orders admission to view the spectacle from the stands already under construction—was a wise one. Lord Musgrave pointed out that sailors and the girls they might bring with them, would quite spoil the spectacle. Nobody, it seemed, reflected on the fact that the sea was a considerable distance away. In any event, to preclude the possibility of such persons being able to afford the entrance fee and spoiling the effect, the stands—whilst not affording too convenient a view—were placed well clear from the pavilions of the aristocracy.

Royalty had declined to accept invitations to the tournament; Queen Victoria confiding to her Prime Minister, that it was a great folly and an even greater wastage of money.

13

MEAT AND PICKLES

THERE was little chance for Celandine to consult with Maudie about the situation of the children during the omnibus trip. The bus was full right up—from the two passengers on either side of the driver to the 'cad' at the back taking the fares. One flighty young 'dolly-mop', rather than be left behind, even joined the men on the curved roof, to the delight of the men below and the outrage of public morality—for there was no decency screen to protect her on her climb up the straight iron ladder. No doubt her charges are left fully drugged with poppy juice, thought Celandine waspishly. The dress of the passengers had not put her in a good mood, for although they were of the lower orders, mostly servants, it would have been difficult to distinguish the maids from their mistresses. Perhaps the cloth was not of such a good order, but for hue and variety they outdid their betters. And Maudie, sitting opposite Celandine, outshone them all. Her pretty face was framed by dark ringlets nestling amongst the flowers she had lain against the pink lining of her green velvet bonnet—until she turned in animated, excited chatter to her neighbours, when the trail of coloured ribbons flew out and the brim of her bonnet covered all but the tip of her little nose. She wore a redingote, with huge funnel-shaped sleeves, of apricot silk checked with pure dark green, and so many skirts stiffened with horse-hair, that she had had difficulty in walking to the omnibus stop, and now could have called forth some censorious comment for their discommoding volume, had she not engaged the male servants on either side of her so charmingly.

When they alighted at the small cluster of houses called Rottingdean, Celandine was very quiet, until Maudie made straight away for the 'Haunch of Venison' public house.

"Does your aunt stay here?" she asked surprised. Maudie winked, "The old dear is very fond of her creature comforts."

They went to a side door, which opened to Maudie's knock, and were ushered into a small parlour by a maid who exchanged greetings with the older girl and said:

"I doubt you'll have long to wait, I'll bring you some refreshment."

It seemed a respectable place. An aspidistra stood on a table in the sun streaming through the netted windows, there were two big chairs and an overlarge sofa, and despite the warmth of the Indian summer, coals burnt cheerily in the grate.

The door opened again and a portly gentleman of some fifty years entered the room in a very deliberated fashion.

"How nice to see you, my dears. Maudie you are looking delightful." He took her small gloved hand in his big white fingers and she put up a cheek for a respectful buss.

"You are too kind, Jem. I'd like you to meet my friend, Miss Spencer. This is Mr. Pickles."

Celandine bobbed a curtsey which Mr. Pickles acknowledged with a dignified inclination of the head.

"Charmed," he said.

"I fear I have much maligned my dear friend Mr. Pickles, in referring to him as 'my poor sick aunt', in that he ain't neither related nor of the gentle sex, and as you can see is really quite hearty."

"I fully understand the subterfuges that one must practise in service," rumbled Pickles in a rich fruity voice, "having never engaged myself to gentlefolk who were not of the opinion that servants should stay unmarried, and should also hold themselves clear of any form of alliance with the opposite sex. Any dereliction from the paths of propriety being visited by the heaviest displeasure and usually summary dismissal."

"Are you then in service, Mr. Pickles?" asked Celandine. She could not believe that this, the most august gentleman she had ever encountered, would bend the knee to anyone.

"I studied the nobility at first hand in my early years, Miss Spencer, for want of another form of education, until I was ready to set up on my own. And I have been very successfully in business for many years now."

Jem Pickles saw no reason to reveal that as a butler in a noble house during the railway boom of 1845, he had bought scrip on credit—by writing away on his master's crested paper —and had been so successful in disposing of the railway scrip, that it had put him in the way of making a fortune. He was now a director on the board of the South Eastern Railway Company.

The serving maid brought in soda and brandy for Mr. Pickles, port for the two girls, a plate of raw beef sandwiches and some pastries.

Maudie giggled. "Can you imagine, Spencer, Mr. Pickles started in the olden times as a running footman, short-cutting across the fields to prepare the inns for the arrival of his master's coach. His refreshment, then, consisted of a boiled egg and a small quantity of wine in the head of his stave."

The girl faltered as she looked at Pickles, as well she might. The look he bestowed on her, down his great hawked nose, was the look of complete disdain that had quelled dukes before now.

"It is such a credit to you, Jem, that you are now so powerful in the city," she added.

When the servant had gone, Maudie passed around the meat and bent her talents to flattering Pickles.

"I am quite sure that visitors to the 'ouses where you were situated, must 'ave 'ad great difficulty in deciding who was the master."

"Shall I say," said Pickles, somewhat mollified, "that the influence I was able to bring to bear in the conduct of some of our most stately homes was not inconsiderable. The tables of the nobility were lamentably poor, until I set a standard in my kitchens that was the envy of kings."

Maudie played the coquette to such good effect, that by the time their glasses were empty, Pickles had seemed to forget the existence of Celandine and was devouring Maudie with his slightly bulbous eyes. Feeling Celandine's gaze upon him, he started, and ponderously felt for his watch, secured across his bulging waistcoat by its gold guard, and holding the time-piece at arm's length, grunted :

"I have another hour, Maudie, perhaps Miss Spencer would care to take a walk along the cliffs. It is most healthful." He reached into another pocket in his waistcoat and taking out a sovereign, handed it to Celandine. "You might wish to purchase something from the purveyors on the beach, child."

For an awful moment, the memory of the other man who had given her a sovereign outside the Rev. Mr. Blackstone's rectory came back to her. The man with the yellow eyes of her nightmares. She sat weak and unable to move looking fearfully at the surprised Mr. Pickles.

"Come, Spencer," said Maudie sharply, "show Mr. Pickles some gratitude and be off. But be back by five o'clock."

"You're very kind, sir," said Celandine rising mechanically.

"Look cheerful, child," said Mr. Pickles with an attempt at joviality, "here, take this glass. I'm sure you'll find some interesting observations on a clear day such as this." He handed the girl a folding telescope that he took from the pocket of his frock coat.

"Take no notice, Mr. Pickles, she's a caution and no mistake."

"Quite, quite. Might I finish that last confection, if you are not desirous of it. Capital pastry." Celandine heard Pickles say as she closed the parlour door behind her.

The stiff wind of Rottingdean soon blew away her melancholy and threatened to blow the parasol, that Maudie had loaned her, inside out. It hardly compared with Maudie's own fringed parasol that matched her little lemon gloves, and the cheap print dress Celandine wore was hopelessly out of fashion, but not all of the servants out that sunny autumn day were as well fitted out as Maudie, not by a long chalk. She doubted that they had such rich friends. To think that she should have come by a sovereign so easily, a sum that she would need to labour more than a month for. Did Maudie do it with him, she wondered, it would be nothing to her consternation after this day's events.

Some gentlemen were grouped together not far away at the cliff edge, using opera glasses with evident enjoyment. It seemed quite the fashionable thing to do. She came as close to them as she dared and took out her own glass, pretending to herself that she was one of the party. She examined a fishing boat, far out to sea, holding the glass with her little finger crooked, in a manner she considered quite elegant. Then she took to studying the women using the bathing machines on the beach below. Puffed with their layers of skirts, they disappeared into the machines coyly, like doves into their cotes, and the long trundle down to the beach began, until they emerged again with shrieks of fear at the water's edge : less voluminous but just as modestly covered in their bathing dresses. Celandine imagined the frantic struggle with tapes and buttons, hooks and eyes, in the narrow confines of the lurching hut, and the fearful danger of arriving at their destination too soon, the door being flung open and of being exposed to the ocean improperly attired.

The 'dipper' intrigued Celandine—a strong woman, built much like a man, she plodded along from hut to hut, seizing each helpless bather as she emerged, and despite their pitiful cries and remonstrances, dipping them mercilessly in the seawater for their health and invigoration. There she left them spluttering to regain their breath, when they would return in tears to the protection of the machines. It seemed very strange to pay money to endure such torture. Not all of the bathers were so timid, however. One well-built woman lay on her back in the shallows quite contentedly, allowing each wave to lift her costume to her neck so that she showed everything she had, a large part of which consisted of a mass of black hair that reached up to her stomach. Celandine sighed. She would not wish to be so liberally endowed, but had no such sign of womanhood herself as yet. Of a sudden she realized that this was what the gentlemen with the opera glasses were so intent on. Blushing she hurried past them, but they paid her no attention. How she wished she was that full-bodied woman down there, knowing, as she surely must, of all those admiring gentlemen.

Further down the beach the men were bathing, and it appeared, without a stitch of clothing. Surely not, for even at this distance she could discern the squat, crinolined dresses and nodding bonnets of ladies moving amongst them. Curiously she followed the cliff top, her heart beating more rapidly. She had not the courage to go down on the beach, but with trembling hand and quite forgetting to crook her little finger, she raised the telescope. Not all of the gentlemen covered themselves discreetly with their hands, and her first thought was one of surprise that they were so small—from what she had remembered of Dick, she imagined that all men were so equipped. She giggled hysterically to herself, perhaps that was why the village children had called him 'Big Dick'. And how the women, arm-in-arm, strolled between the naked men for all the world as though nothing untoward were taking place, laughing and chatting, but with many a secretive sideways glance.

She swung her glass on a large congregation of fair promenaders, gathered—it would seem—quite by accident, on that part of the beach where a diminutive moustachioed fellow proudly stood with the most amazing vertical engine. Could it be, thought Celandine, that the nip, creeping into the late afternoon, had contrived to reduce and shrivel the other gentlemen. She was reminded that she was overstaying her excursion, and reluctantly folding the telescope, Celandine retraced her footsteps on the cliff top and made her way back to the 'Haunch of Venison'.

14

LET ME, FOR A SOVEREIGN

FOR the first time since she had been at Brighton, Celandine did not immediately prepare for bed when she reached her attic room. Everything seemed out of joint and she was restless.

A letter waited for her propped up against the candlestick, which she promptly tore open. It was from her mother and read :

My dearest child,

I feel I must tell you of the great decision I have come to. It has been in my thoughts for some time, that I could be of more service to God than in my present situation, for in true humility I am yet a young woman, and with you in safe hands—for which I give grateful thanks to Him— the call has been more urgent than heretofore.

The Rev. Mr. Blackstone has been persuaded, by an agency greater than his own weak soul, to recommend and bear the expense of my training in a missionary school in London.

I do not desire great things for myself but only wish to serve the Will of God. My one sadness is that we are not together, that I might lead you too down the same path, for which I am sure Mrs. Arkwright's establishment is an admirable training.

As soon as I am arrived in London, I shall appraise you of where you can send to me, and I shall expect an account of your doings at once.

God grant that you are well. Lord, Thy Will is Everything.

From Your Affectionate Mother,
Lucy Spencer.

The letter made Celandine feel very much alone and only served to confuse her more. Mamma would certainly never approve of Maudie Bates, yet she was truly the only friend she had in the world.

On the way back from Rottingdean, Maudie had made no bones about her lover, Mr. Pickles. He was already married, but planned to set her up as his mistress in an establishment in St. John's Wood and as soon as the arrangements were complete, she was to fly to him.

"But what of your respectability?" Celandine had asked.

"Pickles' money shall buy me enough respect for my needs, and for the little I lose I shall have fair recompense. Why should I be always in collar for next to nothing and always at someone's beck and call, when I can take my ease, have all I require and be my own mistress?"

The day before, Celandine might have tried an answer, but now she was less sure of her argument.

"I shall need a maid," Maudie went on, "and I would sooner a friend if you would come with me."

It was a tempting offer, but Celandine could not make up

her mind. Of a sudden she felt that she must be out of the house so that she could think. The gas was still turned down low on the landings—signifying that Mr. Arkwright had not returned home as yet—and providing sufficient light for Celandine, wrapped in her Sunday cloak, to brave the stairs. The house frightened her at night. The gas lights moaned and flickered throwing double shadows of herself, that advanced and retreated on the walls, so that she dreaded what awaited around each corner. When she had negotiated the stairs, the kitchen proved just as eerie—the moonlight coming through the semi-basement windows turning objects that were so familiar by day, into shadowy, lurking figures waiting to pounce. As last she reached the back door. The lock and bolts moved quite silently and the door hinges seemed well oiled. With what she now knew about the household, it occurred to Celandine that this was not the first time that one of the servants had come out at night.

Soon she was making her way along the path that ran behind the gardens of the crescent, and she was more at home with the musty autumn smell of the country in her nostrils. The path wound around the end of the houses and turned off down steep steps leading into a brick tunnel. A gas light beckoned beyond and she could hear the sea very near. Celandine hesitated a moment before she lifted her skirts and ran quickly down the steps, her boots making a fearful clatter that echoed after the girl like a pursuer, speeding her even faster on her way. The tunnel provided ready access for the residents of the crescent to the bracing sea air—passing under the coast highway down through the cliffs. Celandine burst breathlessly on to the promenade and leant panting on the stone wall overlooking the sea. Now that her footsteps had finished there was no sound but the sea dashing against the rocks below her. A faint mist rolled tentatively over the edge of the wall, yellow in the flare of the gas light. Further along the parade, another lamp dimly speared the gloom. Slowly she walked along by the sea wall, listening to the smash of waves breaking in the dark and tasting the salt on her lips from the light spray.

She could never put Mrs. Arkwright into the way of understanding things if she should intend to go away with Maudie, thought Celandine, nor yet would her mother forgive her for such an action. If only she could find the courage, she could go to London and have nice clothes to wear. How she envied Maudie the elastic-sided boots she had on today. She screamed suddenly as she walked into a tall figure, and her arms were seized.

"Careful! my dear, are you so soulful after your lover, that you watch not where you go?"

"Oh, sir, you gave me a start, I was thinking very hard."

She could not see the man's features, his back was to the light, but she could tell by the shape of his tall hat and cloak, and the cane he carried, that he was a gentleman.

"Then I was right, young girls only think hard when there is a lover."

"Oh no, sir! I have no lover."

His gloved hand came up and turned her head a little to the light.

"A pretty little thing like you and no lover, I can't believe it. What's your name?"

"Celandine, sir."

"Celandine. A humble little yellow-headed flower, tumbling in the hedgerows, and no yokel with the sense to pluck it."

"What are you at, sir?"

"Don't be foolish, child, I'll give you a sovereign if you'll let me."

Celandine struggled with the man and he ceased trying to lift her skirt, instead his hand went to the vest pocket of his waistcoat and Celandine saw the dull glint of gold.

"No sir, I'll not," she said sullenly, but she stopped struggling.

"That's better, my dear, this shall be yours if you do as I say."

There was nought but gold sovereigns popping out of waist-coat pockets today. It appeared a very easy way to make money.

He took her hand and passed it beneath his cloak. Celandine's heart was beating so furiously she could scarce breathe. He had it out beneath his clothes. Hot and dry and thicker than her own wrist. No! she could not, it was too massive. But she did not reliquish her hold.

She heard the stolid tread behind her at the same time as the light from the policeman's bulls-eye lantern fell on her partner's countenance and she recognized the features of Mr. Arkwright.

Twisting away from him with a cry, Celandine dodged around the surprised constable and ran for the steps, but neither of the men gave chase. She looked back to where she could dimly see the shape of the two tall hats. Mr. Arkwright's soothing voice came to her through the mist, and she fancied she saw the glint of money passing hands. Celandine stayed for no more but sped up the stone steps.

Over and over she asked herself the question as she ran: Had he recognized her? And if so, would he follow her home and pursue her even there? How could he be so faithless to his wife, who seemingly alone in the household was a respectable Christian? The fears of the long tunnel, the lonely path and the poorly-lit stairs of the house were as nothing to the fears in her head and of that which lay behind her. She regained her attic room and sat fully clothed trembling on the cot, waiting for the sound of Mr. Arkwright's key in the front door.

Would she have succumbed to Mr. Arkwright's demands, the girl wondered, if the policeman had not made an appearance? Yet the law would seem to be in league with him. It wasn't long before she heard the front door go, and Mr. Ark-

D

wright's heavy steps on the stairs. When she thought that they must continue right up to her room, they stopped outside his own. There was a long pause in which she conjectured what he was about: was he standing there listening on the landing, or—she swallowed nervously—was he creeping silently to her. Then she heard the door close as he at last entered his room.

Somehow Mr. Arkwright had not recognized the girl on the promenade as one of his own housemaids. Celandine waited, tensed, with her mouth open to catch every sound. But after ten minutes it was still quiet, he had gone to his bed.

Numb with relief, Celandine slowly took off her outer clothes and reached for the chamber pot beneath her cot. She badly had need of it after the nervous strain she had been through.

The door opened and Mr. Arkwright entered, wearing a quilted morning dressing-gown. He struck a lucifer and took it to the candle by her bed, to view her better—sitting in the middle of the naked oil-cloth with the skirt of her petticoat spread around like a mushroom.

"I heard you piddle, my dear, else I wouldn't have known you were back. There weren't no need to bolt off because of a bobby yer know."

Unable for the present to move, Celandine feared that her posture would give him cause for encouragement, but she could not prevent her colour, courage and all draining away. To answer him while in such a predicament would only put the seal on the easy relations between them, that he seemed so skilful in contriving.

"Let me give you a hand, darling."

Celandine was forced into an answer.

"I cannot as yet."

"Don't bother about that," said Mr. Arkwright reaching down to her. Celandine considered the introduction of the helpful hand he offered rather an impediment than otherwise in managing a task she felt quite capable of executing without his assistance. In their struggles the chamber slopped across the room. Celandine could not but laugh aloud at the master's look of consternation.

"Quiet, child," said Mr. Arkwright softly, the sleeve of his dressing-gown dripping on to the oil cloth, "you'll have the mistress down upon us."

The girl sobered as she thought of that upright woman, stiff perhaps, and sometimes hard, but who had always been fair and honest with her. Someone for all her faults whom she had grown to admire and even love. And here she was breaking faith by entertaining her husband at night.

"I shall scream loud for her this instant unless you leave this room, Mr. Arkwright," said Celandine, wondering what it would be like to be kissed by that silky moustache.

"But of course, I was forgetting," smiled Arkwright, taking out a gold piece and placing it on the washstand, "this shall be yours."

"I don't want your money," screamed Celandine, flattening herself against the wall as he came for her. Did he think that all she wanted was his gold like some gay woman? "I have never done such a thing, and you have no right to serve me so."

Arkwright halted at her vehemence and whispered furiously, "You little fool, to stop me, don't you know that a celandine is just a common pilewort, a weed. A girl in your station should be grateful to be noticed by a gentleman. What else is there for you in your life?"

"Go away!" sobbed Celandine loudly. The man looked towards the door, as though he fancied he heard some movement in the house from her outcry.

"And don't think the mistress shall hear a word of this or I shall bring Lottie to tell how she discovered you abusing the child."

Celandine blinked through her tears at him.

"I'll not give up so easy on another occasion. You have

taken my money and I shall expect my due." He went to the door. "Think on it," he hissed, "and you'll see that you might as well sell it to me for gold as give it away to some snotty boy."

The girl sat weakly on the cot. It seemed to her that in private all men were the same, young or old, whether dressed as priest, or gentleman, or navvy, their main intention was to get a female's skirts up.

Howsomever, the master had made her position quite clear. She must accept a situation of impecunious drudgery, fending off the master's advances, or one of drudgery combined with extra services for Mr. Arkwright and a leavening of gold.

There was a third course open to her that Maudie had suggested. She determined on the instant to take it. She had two sovereigns and would go to London and wait for Maudie. Furthermore, she would do it this night, whilst they all slept.

The first light found Celandine at Brighton Station which she had reached by following the coast road through the night. There were still some hours to wait for the first up-train that Sunday. Using a sheet from her bed, she had wrapped her belongings in a large bundle, in the same manner as 'Puffing Billy' travelled—since she could not have moved her box without help and without rousing the whole household.

She waited, wondering if her absence had yet been discovered, and whether Mrs. Arkwright would send the police to take her up for the theft of the sheet and one black velvet Sunday cloak. But then, she salved her conscience, there was money still owed for her labour. Tired, cold, friendless and fearful, Celandine considered whether she had not been too precipitous, and tried not to think of the fate that awaited her in London if she was unable to secure her position with Maudie.

15

ENTICED IN LONDON

AT eleven o'clock that Sunday morning, the arrival parade at London Bridge was deserted. The great station dozed in the pale sunshine percolating through the glass of the covered promenade, the massive bible hanging, unused, from its chain in the concourse—whilst outside, the church bells called to each other across London.

A line of vehicles waited next to the long platform—from the most well-appointed equipage to the meanest: all manner of private carriages, gigs and dog-carts, omnibuses standing opposite the ugly black projecting boards posted: 'Cheapside— Fleet Street—Holborn', or 'Charing Cross—Regent Street— Oxford Street', and the humblest and speediest of all conveyances—the common cab.

In one of these awaited a respectably dressed woman in black silk. Her strong features were somewhat marred by a wart to one side of her mouth, nonetheless, she was a handsome woman and something about her tokened that, had she not business at the station, she would have been at her devotions now and not skulking in her bed. Her name was Miss Harriet Grigg and though she had never met Celandine—or even knew of her existence, it was Celandine that she had come to the station to meet.

On a sudden the telegraph man in his box touched the trigger of his bell, violently convulsing the station to life. The horses pricked their ears and twitched their muscles as though they were aware that the period of inactivity was almost over. The powdered footmen stood up behind their carriages and the drivers of the cabs, who had been nowhere in evidence before, were suddenly on their boxes.

As the orange and green 'Jenny Lind' locomotive—named after the Swedish nightingale—puffed into the station, the company porters took up their positions, holding the handles of the carriage door to prevent the passengers escaping.

The *mêlée* of screaming newsvendors; porters unstrapping luggage from the roof or taking it from the van; descending travellers—seeking friends, being greeted, searching for cab or carriage : were gone almost as quickly as they had appeared —when Miss Harriet Grigg spied Celandine left in bewilderment on the parade.

The girl had invested in a third class ticket—not wishing to arrive at London in the state she had reached Brighton. Although the carriage gave more protection against the elements, the rough planks provided for seating were not much conducive to rest, and she was tired, cold and hungry when the train stopped at the Dartmouth Arms* after an hour's travelling. Deducing, correctly, that they were not far from London Bridge, Celandine made herself tidy so that tired as she was, and poor though her clothes and bundle might appear, she at least had the aspect of respectability. But it was quite apparent to Miss Harriet Grigg's discerning eye, that she alone of the travellers had no direction to follow.

"Come this way, child !" she said commandingly, "I have a cab waiting."

"Really you must make a mistake, Madame . . ." started Celandine.

"*Miss* Grigg, child, and I don't make mistakes. You are cast on this town and without lodgings are you not?"

"That is so but. . . ."

"No buts, the cab won't wait for ever."

"No, ma'am." And Celandine found herself ensconced with her bundle next to the forceful woman.

* Forest Hill.

"Number free six five bound fer 'The Young Workin' Wimmin's Pertection League', Stamford Street," sang out the driver as they trotted out of the departure gate. Which information was duly noted down as a precaution against mistreatment of the railway company's passengers or their luggage. All of which was a great comfort to Celandine, and allayed the last of her misgivings.

A wintry smile crossed Miss Grigg's countenance as she observed Celandine's reactions. She put an arm around the girl's shoulders.

"Have no fear, child, you'll not need to roam the pavements, I'll find you a good house with rewarding labour."

Half-dozing on Miss Grigg's shoulder, in the pale London sunshine, the girl answered the woman's probing questions quite truthfully as the cab clopped through the light traffic in Southwark Street to Blackfriars. She had thought London to be more beautiful and was unaware that this was the meaner, transpontine side of the city.

The Young Working Women's Protection League, was a building in better order than its run-down neighbours, but Miss Grigg, when she had paid off the cabman, took Celandine past its portals and turned into a side street.

"Before we find you employment you shall eat and rest yourself. You are yawning on your feet child. A good friend of mine who lives nearby shall serve you very well."

"You are very kind, ma'am."

The way they took twisted and turned into dirtier and more evil smelling alleyways. Withersoever they went, thought Celandine, it mattered not, if there was food and a clean bed at the end of it.

"Good day, Miss 'Arriet," said the bully lounging in the doorway. He stepped back respectfully to let them in, taking the short pipe from his mouth.

"Quite a reformed type," whispered back Miss Grigg to Celandine as they mounted the uncarpeted stairs.

An old woman met them at the landing.

"Another unfortunate, Miss 'Arriet, Lor' bless us, don't you never rest. Come in, do. You too, my dear."

If it had not been for the presence of Miss Grigg, Celandine would have fled the place. She did not care much for the old woman whose eye, rheumy with the film of old age, flicked expertly over her, seemingly taking in every detail of shape and dress.

"You looks like you could do with some grub to fatten you up a mite," said the old woman. "What would you say to a nice hot pie and pastries."

"That's very kind of you. I am quite famished and have money to pay you."

"Lor' bless you, pet, that ain't required of a friend of Miss 'Arriet's. I'll send out for a glass of porter, you look that peaky."

"No, really!" protested Celandine feeling ashamed of her churlish thoughts. But the old woman had opened the window and was shouting down into the alley in a singularly powerful voice :

"Alfred ! a glass of the special porter, quick !"

"She's a good sort, is Mrs. Perkins," whispered Miss Grigg, "you'll see."

The old woman brought forward the victuals and Celandine set to.

"Can I offer you a glass of white satin, Miss 'Arriet?"

"Thank you Mrs. Perkins, there is a distinct nip in the air. I'll take just a little gin, with water."

When Alfred the bully arrived back with the porter, Celandine was half-asleep on her elbows at the table.

"She ain't away already, is she?"

"Hold your jaw," hissed the old woman.

"Alfred," said Miss Grigg, with a sweet smile, "Pray take a message to the Captain that I might well have a young female most suitable to his needs."

"The Cap'n," muttered Alfred as he shuffled out, "there's a cove as gives me the uglies."

"You needn't frighten yourself," said Miss Grigg to Celandine, who had only dimly comprehended the conversation. "The Captain keeps a good house and is not the bear that Alfred pretends. But come now, Mrs. Perkins has fixed you a bed with clean linen, away to it with your porter, before you sleep amongst the empty dishes."

Harriet Grigg led the girl into another room and helped her off with her outer clothes. She would not leave until Celandine was tucked between the sheets and had started to drink the porter.

"I'll be back to see you've drank it all. The motto of our league is that good health is a girl's best protection."

Celandine made a face when the woman had gone. The draught had a strange taste and she did not care for it. Feeling beneath the bed, she found a chamber pot and poured the stuff away.

Her adventure had started well enough, thought Celandine, with a situation in the offing and already a roof over her head. She must write to Maudie at the earliest opportunity and tell her everything. Her head was swimming with fatigue and very soon she was asleep.

Celandine awoke to discover that the sheets had been taken away, and that a most intimate examination was being conducted of her. Not daring to move or open her eyes, she listened to the voices of those foregathered around. The hand was withdrawn and a voice she recognized as Miss Harriet Grigg's said :

"She still has her maidenhead and could be passed as nine years of age without difficulty."

"Capital !" said an unknown male.

"There won't be much in it I'm finking, Cap'n," was Alfred's coarse utterance, "not wiv no more flesh than a skinned rabbit and that spotty mug."

"You're a stupid oaf, Alfred," came the cold intonation of the stranger. "The qualities you so demean, are just those that many clients will pay very large sums indeed for."

There was silence for a while and Celandine's flesh crept, feeling their eyes upon her.

"Do yer want me ter break 'er in, Cap'n?"

"Hold yer jaw till the Cap'n speaks to yer, you dolt," said Mrs. Perkins.

"What do you intend, Captain?" asked Miss Grigg. "She's well-drugged now, and the sooner we get her in the way of it, the better. Her virgin purity can be made a marketable commodity, six or seven times over, to suit your customers' tastes.'"

"Not this client, Harriet. He's a suspicious old lecher and he'll not pay for tampered goods. Have her taken over to 'The House' to stay with the others for a while. I'll let you know how we'll manage it later."

There was the sound of movement from the room, and Celandine almost started as she felt a rough hand on her again—then Mrs. Perkins' voice hissed out : "Leave 'er Alfred. You fool with 'er too soon and you'll 'ave the Cap'n's bullies to reckon with."

The door closed, and when the girl was quite sure that she was alone, she opened her eyes. She had not understood all that had passed, but their main intention was quite clear, and Miss Grigg, despite her high-flown manner was no more than a common enticer. They had taken all of her clothes but she must leave this place if she had to run from it naked. Celandine flew to the window. It looked out over a narrow alley, where the rain falling—from the now darkened sky—had burst the mud banks which commonly kept the contents of the central gutter in its place : flooding quantities of putrefying animal and vegetable matter, potato peelings and refuse of all kinds into the alley, turning it into an open sewer. Softly she lifted the rotting sash window and looked down the side of the building. There were drain pipes a-plenty to help her to the ground if they were not too rusty to bear her weight. Celandine sobbed with fright, less certain now of going out quite naked into the world. She determined at least to take a sheet from the bed, as she made to do so, her chemise came into sight, overlooked by those who would use her so cruelly. It would serve better than a sheet. With her heart thumping so hard it threatened to choke her, she hastily pulled on the chemise and climbing from the window, swung out on to the drain pipe. Ten feet from the ground the pipe came away from the wall and fell with Celandine to a frightful clatter amongst the wet debris of the alley. Celandine bolted off like lightning without checking her bruised limbs or daring to look back. Through the slimy nest of alleys she ran, on and on, until she came to a wide dimly-lit thoroughfare where a single figure weaved drunkenly towards her. Dodging him easily Celandine plunged into the slums and stews on the far side of the street. "Bitch!" screamed the man and sat down suddenly on the greasy road.

Celandine ran until she could run no more—when she staggered to a doorway and squatted out of the rain, her small bosom heaving for breath.

Her tears flowed into her drenched chemise for a long time until she quietened. With sudden clarity came the thought that she must look out for herself for no one else would. Celandine began to take stock. She looked more like a mudlark than a housemaid, her clothes and money were all gone, stolen, and even if she could find the place again, she would never dare take herself to the police. But she must have money to buy food and who would give her employment now in her state and without a proper certificate of character. Slowly came the thought that she still had her honour to sell. It had been enough sought after. If she must, she would, but not, she decided, for pennies or a crust of bread. Celandine's hand went to the hem of her chemise where something pressed uncomfortably against her leg. Something round and hard sewn

into the skirt—and she remembered. It was the half guinea
her mother had put there before she left home. The last of her
tiny fortune. She would not have to sell herself just yet. She
fell into a damp miserable sleep clutching the hem of her
chemise.

16

THE 'TIN' TOURNAMENT

THE armour had been made—or taken from musty halls,
oiled and polished—the horses trained and the knights had
practised. The ladies reappeared from furious bouts of dress-
making, concerning themselves with velvet and ermine, wim-
ples and tippets. The pavilions were erected and the silken
banners flew bravely above the shields hung before each
knight's tent. An army of servants, cooks and caterers stood by.
In short all possible preparations for the fullest panoplied
chivalric tournament of the century had gone forward.

The tickets to the event had long since been sold, and all
accommodation for seven miles around Marlow Hall had
been taken—still train loads of would-be spectators were arriving.

Billy Miles cut a tremendous dash when as 'Master of the
Tournament' he rode furiously up to the 'Queen of Love and
Beauty' and leaping to the ground sought permission on behalf
of Lord Musgrave to open the tournament.

His skill at horsemanship evoked a cheer from the spectators,
who had been unimpressed by the clumsiness of the knights
in their full heavy armour. Billy was only in half armour with
slashed doublet and plumed helmet. He had pleaded his duties
as reason for not becoming involved in the combat—accepted
with alacrity by the Musgrave family, uneasy at allowing a

commoner to participate on equal footing with what was quite the most select gathering of good birth and breeding in England.

The 'Queen of Love and Beauty', gave her permission to the dashing horseman, and murmured that she hoped they might meet later at the Ball. Lady Aylesbury was certainly very beautiful, but some thought rather over-ripe for her role as Queen, being well into her mid-years. She at least had no doubts regarding Billy's suitability in personal combat.

Lady Honoria Musgrave, whom many thought more suitable for the role, was also considerably affected by Billy's *élan*, so much so that she would have thrown him a favour to wear, had she not been uncertain of the correct form, and whether the 'Master of the Tournament', was entitled to carry such a favour.

At first the crowds were so dazzled by the colour and pageantry : the bedecked coursers and the knights with their plumes and war-like accoutrements of armour, shield and weapons; their retinue of squires, grooms, gonfaloniers, and men-at-arms; their wimpled ladies mounted on splendidly caparisoned palfreys; the archers, heralds, trumpeters and marshals, all properly uniformed—that the lack of skill in the lists went unremarked. When, however, the spectators had become more used to these novelties, then there were grumbles at how often the ungainly knights charging down the courses at the tilting, missed each other entirely with the lances. Later, when lance began to find shield, the complaint was that the lances shivered too easily. They had indeed been made of a cross-grained wood so that little danger could be done to the combatants.

The Knight of the Black Falcon, Lord Musgrave, Earl of Swayneflete—otherwise Freddy, at length located Billy Miles in the refreshment pavilion, drinking sherry and water, surrounded by an admiring group anxious for any tidbits of news he might drop of the city.

Impatiently Freddy drew him aside.

"What is this I hear of gold being discovered in New South Wales?"

"Pray, sir, be more cautious," warned Billy drawing him further away from the sprouting ears. "It will be public news soon enough. Yes, there would seem to be some basis to believe that gold-fields of even greater promise than those in California have been discovered."

"And you are heading up a company, seeking directors and putting out shares?"

"I have been asked to be Chairman of the New South Wales Auriferous Mining Company."

"Why then, as a close acquaintance, I am surprised that you did not appraise me of this situation."

"The truth is my Lord, I am not convinced entire. The news comes from France which gives me some misgivings. Whilst I am prepared to gamble a few thousand, it is not investment I would recommend to a friend who might not be able to stand a loss."

"I believe you are prevaricating, sir. Will you, or will you not make me a director of this company?"

Billy suddenly became effusive. "Of course I will, my boy, the thing is done but take my advice and wait before you put any tin into it. Now, let us rejoin the company. They are devilish suspicious customers."

At the first opportunity Freddy slipped away to telegraph his broker in London. Messages to buy into the New South Wales Auriferous Mining Company were beginning to pour into London from the countryside.

Billy observed Freddy's exit with satisfaction, only to become curious to see that Joe Salt had left his side and stood talking at the entrance of the pavilion to an unlikely pair of acquaintances. One he recognized as Lord Furlingham, whose austere figure soberly clad in black he hardly expected to see in this company, the other was a tall woman whose equally plain dress could not conceal from Billy's eyes the indication of a voluptuous figure.

There was a sudden rush outside the tent to view the river, where, heralded by the pure singing of two hundred floating choirboys, Bishop Musgrave's barge was slowly coming down river from Bisham Abbey. The bishop himself stood at the prow, mitred and sceptred, blessing the gathering as he came. As the landing ceremony proceeded, Billy searched for the brawny figure of the pugilist. He was nowhere in sight, yet Billy had warned him he would have need of his close presence in the next few weeks.

Just as the sky was turning red and guests were making a move to Marlow House or their lodgings, a cry went up, and all eyes followed the many pointing fingers to a rise, where between two trees the motionless figure of a mounted knight could be seen—black against the setting sun, watching the scene below him. When he had their full attention, his lance dipped as though in salute and he was gone. 'The Black Knight' went up the cry. There had been rumour of an unknown knight at the tournament but none had yet seen him. Many laughed that it was a joke, yet none stayed on the meads longer than they had to.

The opening ball and dinner at Marlow House was a great success. The ladies being much admired in their fifteenth-century creations of cloth of gold, point lace, brocaded satin and ermine, and their head-dresses of diamonds and pearls. Billy Miles, in company with the other gentlemen, wore hose and knight's costume—the financier being one of the few whose splendid thighs and calves owed nothing to the theatrical costumier's skill with lambswool padding. There were military dress uniforms and kilts and tiny Horace Birket, the poet, dressed in jester's garb, attended by his enormous beturbaned Indian servant.

Billy Miles joined in the quadrilles, and gallopades and did the agreeable with all of the attractive ladies in sight. Lady

Honoria Musgrave was much engaged with her guests—and owing to the sharp attentiveness of the husband of the 'Queen of Love and Beauty', Lord Aylesbury, Billy was unable to bring forward any plans to take advantage of the promise she had offered in her eyes that morning.

After the ball Billy retired alone to his room at Marlow House, where a great deal of paper awaited his attention.

The disappointment had grown daily with the jousting, which was a dull affair indeed, and remarks were passed that it was as well that the age of chivalry was dead, if this is what it had come to. Billy was amused that the aim of the young noblemen to prove that they were not just idle good-for-nothings, set against reform, and to show their invincible superiority over the common people, had unaccountably recoiled. He had not considered it without the bounds of possibility that this should occur. At least the arrangements were faultless. William Miles, Esq. was emerging as the single victor.

The third and last day of the Tournament arrived and still there had been no sign or word from Joe Salt.

Spirits lifted somewhat at the auxiliary sports in the afternoon, the ring, and the quintain, where the figure of a Saracen swung around and dealt the knight a sharp blow if he was not struck squarely, and the *mêlée* in which six knights fought an equally opposing number. At last, Sir Thomas Graveney, the Knight of the Golden Lion, rode forward to desultory applause, to collect his honours as Champion of the Tournament from the 'Queen of Love and Beauty'. When, from out of the sun, came the thunder of hooves and the shout of 'The Black Knight' went up.

Poor Sir Thomas readied himself for the onslaught, squaring his shield and setting his lance, but all the advantage was to his opponent. With a tremendous crash, the Knight of the Golden Lion was unhorsed, and wheeling his courser the Black

Knight raised his unshattered lance and rode back into the sun.

Close to where Billy Miles stood, Horace Birket had to be held up by two spectators. It was not clear what had caused him to collapse, but to Billy it sounded suspiciously like an excess of delight. Birket's huge Indian servant, for once, was missing from his side. Could the joke be that the servant and the Black Knight riding off into the distance were one and the same person. Billy smiled grimly to himself.

One of his servants pushed through the crowd to the financier and whispered that Joe Salt had been found fighting drunk in a small country pub in Wycombe. Taking two of his largest footmen with him, Billy made all haste to ride there.

Joe Salt was drunkenly haranguing the frightened landlord in the taproom when Billy Miles arrived.

"We were 'appy in the country, 'til 'e arrived with his Lunnon trickery. 'E's the devil's spawn, there ain't no denying it. Damn 'em to 'ell! that cursed Mr. William bleeding M——" Billy hit him hard across the face. Joe Salt sprang up to a fighting crouch, his face in a toothless grin, his body hard as nails ready to mill for fifteen rounds. The footmen stepped back as the skin over his great knuckles tightened.

"Cut it, Joe," snapped Billy. Slowly the rheumy eyes focused. The huge hands relaxed until they seemed to pray to Miles.

"She's dead Mr. Miles, Polly's dead of the cholera in Lunnon."

He sank slowly on to the wooden table and sobs shook his huge frame.

"Get outside," said Billy to the servants. The landlord melted away behind the bar.

Of a sudden Joe Salt stopped sobbing and looked up at his master dry-eyed.

"You'll rue the day you struck me, Mr. Miles," he snarled.

"What of the children?"

"Dead, all of 'em dead."

"Who told you this?"

"Why Lord Furlingham, came by out of 'is way ter tell me. 'E was doing missionary work in Shoreditch and they knowed where I was."

"How do you know Furlingham?"

"'E was my landlord weren't 'e? On the worst day in my life when I first set eyes on you."

That's why they were talking together outside the refreshment tent, thought Billy.

"Ain't you concerned at all you 'ard beggar. I kin understand about poor Polly. Put on a little weight she 'ad, and weren't no more ter yer liking, but yer own son, 'e was yer own son damn yer."

"Sober yourself, Joe. I'm not paying you to swill beer all day."

Billy walked outside to his sweating horse.

"Stay with him," he ordered the two nervous footmen, "and take him back to London tomorrow."

At the final banquet that night, Billy said little to the usual admiring group around him, but he drank copiously. Slowly the numbers of hangers-on diminished as his temper grew more foul—deciding their absence would be the better part of valour. Sought after, courted and admired as he was, the smiles became a little frozen as Billy swayed from group to group, argumentative and insulting. He was approaching Lord and Lady Aylesbury fully intending to tell his Lordship how he would dearly love to roger his wife, when another thought struck him. Veering off course he stumbled through the last remaining guests in the banqueting hall and took himself to his own room. There, he sat at his writing desk and put pen to paper. He was determined that there should be no mistake or blot in the note and that the writing should be clear and even. A pile of crumpled paper lay on the floor, and the house was silent, when he was at last satisfied.

Unsteadily Billy went out into the corridor and carefully counting the bedroom doors, arrived outside Honoria's room. Gently he knocked, until he heard a movement. When he observed a glim of light, Billy slipped the note under the door and returned to his room.

The note simply said:

Dearest Honoria,

Pray excuse the lateness of the hour. Believe me I should never have countenanced such an action unless it were of the utmost importance. It concerns the honour of your family and only you can resolve the matter. Please come at once to my room. The morrow I fear will be too late.

Most sincerely yours,
WILLIAM MILES.

Billy had but a short time to wait before a light tap told him the girl had arrived. Quickly he let her in, and closed the door behind her. She had pulled a redingote over her nightdress but yet had contrived to tie a ribbon in her hair.

"Whatever has occurred, William?" gasped the girl.

"Why my love, I decided that I could not pass another night beneath the same roof as you, without your sweet presence."

"William, I do believe you are drunk."

"With desire for you, my dear."

"You are a liar, sir. There is no threat to the honour of my family."

Billy moved closer to the girl.

"There most certainly is. The Lady Dowager of Brighton sleeps to one side of this room, and the Countess of Dilroy the other. If you were to make an outcry there would be a most famous scandal."

"But . . . but you have lured me here."

Billy shook his head slowly from side to side.

"You came of your own free will. What respectable young lady visits gentlemen at this hour? Who would believe you? Come my dear, your honour can either be lost in public, or with more satisfaction to both our tastes—in private."

As Billy took the girl into his arms she suddenly became limp. She had quite fainted away. Billy had never seen so much swooning. Such continuous loss of consciousness could only be due to the restriction of whalebone restricting her circulation. Since stays were also effectually unpropitious to dalliance and enjoyment, Billy laid the unconscious girl on his bed and proceeded to remove the offending article.

The fact that William Miles continued to examine papers behind his large desk during the interview and the continued presence of Joe Salt standing threateningly by in the room— were not conducive to Freddy's ease. Neither was he in sympathy with the duty which his sister had sent him to perform, having no great wish to see the financier as his brother-in-law.

"This is a personal matter, sir, that I would treat of, and I should be grateful for your ear alone."

"I conduct *business* from my office, sir," growled Miles without looking up, "in which Mr. Salt is my complete confidante."

Freddy hesitated. The power of the man had never been so evident to him as now, in this room, where millions of money had been managed. Where the fate of his own large investment in the New South Wales Auriferous Mining Company would be decided.

"I have persistently called at your residence, sir, only to be told you are not at home."

"Then pray, sir, speak, but be brief, for you are aware there is a director's meeting to be held shortly."

"Very well, sir. I shall speak. I should like to know, sir, what are your intentions in regard to my sister?"

"Intentions? I have no further intentions. Having become

somewhat intimately concerned with your family's fortunes, it is quite clear to me that a suitable settlement would not be forthcoming."

"Indeed, sir. I consider that a poor excuse from a gentleman of your wealth and position, who has given such continuous undivided attention to a lady. It is in the highest degree dishonourable to trifle with a lady's affections, sir."

"Has she suggested that she has been compromised?" asked Billy at last looking up.

"Why, no," said Freddy uncomfortably.

"Then be content with my excuse. For if I put about the truth, that I find her uncommonly inactive between the sheets, she'll never be wed."

"You toad, you turd, you turk, sir."

"Quite so," said Billy mildly, returning to his papers and indicating to Joe Salt that Lord Musgrave, the Earl of Swayneflete should be shown out.

The special meeting of directors and shareholders had an unduly large sprinkling of nobility amongst it, who were usually at this hour, either in bed or just returning from Crockfords.

Rumours were circulating wildly; that gold had actually been shipped and arrived in England, that the yield was superior in quality to that from California, and the most persistent rumour of all, that a dividend of nine shilling per share was to be declared.

A small burst of applause went up as Billy Miles appeared and took his place with Joe Salt standing in close attendance behind him. The minutes of the last meeting were read. There was a general murmur of assent that they should be signed. William Miles got to his feet.

"My lords and gentlemen. I feel called upon to make a statement at this time, due to public expectations of a large dividend. I can assure you that our enterprise is going forward as a sound commercial enterprise and that few others can eventually hope to yield a better dividend."

Here there were cries of delight and cheers quite unlike the usual decorum of a business meeting. Miles continued gravely:

"It is not my way to falsely stimulate further outlay, however, by a disproportionate return on investments, and we shall not be declaring a dividend at the present time." There was a shocked silence as the meeting slowly comprehended the burden of his message, that there was to be no immediate return on their investment, which they had all heavily embarked on. Miles gathered up his papers. "That is about all. With your permission, gentlemen we shall adjourn the meeting."

"I demand, sir," cried Freddy leaping to his feet, "being equally responsible with yourself for what is done, to know what has brought you to this extraordinary decision."

"You do, do you?" rejoined the financier, "then you shall not."

There were loud howls from the body of the meeting, shouts and hisses.

"I am accustomed, Lord Musgrave, to have gentlemen with whom I am associated, satisfied with my arrangements, and if you are not then I'll retire and leave the affair in your custody."

"Your resignation is accepted, sir," cried Freddy, flushed with triumph. "We shall convene an immediate board meeting and elect your successor."

Uproarous cheers followed this little speech. So delighted were the shareholders to be relieved of their disappointment at the disappearing dividend, that they overlooked the fact that when William Miles walked out of the door, all public confidence in the company went also.

He was followed almost instantly by the comparatively few at the meeting who knew something of the city. Billy had no reason to hare to the stock exchange. The 2,000 shares he had in the company were selling at premium this very moment, netting him some £58,000.

17

SAWNEY

"SHE must be 'alf witted ter sleep aht larst night," said the smallest of the ragged boys.

"Couldabin 'alf witted wiv the drink," said the tallest.

"Nah!" said the 'Snob', their leader, "she'll do I tell yer. I've 'ad to pad the 'oof 'til daybreak meself on occasion, besides I gotta feelin' in me bones abaht 'er."

He shook Celandine roughly by the shoulder.

"Vanna yarn a crust, gal? Vake up vill yer!"

It took Celandine some few moments to comprehend where she was, remember the events of the previous night, and come to the conclusion that the ragged boys were no emissaries of the Captain.

"I'm hungry," she said.

"See!" said the Snob, looking around him as though he'd proved the point. "I told'ja. I mean—it stands ter reason, don't it?"

"What must I do to earn this money?" asked the girl studying him. He was a year or two younger than her, she judged, with a young old face, wise in the ways of the city.

"Talks like a bleedin' swell," said the lanky Nobby with awe.

A servant girl from the country, out of place, deduced the Snob.

"Useful, werry useful," he said, "there's nuffin' a swell likes better than ter drink down an 'ard luck tale in 'is own lingo. I mean, it makes 'em feel like bleedin' saints 'emselves don't it? Look, gal, ve're goin' thievin' on the stairs and are after a 'passer' and it strikes me you're just the ticket. So what do yer say?"

Celandine got stiffly to her feet with decision. If she was to survive in the Metropolis, she needed a protector and God had provided her one, in the shape of this young felon.

"You must tell me what I should do."

She stood a head shorter than Ralph, the smallest boy.

"Oh, my, ain't she prime? A lickle fallen angel, 'nuff to melt the 'eart of the 'ardest of beggars." The Snob surveyed her thoughtfully. "You could do wiv a shawl, I thinks."

"Yes, indeed," said Celandine, "and some boots, the pavements are very cold."

"Boots!" sneered the Snob. "You really know nuffink, 'oose ganna take pity on a gal viv boots? The shaw's not fer to keep yer varm, but to 'ide away the stuff ve pull. Come on else the steamer'll be gone and the pigeons flown."

They made off towards the Waterloo Road and the river.

"Ere's a try out, then," said the Snob, spotting a servant girl leaving a house on some errand. "Go and ask 'er the vay to Dook Street." He looked at Celandine slyly.

Fearful of the outcome, Celandine approached the girl. But for the vagaries of fate, she might have been this well-fed, well-clothed servant.

She asked her question of the maid and took the instructions and still her new blackguardly acquaintances did not appear. With inspiration she broke into a flood of tears that was only half simulated. As the kindly woman bent down to her, she was bundled head over heels by Ralph and Nobby shouting and fighting as they came.

"Oughta be locked up, the ruffians," screamed the Snob, appearing beside the unfortunate servant shaking his fist. Soli-

citously he helped the woman to her feet managing to dislodge
her shawl in so doing. Celandine took to her heels as the shawl
was immediately gone somewhere into his rags. He began to
brush the victim down in an unnecessarily intimate fashion,
much to her outrage. Apparently affronted at her protestations,
the Snob stepped back a pace.

"Vat a werry pecoolier way to carry on, to be sure. *Some*
people don't 'ave no gratitood," and off he sauntered whistling
carelessly.

"Smoove as silk," said the Snob as they crossed the bridge,
"I reckon as 'ow you'll do." He produced the shawl and placed
it around her shoulders. "Don't know as I cares fer yer gar-
mint all of one piece like that," he said critically. "Should
'ave a few 'oles to show yer poor freezin' skin froo."

"I'll not rend it, and that's that," said Celandine indignantly,
and tears came to her eyes. Wasn't she a sufficiently pitiable
sight, this cold day, dressed only in her chemise sullied with
the filth and offal from the alleys, that she must make holes in
it too?

"Now don't get wexed," said the Snob hurriedly, "I'd say
you've done werry well, werry well indeed. Now 'ere's 'ow our
gentle bunch of lambs goes about the art of stock buzzing,*
in which I may say, I'm no mean hexpert."

When they reached the Adelphi Steps, the travellers were
already being disgorged from the steamer on to the landing
place, pushing amongst the would-be vendors of sweets and
nuts, and men and boys demanding to carry their bags. Celandine's band wasted no time. The Snob chose a 'plant', an old
gentleman with white sideburns and large straw hamper.
Ralph pushed before him shouting, as he walked backwards.

"Carry yer bags, sir. Right up the steps, sir. Only fu'punce,
sir."

The other two boys positioned themselves close behind the

* Stealing handkerchiefs

gentleman, Nobby looking about alertly while the Snob was at the gentleman's tail-coat.

"I'll carry it meself, thank you, young man."

"Only fu'punce to the top of the stairs, sir."

"Very well, you young scamp. Make sure you don't drop it."

Celandine concealed in turn a yellow silk handkerchief and a snuff-box, passed to her by the Snob.

Momentarily flushed with the success of their enterprise, she envied not at all the secure but dull lot of the servant girl they had robbed. She was free, and had at least friends of a sort who relied on her. If the choice was between selling her virtue for bread, or stealing—surely God would approve the latter course.

18

BLEEDING JACK'S

AT five o'clock, when the evening was drawing in, and the small band of robbers trudged back to their mean lodging house—Celandine was less pleased with her lot. Her feet were cold and sore, and she was weary to the bone from her day on the streets.

The Snob, however, was exultant. Never had there been such a day. They had stolen handkerchiefs with rare success, fruit from the stalls and fresh meat from Smithfield—or nearly fresh, Celandine's tiny nose had quivered with disgust when she placed it to the bacon. And to cap it, to the immense awe and admiration of Ralph and Nobby, the Snob had achieved his burning ambition, in taking a watch from the vest pocket of an elderly gentleman. Admittedly the gentleman was very old and nearly blind, but then, reasoned the Snob, suchlike could prove to be the most dodgy of customers. How-somever, the Snob now considered he had joined the nobility as the Prince of Thieves; a pickpocket. Nor could it have been achieved, but for his charmpiece Celandine—turning away the wrath of street traders and the suspicious eye of Gentlefolk, Celandine, whom he insisted on calling 'Anjool'.

The girl's spirits sank even lower as they entered the filthy common lodging house in the Borough that the ragged boys frequented.

Bleeding Jack, so called for his propensity to that adjective and an inclination of letting blood with his fists, greeted them with an aggressive growl.

"Wotcha got 'ere then, anivver bleedin' lodger, the terms is the same, tuppence a night fer a bed, or one brownun on the floor. And if yer ain't got the needful outcha bleedin' goes, quick as yer like."

"My good sir," said the Snob, inflating himself, "this young lady—'oo you'll find answers to the name of 'Anjool'—is a werry prime member of our concern, and vill be the makin' of our fortune one day. I took you for a werry knowing card, Bleedin' Jack, but ve'll be orf elsewhere if yer ain't hinterested in our business. The short and the long of it is, we already 'as a goodish fortune to do trade wiv, this werry minute."

Celandine studied Bleeding Jack's sharp-edged countenance, raw and angry at the corners. He was seemingly undecided whether or not to take off the insolent boy's head.

"Yer can show me the bleedin' merchandise," growled Jack at last, and led the way down to his basement. The atmosphere was thick with the steam coming from a black pot containing a stew that Jack prepared to sell to his lodgers—mingling with the damp odour of newly-washed handkerchiefs, of all colours, dependent from a line before the fire.

The children emptied their rags of the day's pickings from the streets, on to a scarred table.

"It's 'ardly worth the bleedin' trouble," said Jack shaking

his head sadly, as the fruit, meat, vegetables and handkerchiefs rained down.

"Wodja mean, yer skinflint!" said Nobby hoarsely, "that's the most we've ever pulled." Ralph joined in, falsetto with rage, "'e's up to his old tricks, Snob, I'd as lief go ter the workus as trade with this leary cove."

Bleeding Jack was coming round the counter, with a fistful of knuckles and a rumble in his throat that boded ill for the band, when the Snob held up his hand and from it hung the silver watch.

"Do Bleedin' Jack the courtesy pals, 'e's a werry discriminatin' gentleman." He laid two snuff boxes next to the watch on the counter.

"Vell, vell," said the lodging house keeper, with a smile like a knife wound across his visage, "now a silver frying pan is worth the takin' in. 'Course I wants ter do business wiv you boys, but the Cap'n's percentidge is up and I 'as ter be werry cautious."

The Captain again, thought Celandine, was she nowhere safe from his influence in London. She doubted, however, even should he walk into this thieves' den, that he would recognize 'Anjool' the ragged fogle-hunter,* as that same virgin Miss Harriet Grigg had 'ticed away.

After considerable haggling a figure was arrived at that was agreeable to all concerned : sixpence each for the handkerchiefs, one and sixpence for the black ones—being more valuable on account of being much sought after by the costermongers for their necks—ten shilling a piece for the snuff boxes and one guinea for the silver watch, making a grand total of two pounds nine shillings. A sum exceeding the amount the boys had made the whole previous week, before Celandine's advent to their band.

The food they could not agree upon and decided to share amongst themselves and sell to the other lodgers. With enor-

* Watch stealer.

mous magnanimity, and much to Celandine's relief, the Snob
tossed the 'sawney'—the now extremely powerfully smelling
piece of bacon that he had kept warm next to his unwashed
body all day—accurately into the black pot. In return for
which, Bleedin' Jack hurled a suitably opprobrious epithet at
their departing heels.

Heavy with the unwashed smell of humanity, their sleeping
quarters were even more offensive than the fence's basement.
The room was some twenty foot by thirty on the third and top
floor of the house, lit by candles placed on the floor; which
fortunately only illuminated the vermin that dropped from
the ceiling in its vicinity and the rubbish that immediately surrounded it, tactfully concealing the mouldering walls from
sight, and the plentitude of bed bugs, body parasites and
roaches that populated the floor and bed clothing. Older
people and families had appropriated the first two floors, leaving the last for three dozen or so of the youngest lodgers—a
collection of boys and girls, none much above the age of sixteen; servant girls out of place, young prostitutes and their
chaps, orphaned children, runaway children, poor Irish girls
and a displaced mechanic and his wife, shocked to find themselves sunk so low. And all bound to turn to dishonest pursuits
if they should wish to continue to take advantage of the doubtful benefits that the establishment had to offer.

The floor was marked out in a series of chalk squares, most
of which contained mattresses filled with straw or rags. The
sole coverings were dirty canvas quilts made from the same
stuff as potato sacks. Only one of the beds was raised from
the floor, a broken four poster in the furthest corner, through
the filthy torn curtains of which the watery eye of the deputy
lodging master would occasionally appear, but without inter-
fering in the proceedings.

The room was already fairly full with children in various
stages of dress and undress; lying on the mattresses smoking
short pipes, cooking putrefying herrings over the small fire,

eating scraps of bread—or the less fortunate, just eyeing morosely those that were engaged in these pursuits. And more were arriving every moment, driven in by the cold night air with their day's gleanings.

The Snob made direct for the reserved place that they shared with two prostitutes, sisters, some years older than Celandine, who were sitting on the floor by the mattress.

"Anjool, I'd like ter hintrodooce yer ter two of the fairest in'abitants of the rookery: Buntin' Bett and Mary the Merry Mot."

The girls were in their petticoats with their arms and shoulders bare in what was, to Celandine, a most unseemly fashion, as they laughed heartily with pleasure, their bosoms quivered immodestly, threatening to part company from the bodices that constrained them.

By way of greeting, Bett gestured with her pipe to the Snob and said:

" 'E's a precious caution is that one."

'They 'elps us," he continued, "when we're short on the necessary and wicey-wersa when we're in the rhino. Due to the inhestimable good offices of the aforesaid 'Anjool'—the sweetest little shallow cove who ever dropped a crocadile tear—we're flush enuff to enjoy a small celebrashun. So down to the 'am and beef shop, Mary, for the grub. We'll 'ave saveloys, sausage rolls, fresh bread and a jug of gin."

"Oh, ain't 'e a caution," laughed Mary to Celandine as she went on the errand.

Celandine sat down and discovered from Bett, while the boys were hawking their fruit amongst the lodgers, that the sisters were from the country and came up for no more reason than they were bored with hard farm labour and their stern step-father. It being generally agreed that they were the prettiest girls for miles in their locality, they thought they would have a better choice of a husband in the city, than from the dull country boys they were used to. Their money, however,

had run out before the protectors appeared. For some months
they had stayed at lodging houses and run away each week
without paying the rent—when Bett had acquired the nick-
name of Bunting Bett—until their clothes had gone to the
'dolly-shops'* for food and they were reduced to their present
circumstances of the lowest of lodging houses. The money here
was demanded each night and they had been forced to turn
gay on to the streets for their livelihood.

Mary, the Merry Mot, had returned with the victuals during
this narrative and added in her country burr.

"Lor' we'm baint spending our life hereabouts for always,
me dear, we'm saving our tin for good clothes, then we'm
off up West for ter pander ter the swells."

"Do you like the life?" enquired Celandine curiously.

"I loikes it well enough. Bett there bain't so keen on that
part of it—though I always did. I reckons we'll do well up
there, both being flaxen and sisters, it's more of a pair loike."

The Snob, Nobby and Ralph returned for the victuals and
they passed the gin amongst them. The air had become quite
blue with the tobacco and the fumes from the cooking, and
Celandine felt that the overcrowded room was becoming over-
bearingly hot and oppressive. She was not prepared for Mary's
solution to the humidity however, nor to seek relief in that
manner, which was to pull off her petticoat and plump naked
on to the mattress with a relieved grunt, her large white rump
proud in the air, her breasts pressed out flatly beneath her.
The rest of the diners continued eating and drinking, paying
no special attention other than to divest themselves of some of
their rags. Looking around through the blue haze, Celandine
could see that many of the lodgers were undressed now, and
the liquor—that most of them had consumed—had raised
their spirits and their voices, and the most obscene language
was being bandied to and fro. A group of younger children
were capering about quite unashamed of their nakedness and

* Pawn-shops.

many had already gone to their beds, half-a-dozen or so boys and girls all jumbled together and engaging publicly in the most wicked practices.

Celandine thought of her mother and Mrs. Arkwright. How she would be ridiculed here if she knelt and said her prayers, whilst girls discussed over her head the number of times they had been obliged to take treatment at the infirmary and boys boasted of their young conquests.

Fatigued almost beyond endurance with the long day, the gin and the heat, Celandine hardly cared what was practised around her if she could but creep beneath the quilt and go to sleep. She pulled back the cover and shuddered at the vermin crawling there.

"Bide awhile, Anjool, if you're desirous of a night's repose, we 'as first to engage in a little varlike activity. Come on pals, let's be at the blighters."

The Snob whipped off the quilt and with drunken whoops the company fell upon the exposed creatures, scooping up handfuls and crushing them beneath bottles, and porringers with the dinner still in them. Nobby, hardly decent now in the merest of rags, somehow became entangled with Mary, and Celandine—despite the knowledge that she should avert her eyes—could not help but be fascinated as they became engaged in a more personal combat.

"I reckons they'll finish off vat's left, between 'em." laughed the Snob, throwing the canvas upon them. He turned to Celandine. "You'd do best to strip afore yer joins 'em under there. The wermin is a dooce of a job to find in yer clothing, but they comes off skin easy enuff."

"Oh, I'm not ready yet awhile to take myself to bed," answered the girl airily. In truth she was afraid to stand before them all naked, not only for shame, but that the other girls all seemed so womanly.

A great deal of laughter and shouting of odds came from a group of boys and girls in one corner.

"Is that a shooting match coming off," said Ralph, "Oo's backs-ter-the-wall?"

"I fink it's Purty Pete and the Parson," answered Buntin' Bett.

"I fancy the Parson meself," said the Snob. "Not that Pete ain't a werry pretty performer, but I've seen the Parson make a five footer wiv no trubble at all. Let's join in the sport pals and 'ave a little vager."

As soon as they had taken themselves off, Celandine slipped out of her chemise and got beneath the covers at the other end to Nobby and Mary—still busy at crushing vermin it seemed. She curled into a ball away from them and saw through sleep-weary eyes, the backs of the company giving their encouragement at the shooting match. Just for a moment the spectators parted and Celandine had a clear view of the vigorously engaged contestants and saw what they were at. Celandine blushed furiously and closed her eyes. She opened them again immediately—but Purty Pete and the Parson were lost from sight behind the enthusiastic company. Celandine drifted off to sleep, quite unable to bring herself to say her prayers.

Sometime during the night, she was awakened by the importunate writhings of a thin, cold body insinuating himself next to her.

"What do you think you are at?" she demanded with annoyance.

"Vell, vat d'yer think," came the Snob's surprised voice; for it was he.

"Indeed, you do no such thing with me," she said spiritedly. There was a pause, and then the Snob said, rather plaintively.

"Butcha gotta."

"Why is that pray?"

"'Cos I'm yer bloke in't I, an' they all do it, I mean—it stands ter reason."

"Well it will just have to unstand to reason, for I shall do no such thing with you."

E

"Keep yer jaw darn, can'tcha," whispered the Snob hoarsely in her ear, "yer don' acksherly 'ave ter do it, jest don' you blab to me pals, see."

Celandine thought it wisest to suffer his close proximity, but she whispered sharply back. "Very well, but do keep still, you are all on wires and I would sleep."

19

A DECLINE IN STOCK-BUZZING

IN the following weeks the band followed their calling as common thieves, but never with quite the success they achieved on their first day out with Celandine. The girl had decided, from her discussion with the two young prostitutes and after due reflection, that she too must save her money and purchase decent wearing apparel. Not in order to ply the trade of a gay woman up West, but perhaps to secure a position with a milliner or in a shop or mayhap as a servant to some poor but respectable family, who would not be so particular as to her deficiency in regard to a certificate of character.

She had sent off a letter to Maudie and went daily to the Borough Post Office expectant of a reply but none had been forthcoming. Having no way of knowing if her mother had yet returned to the country, she had delayed writing to her, hoping also that when she should write, there would be a more favourable address to place at the head of the communication.

Much to the Snob's chagrin, she insisted on covering herself more adequately and spending a little of her money at the dolly-shop, purchasing a pair of boots and a second-hand gentleman's frock coat of blue linsey with large wooden buttons down the front. The tail of the coat reached to the ground on Celandine—which was to her complete satisfaction since it had become quite cold with Christmas only a short distance away.

With her savings gradually accumulating and the daily excitement of living on her wits, Celandine would have been reasonably content with her temporary existence, but for the squalor of their accommodation, to which she could not accustom herself. The Snob had proved an adequate protector and although the couples were quite prepared to swap partners on occasion, no such suggestion had been put to her. After a gin-induced sleep—she found this remedy to be the best to ensure respite from the bugs and foul air—Celandine sometimes wondered if anything had occurred that she was unaware of during the night, for the Snob always insisted on her company. At first there had been occasions when she had awoken severely discommoded—but had put it down to the uncommon amount of walking they daily practised. She could not believe that the Snob would take advantage of the situation after giving his word.

She liked the evening best of all, when they walked home through the New Cut from a day's dishonest toil. The incomprehensible raucous cries from the costermongers greeted them as they left the stench of the river behind. The receptacle of most of the refuse of London, or the 'Big Stink' as Londoners called it, had been exceptionally virulent that year, and the cholera epidemic had only just now somewhat abated. But here where the gas jets on the vendor's stalls flared up white to the red night sky, where the colza oil lamps swung from the barrows, their orange flames turning to black smoke and the ragged street sellers held home-made tapers to light their wares —here the 'Big Stink' was lost amongst the myriad smells.

As they walked through the crowds, besieged it seemed by all the street vendors in London—where the Snob still kept his eye skinned in the 'push' for the come-down gent amongst the ragged throng—Celandine inhaled the emanations from yellow haddocks, Yarmouth bloaters, whelks and vinegar; the greasy effluviums of fried fish, eel pies and kidney stews from the coffee shops; the aroma of the dishes of boiled potatoes and sheep's trotters from the street vendors mixing with the sweeter odours of baked potatoes and hot chestnuts—all overlaid with the spirit and beer-laden breath of the passers-by.

But amongst this multifarious assault she was refreshed with the scent of apples and pears, and the wet leaves thrust in her face by the watercress girls, and touched by the sad pungency of three onions, the sole stock of one half-naked guttersnipe squirming through the throng. The smell of greens and pickling cabbage came to her like the sweetest fragrance as did the familiar earth smell from a cartload of turnips, lit by a candle in the hollowed-out recess of one of the vegetables, burning in benediction to her memories of the countryside.

Further down the New Cut was the 'Vic', the Royal Victoria Theatre, to which they usually repaired on a Saturday night, where the most melodramatic histrionics were played out; to the accompaniment of hisses and boos of the sweating shirt-sleeved costermongers and their wives and girl-friends; to the sound of crunching walnut shells and the exhortations from ham sandwich sellers, and vendors of pigs' feet, sheep's trotters, periwinkles and porter. All of which was punctuated by the interpolations of witticisms from the inevitable imitators of Mr. Punch amongst the audience.

His Grace the Archbishop of Canterbury, barely a mitre's toss away in his sumptuous ecclesiastical retreat, took his pleasures rather differently. This was not the same archbishop, Dr. William Howley, who had so nearly put in an appearance at Celandine's birth, for he, after spending £80,000 on restoration and additions to Lambeth Palace had expired the previous year.

His successor, John Bird Sumner, the ninety-first Archbishop, was at that time amusing himself with a petition 'praying that bone-crushers be henceforth forbidden to ply their trade, in the belief that the Miasma generated from the decomposing bones aggravated the cholera epidemic'. Showing a laudable concern for the welfare of his neighbours—if not for the livelihood of the bone-crushers—as befitted the senior resident of the parish, whose palace and gardens covered just about the same acreage as the New Cut district, where some 8,000 of his fellow Londoners fought for food and dwelling.

"I'll go to the magistrate and tell 'ow me money's been took," screamed Bunting Bett, "and I know 'oo. I've a seen 'im squintin' thru' 'is curtains when I goes to me bed."

"Say yer naught, that be my advice," murmured Mary, her more phlegmatic sister, "oo's to tell it was 'im. 'E'll call yer a lying stiff and ow'dja tell the bobbies 'ow yer come by the money. No, say yere naught, no one wants the peelers 'ere. Wem'll start over, and be more cautious with our silver."

But Bett was not to be comforted, she moaned with anguish, beating the mattress with her fists until the other occupants, hidden beneath the quilt, stirred uncomfortably.

It was the early morning of Christmas Eve. Snow was drifting through the broken roof with the first light and settling unmelting in small piles amongst the sleepers.

Celandine listened sleepily to this exchange, when she suddenly came to her senses, leaping naked from the bed, unconcerned for the freezing cold or modesty, she searched frantically amongst the pile of clothes for her petticoat. She soon found it : the hem had been torn out and her fortune too was gone.

'Somefing was very upsetting to Anjool,' thought the Snob. She had not spoken to any of the band that morning and their luck was out. They had trudged through the slush and not pulled a single silk yet, and already it was noon. He was sorely tempted to call it a day. His instinct told him that some misfortune would befall them if they tried to run against Lady Luck.

"Ve've enuff rhino to tide us over. Ve'll knock it off for the day."

Ralph and Nobby nodded gloomily in agreement.

"No!" said Celandine fiercely, "if you want to give it all up, I shall carry on myself."

"Vat'choo frettin' abaht, Anjool?"

The girl walked away with her face set.

"Anjool, ve ain't a giving up. Tell you vot. Ve'll try a new district ter change our luck."

A flurry of snow followed them as they made their way to the Strand. The Snob pattered away with his usual good humour but he was nervous, they were out of their rookery and the folk were too well dressed.

The assemblage of ragged children set behind the tail coat of one ruddy-faced gentleman when he suddenly turned and shouted irrascibly.

"Be off with you, you young sneaks or I'll call a constable."

The Snob was visibly shaken by this.

"It ain't no good Snob," said Nobby, "we stand out 'ere like a bloodied thumb, I'm orf."

"Me too," joined in Ralph, ashen-faced, "we'll be taken if we carry on this gate."

"But I *mean*, we can't just leave 'er, can ve," said the Snob desperately to their departing backs. He hurried after the erect figure in her blue frock coat, marching determinedly forward into the snowflakes.

"Here's a plant," said Celandine as he joined her, "if the other two are off I'll be passer and lookout."

A portly gentleman was handing down a young woman from a cab. The Snob became a little more optimistic. The gentleman seemed absorbed in his young companion and the thickening fall of snow would cover the Snob's movements. Celandine hung back keeping an eye open for any likely observers while the Snob crept up to the coat-tail. As he came nearer he felt all the old confidence return. There was the silk, already half hanging out. A black one too. And a free show from the plant's lady friend, lifting her petticoats very high behind her above the slush, for fear of passing as a draggle-tail, showing the prettiest pair of calves he'd seen in a while. So attentive was the gentleman, that after he'd pulled the silk the Snob thought he might pop round to the front, slip his watch from the swell's vest, divest him of his pocket book and rifle his pockets for any loose change.

He took gentle hold of the handkerchief as the girl turned around, looked him straight in the face and screamed: "Stop thief! Police! Murder!"

The Snob was so surprised that the large man had taken a firm hold on him before he could move.

"Pray give me no inconvenience you young villain, I intend to put you in charge."

The Snob looked round in dismay, there was no one in sight, the snow had driven them off the streets, even Celandine had disappeared to crouch trembling in a doorway.

"Anjool!" cried the Snob as the gentleman marched him past her hiding place. "'Elp me, Anjool!"

What would it profit the Snob for her to be taken up by the police as well, thought Celandine.

"It would seem the capital is suddenly bereft of police constables," said the gentleman, becoming somewhat puffed.

"Never is when you wants 'em. Down in the areas keeping company with cook out of 'arms way I shouldn't wonder," said the young woman.

"I do hope that we can arrive at a speedy conclusion to this distressing matter," rejoined the man, uneasily contemplating the crowd that was beginning to foregather.

"Lemme go, mister. I won' nivver do it no more. Go on mister. I *mean* it's Christmas Eve in'it?"

"Don't you worry yourself, we'll find a bobbie, the likes of you should be locked up," persisted the woman.

"Please 'elp us Anjool!"

He'd have to charge the boy, supposed the gentleman, and the policeman would convey it all down to his notebook, and the names of the witnesses. Could it possibly come to his wife's ears? He wouldn't fancy at all to come across an account of it in 'Paul Pry', or some such scurrilous journal. Where would his respectable reputation be then? Anyway the scamp hadn't actually stolen anything.

Reluctantly Celandine emerged from the doorway and approached the group.

"Why 'pon my soul," said the gentleman, "the boy has made his escape."

"Jem, you did that a purpose, lettin' 'im go. You're an old fool he should've been taken up."

The military man said: "The divil with the police, sir. Should 'ave flogged 'im yourself, sir. Best thing for a chap like that, a good flogging, sir."

"You're an 'ard beggar," said the slightly tipsy girl from the milliner's shop, "ter flog a fellow human on Christmas Eve."

The soldierly gentleman looked down at the girl admiringly. "Sometimes a man 'as ter be 'ard yer know, my dear," he said, squeezing her plump arm.

As she came up to them Celandine recognized the couple who had seized the Snob.

"Maudie," she said, "it's you, and Mr. Pickles."

"Oh my! Celandine, what 'as become of you. You remember Celandine, Jem, down at Rottingdean?"

"Indeed, yes," replied Jem looking around him nervously as more spectators arrived. "Come, Maudie, I feel we should make a departure. The purchase of your Christmas gift might usefully be delayed to a more propitious moment."

"Well, Celandine's to become the maid you promised me."

"Don't be absurd, my dear. She's quite impossible," he sniffed delicately, examining the girl for the first time, "she's hardly . . . er . . . suitable."

Maudie's brown eyes flashed dangerously. "Yer brings me

out in the perishing cold to buy me a present. Buys me a bag
of chocolate creams and eats 'em yerself. Then ter top it yer
says I'm not to 'ave no maid. If you think I'm staying home
with that old woman Christmas Day while you sucks brandy
in the bosom of yer family, yer can just unthink it. I'll not
stir from this spot without Celandine, and that's a fact."

The sweat was beginning to pour down the inside of Mr.
Jeremiah Pickles' unmentionables as the crowd waited for his
retort, when he spied a cruising cab and waved frantically.
"Then you must have the girl, my dear," answered Pickles,
forcing a smile, "for the pavement would be very cold comfort
over Christmas."

"But *werry* rewarding, Guvnor," shouted a voice, and the
crowd roared.

"Some people," remarked Maudie to the world at large,
"is common as shit."

Mr. Pickles hastily conducted the girls to the waiting cab
before there was a riot. Once inside he removed his beaver hat
and wiped around the inside of the brim with the black silk
handkerchief.

"Do open the window a trifle, my dear. For it is exceeding
hot in here."

20

BROADCLOTH AND FUSTIAN

AMONGST the sea of black hats—for men outnumbered the
women ten to one in Hyde Park—Celandine's eye flew to
the owner of one well-glazed stove-pipe hat. The crown of the
hat was of thick leather strengthened with stays of cane and
its owner carried a short truncheon beneath the long tails of
his swallow-tailed coat. He was taller and thicker of figure—

but it was definitely Dick Blackstone in police constable's uniform.

"Oh, Maudie, that policeman there, at the top of the stairs, d'you see? It's Dick, Dick Blackstone."

"Your sweetheart, the parson's son. So 'e ran off to be a bobby, did 'e."

Celandine felt herself blushing. "He wasn't really my lover, Maudie. We grew up together. I never thought him so handsome then."

"He's a well enough set-up fellow, in truth. But there ain't nothing there. They don't make but a guinea a week. Why Mr. Mayne 'imself, the commissioner, don't earn in a year what my Jem makes a month."

"Money isn't everything Maudie, you know."

"Ain't it? Well, I've seen what the lack of it brought you to."

"Of course you're right. Don't think I'm ungrateful, but I must have a word with him. Wait here, I shan't be but a moment."

She could never repay the debt she owed Maudie, thought Celandine, as she struggled through the visitors towards Dick. Perhaps she wasn't servant maid to the most respectable house in London. But what maid wore her mistress' cast-off clothes, accompanied her out on excursions, shared her bed when the master wasn't there—and had none of the labour of keeping the brand new rosewood furniture clean? Perhaps Maudie always made certain that Celandine's clothes did not outshine her own, but Celandine had no pretensions that she could compete with the fascinating, fashionable little demi-monde that Maudie had become. Nor did she object to her young mistress acting the little madame when Mr. Pickles was at home. That was only her right. Celandine was only too aware that girls who had fallen to the depths seldom regained their respectability as she had.

Police Constable Blackstone had early been assigned to the

new division, created under Superintendent Pearce, to police the crowds at the Great Exhibition. Since May 1st, 1851, he had marvelled at Mr. Paxton's Crystal Palace, at the enormous variety of exhibits: from Queen Victoria's favourite, the stuffed tableau of frogs from Wurtemberg—which he personally considered in very poor taste—to his own favourite, 'The Greek Slave' by Hiram Power, that caused such a scandal at the opening of the exhibition not because the carving was nude but because the girl was in chains—which was precisely the reason for Dick's predeliction. He was fascinated by the new machinery and scientific inventions, all the stands of which he now knew very well, for they were already into October. Most of all he was astounded by the visitors, especially on shilling days, when people from all walks of life, races and creeds mixed together. Not that he agreed with Colonel Sibthorpe's opinion given in Parliament that 'mixed races at the Exhibition would produce a piebald generation, half black and half white', but he had never thought to see broadcloth rubbing shoulders with fustian so amicably in public.

However, nothing had moved him so much in all those months, as when he saw Celandine approaching him. She was not as he remembered her—and he preferred to remember her in her patched, well-laundered smock, than as he had last seen her, naked before his father—but despite her smart ladylike clothes, she still preserved that air of childlike simplicity that had so endeared her to him.

"It's good to see you again, Dick," she said, kissing him on the cheek.

"You look wonderful, Celandine. How I've missed you." He stopped, about to take her arm, when it came to him that the sergeant was not far away.

"Why did you go away without telling me, Dick? And what are you doing in the New Police? Whereabouts are you living in London?"

Dick, looking around for his superior officer, saw the familiar figure of the aged Duke of Wellington, who so loved to visit the Exhibition, coming up the steps.

"I can't speak now, Celandine. We must meet and I'll tell you all about it." He doubted, however, that he would tell her what had prompted him to go away. "I am on duty and mustn't be seen talking to my acquaintances."

A hurrah went up from some agricultural workers nearby as word spread that the Iron Duke had arrived.

"Nobody knows we are acquainted unless you should tell them. You might be giving directions to some poor country girl who has lost her way. I suppose you are allowed to do that?"

"You look neither poor nor a country girl, to be dressed so well. You are not married?" he asked suspiciously. Celandine felt herself colour up.

"Of course I am not. I am rather a superior servant girl. Here is my mistress' card, you must come to me, and I shall tell you how it all came about." At least, that which it is fitting you should hear, thought Celandine to herself.

Dick became uneasy at the growing tumult as the Duke foolishly acknowledged the cheering crowds and waved back to them. The Exhibition was more crowded this day than he could remember it.

"You will come won't you, Dick?" asked Celandine noticing his abstracted expression.

"Of course I shall, as soon as I can. I must go now." He gave her a quick smile. Then he called down the steps in a firm voice. "Constable Martin, would you be so good as to come this way."

Celandine watched as he took the officer aside and they moved off towards the door.

She supposed he had his duty to do, but it seemed very strange to her that she was able to command less of his attention now in her bettermost clothes than she could in the country, wearing her old smock dress. Did the cheering have aught to do with his sudden departure, wondered Celandine.

The distant crowds—hearing the uproar and remembering the anxiety expressed in many papers, that the revolutionary building would not be safe to take the heavy machinery and tramp of so many people—became alarmed and raised the cry that the building was falling.

With difficulty Celandine regained her position with Maudie when there was a rush that carried them clean along with it, much to Maudie's concern for her bonnet and crinoline.

When Dick Blackstone reached him, with five other policemen, the Duke of Wellington said : "There's nothing on earth more contemptible than those damn foreign fellows, unless it's a British mob."

"It's your own presence that has aroused them, your Dukeship," answered Dick, slightly nettled by the Duke's tone towards the crowds that loved him so dearly. "I think your own personal dignity might well be best consulted by taking your departure."

The old man snorted and looked Dick up and down, while the five other liveried guardians of the public peace linked arms, straining back against the press to keep the Duke from being buffetted.

"If you can't follow a gentleman's calling, for God's sake don't pretend to talk like one."

"Would you come this way, sir?" commanded Dick, taking his arm. The Duke shook him off, hobbling along without his aid.

"Dammit man, the best test of a great general, is to know when to retreat and to dare to do it."

There was a further surge from the crowd and the police were forced literally to carry the old campaigner to the safety of a side passage.

The Duke, pale and indignant, stood looking out of the window at crowds streaming from the building.

"See those sentries? First out of the building. I know the British army. That's why you must always allow to hang a few of the beggars once and again." He seemed almost to be talking to himself and Dick did not feel obliged to comment.

"Mr. Cole is come to take you to his office, Your Dukeship. I'm sorry you've been troubled, sir." He saluted the old man's back—but the Iron Duke vouchsafed no reply. Dick returned to his duties, leaving Britain's greatest soldier, now reduced to warring with words against any manifestation of class equality. The last battle of his life he won, combating the enormous sparrow population in the Crystal Palace defecating on exhibits and visitors alike, quite regardless of their rank.

"Try sparrow hawks, ma'am," he advised the Queen.

Superintendent Pearce called Police Constable Blackstone to his office the following day.

"It would seem that you understand your instructions well enough regarding the preservation of the security of person, Blackstone."

"Thank you, sir."

"I ain't finished yet, Blackstone," snarled Pearce, "you can save your thanks till then."

"Sorry, sir."

"'Aven't you read in your manual, that courtesy is to be offered on all occasions to the public? Even if 'e is a Dook. What co-operation are we to expect from the public if we save their precious necks and antagonize them into the bargain?"

Dick stood to attention and said nothing. Pearce rifled through the papers on his desk furiously.

"I'm taking you off detail in the exhibition, Constable Blackstone—in case you decides to save Albert 'imself," he added sarcastically. Dick's heart sank. "You're losing your uniform too. You'll report to No. 4, Whitehall Place, Scotland Yard, for private clothes duty. That's all, you can go."

"Thank you, sir," said Dick delightedly. "With pleasure, sir." He saluted and went to the door.

"Another thing," said Pearce. "The commissioners have decided to give you a reward and it shall be entered in the conduct book. I can't imagine why," he growled, returning to his documents.

Celandine was content to let time slip by. She enjoyed the tasks she engaged in, her excursions with Maudie and her mistress' inconsequential chatter, the long hours she spent reading when Maudie was out with one or other of her increasing number of followers and even the visits of her master, the dignified and ponderous Mr. Pickles.

Whether because of the contentious nature of her introduction to the household or for some other reason, Celandine did not know, but Maudie insisted that she should make herself scarce when Pickles was about. She would appear briefly before him to show in the perruquier from Strathearn's in Prince's Street, Hanover Square, who came by cab which was kept waiting while a tonsor was operated upon Mr. Pickles' not very luxuriant locks. Else the master might send her out to the pastry shop for some of those delicacies he was so partial too. She opened the door to her employers each time they returned from the Park in Maudie's well-appointed equippage —yet she doubted that Mr. Pickles would recognize her if he saw her out in the street.

More and more she inhabited the world she found in the books of Mr. Dickens and Mr. Trollope, where the very streets were cleared of the throngs of gay women before the heroes stepped on to them; where the heroines, waiting for their ever-so-chaste young men to call up a cab, were never inconvenienced by the steaming streams lapping around their shoes from the squatting Cyprians who turned the Strand into a public piss-house.

On occasion she would entertain Dick Blackstone in the kitchen or go out at night to dance and hear music with him at the Argyll or Holborn Casino where they had a splendid band of fifty instruments. But she insisted that Dick should treat her in the fashion that gentlemen treated ladies in her novels and be thankful if he could steal a buss on the cheek. She had seen enough to satisfy her curiosity about the stronger sex and could not see what drove Maudie so hard about them. There had seemed plenty of young and handsome women up West to throw themselves at any gentleman who had the price of another shillingsworth of brandy to set before them, and she saw no reason to swell that number of gay birds. After some months Dick became a less frequent visitor to the house.

21

MRS. FITZGERALD'S NEW SILKEN STAYS

THE advertisement in the 'Ladies' Newspaper' stated: 'Mrs. Fitzgerald's New Silken Stays are guaranteed to promote the tapering waist and emphasize the well-developed bosom and large hips that are the combination of points required for a fashionable figure. The measure must be taken on the person in order to achieve this desirable effect and to produce that close adjustment which indirectly bids its wearer to exercise self-restraint, and gives evidence of a well-disciplined mind and well-regulated feelings.'

Celandine doubted, as she hastened along Oxford Street to the omnibus stop, that the two pairs of Mrs. Fitzgerald's corsets parcelled beneath her arm, would have the useful moral effect on Maudie that the latter part of the advertisement had indicated.

"Oh, I say, My Lord!"

The handsome young gentleman, who blocked her way

on the pavement, could have stepped from one of Celandine's romantic novels. He had the straight nose of a Greek God and sported long, blonde hair and silky Picadilly weepers. He was wearing one of the new hats that used to be worn by cab drivers, called a Hemispherical Hat, made of hard felt with a bowl-shaped crown surmounted by a knob on the top. His bamboo cane was of the slenderest and the shoe-tie passing through the ring at his neck was so narrow it could have served as a boot-lace—this, in its turn, encompassed the tallest of all-round collars. All of which, with the virulent pea-green of the long Noah's Ark overcoat that he affected, suggested that he was no ordinary gentleman.

"I beg your pardon, sir."

"No, oh I say! entirely my fault."

Celandine stepped aside, so fascinated by the glorious apparition that quite immodestly she could not take her eyes from him. He in his turn seemed equally affected by the girl.

"Look here, my dear, I know it's dooced bad manners, but, by George! you're such a stunner, I mean, main't I introdooce myself."

Celandine bridled, he must take her for a common girl of the streets.

"Will you let me pass, sir, for I am in a hurry."

"Please, my dear," pleaded the swell—as she took sudden flight—his long legs chasing after her.

"You needn't frighten yourself, let me put you more in the way of understanding things. You see I am an artist and am at present looking for a model."

Indeed, thought the girl, slowing her step a trifle, he could be so, with his uncommon apparel.

"You may well be what you say you are, sir, but what affair is it of mine?"

"Oh, my dear. Do you ever look in the glass? I would paint you of course. You shall be my Beatrice, and shall make both of us famous."

Celandine stopped and coloured up furiously. Was the beautiful young man poking cruel fun of her? Or merely flattering to gain some dark design of his own? He seemed of genteel birth and polished manners.

"I see that you are suspicious of my purpose, and you are right to be cautious. But I beg you to take my card, and make what enquiries you will as to my character. Think on it—and if you would make both our fortunes, come to my studio at any hour of the day or night."

The pasteboard read Arthur Banks, followed by an address in Millbank. It was certainly very wonderful that an artist should approach her so in the street.

"I pray you, fair lady, do give my proposal your earnest consideration and even if I should never see you again at least tell me your name."

"Celandine, and there's my 'bus I must fly."

Arthur Banks raised his Hemispherical Hat to her display of slimly proportioned ankles as she lifted her skirts and ran.

"Oh, my Lor'," he said, "what a stunner!"

"Tighter," sobbed Maudie, "much tighter mayhap it'll strangle the little bastard."

Maudie would never wear a chemise beneath her corset, she liked to feel the silk and whalebone close around her naked middle and to imagine it forcing the blood down to that seat of pleasure which had been her undoing.

"What's to become of me, Celandine? I never reckoned on 'aving no kid."

Celandine was uncertain whether the tears were of anguish at the tight lacing of the new stays or for fear at what the future held.

"Perhaps it will come to nothing," panted Celandine.

"It will, it will, it's two months gone by now. But I'll not go to no lint-scraper to lose it and maybe my life as well."

"What does Mr. Pickles think on it?"

"I dunno 'e didn't say much, just looked leery. It ain't 'is anyway I reckon, else it would 'ave come about before."

Celandine smoothed out the wrinkles in the silk. "There it fits a treat," she said breathlessly.

"Oh my, ain't that 'andsome," smiled Maudie, turning stiffly before the glass and admiring how Mrs. Fitzgibbon's stays split her plump figure into two bulbous hemispheres, "and not a sign of any swelling," then suddenly she was in tears again, "but it's goin' to 'appen that's for sure. And what gentleman wants a lady wiv all 'er belly swollen up?"

"You'll make your eyes a sight if you carry on so," said Celandine, drying her mistress' cheeks with a towel.

"It's all right for you, Celandine Spencer, just sixteen and a sweet little virgin." The girl was shocked at the unexpected vehemence in Maudie's voice. Surely Maudie was not jealous. Silently she helped draw on the openwork silk stockings. "But what of after, wiv me looks and figure gone, and nigh twenty years of age? You knows 'ow the fine gentlemen carries on round 'ere, they're orf after annuvver sixteen year old."

Celandine arranged the silk garter just above the knee and closing the metal fastening, brought forward Maudie's tiny walking out boots with the square toes and the military heels. Taking a button stick she began to squeeze Maudie's feet into them, fastening down the buttons on the outside of the boots.

"Oh, Maudie, I suppose you are about right, but you have your diamonds and I have a little money. We could go to France. I understand that the French gentlemen do not take a woman for a mistress until she is quite mature, and have none of the Englishman's schoolboy preoccupation with young girls."

Maudie's tousled head appeared through her chemise, with her jaw hanging open.

"'Ere you ain't just saying all that?"

"Indeed no, I have read that is the fashion and I have even

learned a little French myself," she tied on the cambric petticoat, "I believe we could manage very well."

"I takes it all back," laughed Maudie in good humour again, kissing her friend enthusiastically. "P'raps there is some good to come from learnin' to cipher."

Celandine dressed Maudie's elaborately crimped hair from a central parting, down over her ears and twisted it into a bun at the back. Then she arranged the velvet bandeau that prevented the small bonnet, worn well back on the head, from quite slipping off altogether.

"I'm sure we'll not need to go to France. Mr. Pickles is much too kind to cast you out."

"Even if 'e never finds out the brat's not 'is, I wouldn't put my trust in it, nor no man," said Maudie, quite confident in this instance, of the superiority of her worldly widsom over that of any schollard.

When the capuchin hood had been adjusted across her mistress' shoulders and the graceful folds of the highland cloak that measured sixteen yards around had been arranged—Celandine stepped back enviously.

"Oh, Maudie you look so splendidly attired." She felt very poorly apparelled of late, Maudie having a seeming reluctance to pass on any of her clothes.

"You can't attract the gentlemen without you dress spicey," answered Maudie, buttoning her tight-fitting gloves. The small hand had become a symbol of gentility and she was very proud of her own tiny hands. She took the white enamel stick of her parasol. "It's a pity you can't accompany me on this excursion, my dear, but I did tell the dear Major, that I walked alone each Tuesday at four o'clock in the Burlington Arcade." She kissed Celandine on the cheek. "If you must bury yourself in a book, my dear, do make it a French one."

When she had gone, Celandine slowly began to tidy the dressing-room. Maudie never wanted to take her anywhere any more. Surely she was not fearful of the competition from her own maid. It was true that the angry red blotches that had marred her face for as long as she could remember had gone, and that her hair had taken on a new lustre. She felt different too, no longer content to read her romances, she would turn to the works of Mr. Shakespeare or wander the apartment when by herself—one moment as gay as a sandpiper; the next unaccountably in tears. Then there had been the artist. Something had warned her against confiding in Maudie about Arthur Banks. Did that handsome young man really want to paint *her*—Celandine Spencer.

Leaving the debris where it lay, Celandine went to the large pier glass and loosed her hair, letting it fall luxuriously down to her hips. How would she look in one of Mrs. Fitzgerald's Silk Stays? Throwing off her apron, her print dress and her chemise, Celandine stood naked before the glass and examined her limbs dispassionately. Even without a corset, she admitted to herself, the outlines of her figure compared favourably with Maudie in her lacings.

Celandine pulled on the new stays that were in a delightful shade of Aurora Pink. It was a difficult task to lace the garment up quite unaided and she did not hear the hansom cab that pulled up outside the door. Nor as she pulled the last two metal rings together did she hear the master's key in the front door.

Pickles, feeling mildly peckish, and wondering what food there was to be had in the pantry, drew in his breath with incredulity at the charming sight he observed through the open dressing-room door. How had he overlooked this delightful confection in his own dwelling? His hungry eye travelled down the waves of golden hair flowing over her naked shouders, past the short pink corset—that busked in her waist so tight, that he could have encompassed it easily between his two hands— down to where the honeyed tendrils coiled on the broad white shelf of her splendid hips and rested in profusion on the proud swell of her plump buttocks. How delightful were the two dimples, set one on either side and just above the deep cleft between those excellent posteriors. Exquisite indentations, quite as though they had been placed there by a master-cook, delicately pressed into freshly-rolled dough. And then her firm thighs, constrained above the knee, where a silk garter cut delectably into her skin. The white stockings that were so held, did naught to conceal the shapely swelling of her calf. Thence his inquisitive gaze went to the tiny boots—which doubtlessly squeezed small feet commensurate with the rest of her well-turned parts.

"By George!" breathed Pickles.

His examination next turned to the girl's reflection in the long glass, her perfectly rounded knees and the well proportioned legs leading up to her softly rounded belly, beneath which lay those portals—scarcely hidden by the merest brush of gold—that was the pantry of his desire.

Above the silken stays burst forth the rich plumpness of her panting bubbies, each tipped with its over-ripe, succulent strawberry.

Pickles passed his tongue over dry lips and continued his appraisal of smooth shoulders and neck that supported her well-shaped head. Her face was oval, and her red lips trembled beneath a straight nose. The enormous blue orbs of her eyes were wide-set, and staring with affright at Mr. Pickles, reflected in the glass.

"Is this the manner in which you spend your Mistress' time when she is away?" asked Pickles, striding into the room with an assumed fury. The cold eye, the imperious nose and the ponderously sarcastic tone, of the man who had held them in fear and trembling below stairs and was not to be vexed by those above either—bent its full majestic force on the guilty Celandine. Gone were her aspirations to maturity, flown was the dawning confidence in her handsome appearance.

"I thought it would do no harm," stammered the girl.

Pickles' nostrils dilated with scorn. Slowly he drew off his yellow gloves and placed them with his silk hat and cane on an occasional table.

"Indeed!" he snorted. "You consider it unharmful for a modest young girl to bedizen herself like the veriest strumpet?"

What splendid bobbing bubbies, he thought to himself.

Celandine was at a loss for an answer. It would only enrage him further to learn that the garment she wore belonged to his mistress. She reached for her frock, only to stop with fear as he roared at her.

"Be still, and don't fidget! If you wish to dress in that fashion, you shall remain so." Would that I could press forward such a command indefinitely, ruminated Pickles.

Bowing her head meekly, Celandine stood before him, modestly pressing her plump thighs together, and wondering how it was that he seemed not to have noticed the meagre nature of her covering.

"Sit down there!" ordered Pickles, indicating a well-stuffed Coburg sofa. "I would speak to you of your mistress."

Celandine hesitated a moment as a memory passed through her mind of Mrs. Saward the cook, spread out on her sofa, and of a similar article of furnishing in the little parlour at Rottingdean, where she had first made the acquaintance of Mr. Pickles. But the one time gentleman's servant had already turned from her and was majestically pacing the room, his hands clasped behind him, beneath the tails of his coat. Celandine's hands likewise were clasped, quite firmly in her lap. She sat on the edge of her seat, very conscious of her tremulous bare bosoms, as the portly bulk of Mr. Pickles' chained and bloodstone-buttoned waistcoat returned, and bore down on her.

"I have decided to take you into my confidence child, and whilst I would not wish you to be disloyal to your mistress, nevertheless you owe me a duty as your employer to answer my questions. I have had some reason of late to be concerned about your mistress' comings and goings. So tell me frankly and it shall go no further. Where is she at this moment?"

With some relief Celandine could answer honestly:

"Why, sir she has gone on an excursion to the shops, and would surely have stayed, had she known that you were to come this afternoon."

Pickles sat down heavily beside her on the sofa, bouncing the girl in such a fashion that brought a blush to her cheeks.

"Why should you tell me that which might take your situation away?" he said brokenly—of a sudden the hauteur driven from him.

"Indeed, it is the truth, sir," cried Celandine distressed at the change which had come over the man.

"I believe you to be an honest girl," he said sadly, patting her shoulder and absently leaving his hand there, "and I am certain that you believe what you say. She has made you aware of her approaching *accouchement*?"

"Oh yes, sir, may I offer you my congratulations?"

"Would that I could accept them, my dear. It is the dearest wish of my life to have an heir," Celandine was distracted for a moment as Mr. Pickles' other hand rested in a fatherly fashion on her thigh, "but I fear neither my wife, nor Miss Bates, nor indeed any other woman could bear fruit from my seed." He turned his eyes from hers and his head sank on to his chest. "I am impotent."

"Oh, sir!" Was that a moistness in his eye. A sob broke from him. It was a very terrible thing to see such a man broken in grief.

"You mustn't carry on so, sir."

Then his head was on her breast and she was comforting him.

"Oh, you mustn't, sir," cried Celandine, for Pickles was taking his fill of strawberries and searching eagerly for the pantry, from which she endeavoured to deny him proper access by keeping tight closed her thighs. Nevertheless this engagement with her master had produced a most curious inclination to wantoness in her.

"Let me, my dear, I'll not hurt you."

What harm was there in it, thought the girl. Was not poor Pickles' mistress by now divested of her fine clothes and disporting herself in a similar fashion with another man?

Pickles stumbled back from her, panting and wrestling with his clothes.

"Let us make love, my dear."

"How can you suggest such a thing, sir, I must go—the mistress will be returning."

"Don't be a little fool, stay here, there's a dear, I'll give you a present."

Curiosity stayed her for the moment; and the desire to prolong the singular satisfaction to be had from seeing the venerable Mr. Pickles—who had so long ignored her very existence—humbled and pleading for her compliance.

Her undoing was the paroxysm of laughter that she was reduced to at the ridiculous figure Pickles cut with his trousers lowered. Nature had well compensated him for the lack of hair on his head, by a luxuriant matt over his large belly and lean shanks—from which peered a medium-sized spouter for such a stout gentleman, no bigger than those she had witnessed on the boys at 'Bleedin' Jack's'. She lay helplessly on the sofa endeavouring to control any outward sign of the hysteria that had overtaken her as Pickles, impeded by the breeches around his ankles, shambled forward. That great belly preceding his manhood, ceased of a sudden to be a source of amusement—when it fell on her, knocking the breath from her body.

"Oh, please let me up, sir, I cannot breathe."

Panic-stricken, Celandine struggled beneath him—but despite the girl's attempts to extricate herself from her situation and despite his own unwieldy bulk—Pickles found his mark.

"Oh, you shan't, oo-oh you hur-hurt me."

But in truth after the first few lunges it was not so fearsome as Celandine had imagined. She was more uncomfortable from his great weight than from anything else and soon ceased her struggles which were of such little avail. At least there was some small consolation that poor Pickles would not place her in Maudie's unenviable condition. How he laboured above her, and was becoming quite red in the face with it. His motions became more frantic and Celandine was beginning to feel that answering excitement to which Maudie had so often alluded—when Pickles began to splutter.

"Oh-oooo-eeeeeee-yi," he roared, and with that, collapsed inert on her.

"Oh, sir—you crush me."

Pickles slowly rolled off the girl, and despite his flushed and disordered appearance—resumed his dignity with his trousers.

"Come, my dear, don't look so glum, it's not as though it's the first time you've been poked."

He frowned at the girl. "I must confess to some disappointment, Celandine, to discover that your honour was not quite irreproachable when I took you into my employ." Taking the girl's forlorn and tear-stained look as mute acceptance of his rebuke, Pickles examined his watch.

"By Heavens, I shall be late for the board-room. In the city we should really make no appointment when we have occasion to use a carriage. The streets are stuffed up to such a degree." Carefully replacing the time-piece in his waistcoat pocket he turned his attention once more to the girl.

"Give me a kiss, my dear, and I'll be off. Not a word to your mistress, mind. And I'll bring you a present next time I come. There's a sensible girl."

Was that all about it? she wondered, when he had gone. Wherein then was all the to-do?

Celandine lay there trembling as though she were on wires. Slowly she calmed and the full import of what had occurred, came to her. She had done it with Pickles. She had lost her respectability. She was a fallen woman and had contrived it all through the offices of her best friend's lover. Celandine turned over on the sofa and wept long and bitterly.

It was time the gas-lamps were alight when Celandine at last raised her head. Maudie would return shortly. How could she face her dearest friend that she had betrayed? What if Pickles should wish to discard Maudie and install his new young lover in her place?

With sudden decision Celandine flew about the apartment gathering her things together in her box, and what little money she had she secured safely about her.

It was an agonizing moment waiting outside to hail a passing cab, for what if a cab should rattle up, only to put down Maudie before her. But she could hardly do the economical and walk with her large box. She at last attracted the attention of the jarvey of a four-wheeler, and it was not until she had given her instructions to the man and was safely installed inside, that she recalled she was still wearing Maudie's stays.

But Maudie, on returning from dalliance with her lover, was to have more important matters to consider than the whereabouts of Mrs. Fitzgerald's New Silken Stays.

22

THE MIDNIGHT MEETING

At 11.30 that night the sweet forgetfulness of sleep still evaded Celandine. Was this the punishment of fallen souls that she had read about and of which her mother had warned her? If these were the torments that followed close on a damaged reputation, it was indeed hard to bear. Her face felt flushed as if in fever, her pulse raced and her limbs prickled with heat as though requiring some solace of she knew not what.

The lodgings she had taken in Endell Street were clean and respectable—if rather more than her slender purse would allow. But she was determined no matter how she must contrive it, not ever to return to that low-life that Maudie had rescued her from. The very walls, however, at this moment, oppressed her so fiercely, that she felt she must seek relief in the night air. To this end she wrapped herself in a hooded cloak and taking her key, sought the lights of Shaftesbury Avenue.

The pavements were well populated with the unfortunates of the night, and their foolish followers, mostly of the commercial and shopkeeper type, who allowed Celandine to pass unmolested deeming her, from her plain clothes, either respectable or too expensive for their means. Small children were about too, disguising their true calling by selling pincushions, flowers, lavender and other such trifles. Celandine with the dark shadow of a shameful life hovering over her, moved purposefully ahead, pausing only when she passed sixpence to a cross-sweeper still at his post.

Would she be forced to join these poor creatures, she wondered, when her money was gone. She passed a match-girl and her chap—the girl's profession apparent from her glowing phosphorous rolled jaws and decaying gums, all for ninepence a day: the price of respectability. Would Dick Blackstone rescue her from her plight once he had learned how it had come upon her?

The way was becoming better lighted with flaring gas jets from night houses and gin palaces and the paler illumination of the French restaurants, oyster shops and the doubtful coffee shops with their blinds drawn. Her path thickened with fast men and flash women, old hags with fruit and vegetables, male vendors of knives and pencils, policemen and bullies.

For want of breath Celandine at last slowed her pace feeling at least somewhat eased physically if not so in her mind. She found herself before the entrance to St. James' Restaurant,

St. James' Hall, where a large number of women were congregated. It seemed that some kind of midnight service was about to commence for the fallen women who congregated nightly in the Haymarket and the casinos round about.* In company with the pathetic birds of the night, Celandine considered that she too was in need of comfort, and allowed herself to drift with the unfortunates into the building.

Celandine regretted her impulse once she had been shown into the large well-lighted dining-room. The majority of the fallen sisterhood were most fashionably attired, blazoned with finery and jewellery, and despite her understanding that the wages of sin were a debilitated constitution, dreadful disease and an obscure ending in frightful degradation, the well-dressed creatures seemed in remarkably rude health. Their health seemed far better than other women of their class, infinitely more so than the match-girl she had been considering earlier that night.

Compared to their finery, paint and false curls, Celandine felt very plain indeed. Could she, wondered Celandine, ever grow to like the life. There seemed from her experience, very little to it but her modesty to overcome.

The gathering, which must have been well over two hundred, as they grouped in clusters about the tables, partaking of the tea, coffee, bread and butter, toast and cake supplied— would have put a similar gathering of their betters, quite to shame for their beauty.

Celandine read the bills posted up regarding the meeting. The patron, she observed with surprise, was the landowner from her home parish: Lord Furlingham. It was originated by gentlemen connected with the Country Towns Missions, The Monthly Tract Society, Female Aid Society, London Female Preventative and Reformative Associations, and other

* There were enormous numbers of prostitutes in London: 80,000 being the figure most popularly quoted. It has been placed as high as 100,000 – 150,000 out of a total population of 2 million.

societies, anxious to attend to the spiritual welfare of their dear young friends with prayers and admonitions. It appeared from the poster that any woman repenting of her sins would be conducted to a reformatory where she would enjoy a life, thought Celandine, taking stock of those around her, considerably less comfortable than she now enjoyed.

The girl was half persuaded to turning gay on the streets, when her eye went to the gathering of clergymen, gospel grinders and stern women of moral rectitude who had convened the assembly. There next to an aristocratic-looking gentleman, stood the tall handsome figure of her mother.

Celandine fled the hall and hastened through the streets pale and shaken. She would have died if her mother had met her after these years in such company. Nor could she ever be easy in such a life with her mother campaigning the pavements. There was, however, one solution to her problem. She stopped for breath and took out the piece of pasteboard from her pocket. Arthur Banks was young and beautiful and might well be all that he claimed. But had he meant it when he said come at any hour of the day or night? Celandine hailed a hansom and directed it to Millbank. Arthur Banks was her one hope. Sitting in the cab jogging rhythmically along Celandine suddenly smiled to herself. How well mamma had looked and so beautiful even amongst that attractive gathering.

23

MODEL OF IMPROPRIETY

"Do take a look, old fellow," enthused Arthur Banks, "just a peek round the life class door, you know."

Bookbinder smiled tolerantly at his young friend's excitement. Arthur with his inconsequential fancies made him feel very old at times. Owen Bookbinder indeed appeared older than his thirty-three years, this was partly due to the leonine beard he now affected, already streaked with grey, but the ridicule heaped on the Chartists after the Great Procession, had been a heavy blow to him, and one from which the movement had not yet recovered. When the monster petition had been laid out on the floor of the House, pages and pages proved to be written in the same handwriting, with such signatures as 'Pug-nose', 'Flat-nose', and 'No-cheese'!

Feargus O'Connor, unfortunately meeting the bigoted Colonel Sibthorpe at the door of Parliament, remarked that he was 'glad there had been no violence', the irascible Colonel retorted: "Not I . . . if you had attempted to come over the bridge, you would have got the soundest thrashing mortal man ever received."

Bookbinder wondered still whether that would truly have been the situation. How would it have stood with the movement now if he had encouraged instead of quelling the physical-force Chartists. But Owen was content in his own mind that nothing would have been worth the blood that would have been spilt that day.

Only last year in 1852 poor O'Connor—having exhibited such symptoms of violent and extravagant behaviour in the House, that it became manifest his mind was affected—had been conveyed to a lunatic asylum.

Another more personal blow had fallen hard on these events: the death of his father. Owen, leaving the field work to younger men, had taken over the family printing works in Shadwell, where he still printed tracts and bills for the movement, but considered keeping employ for his workmen to be his major consideration.

"If she could draw a little, I might make use of this young woman," said Owen humorously, "but I doubt such a beauty as you describe could wash, let only etch, a plate."

Bookbinder had recruited many artisans into his business from this place, the Working Men's College in Great Ormond Street, and many of the artists who made designs for him, taught in the evening classes to any working man who could afford the twopence a week.

"I tell you Owen, she'll be my inspiration."

"And while you're spending pleasant hours making easel paintings from this young woman, for rich patrons, you could be designing functional things for ordinary folk, carpets, curtains, tables and chairs, and providing useful labour for the poor." Bookbinder was only half-mocking. His thoughts had turned more and more of late to a commune which would build its own model houses and support itself by its own industry, where everyone would be equal, having early gained the conviction that the character of man was formed for him by the circumstances into which he was born and in which he lived.

Arthur had always had a roof over his head and never missed a meal in his life. He would sooner teach someone to draw than think to give them a crust of bread. He found Bookbinder's belief that art and practicality should go hand in hand, curious. Art was surely the avoidance of reality, and he always carefully avoided any discussion with Bookbinder on this topic.

"Do take care, Owen, we must not make a disturbance, Gabriel can be so savage when he is interrupted." Arthur opened the door of the life-room just sufficient so that they could see inside.

Dante Gabriel Rossetti, poet, painter and leader of the Pre-Raphaelite Brotherhood, declaimed volubly in great torrents of words to the bemused artisans, on the transcendant qualities of the model they were gathered about and attempting to draw. His classical allusions and occasional lapses into Italian were quite beyond his unlettered students. Nevertheless, the warm liquid voice and passionate volubility that threw his shoulder-length hair about violently, and the graceful brown hands gesticulating with such feeling, completely enthralled them. And each one was inspired and uplifted by the magic he wrought.

Including Celandine, the startled beneficiary of the poet's laudatory prose. It hardly seemed possible that the famous Mr. Rossetti was describing her own charms. Arthur Banks, too, stared at Gabriel with hero-worship.

Only Owen Bookbinder was not under the spell. A man could use his own eyes to see what was before him, he considered, and did not need another's words to describe it for him. The girl was posed seated in a chair and wore an evening dress of Camayeux silk, printed in alternate stripes of pink and mauve, with a shawl modestly covering her naked shoulders. It was the fierce light of pride that Rossetti had lighted in her eyes which took Owen aback. This was the way a woman should be, he thought, to stand up straight next to a man. She scarce conformed to the type that the Pre-Raphaelites usually favoured, which was tall, willowy and docile.

This was the woman, Bookbinder determined, whom he would marry, if she would have him.

Rossetti's hawked nose turned towards the door, and Arthur closed it hurriedly.

"I had not expected that our tastes would be quite so much in accord on such a matter," breathed Owen, "She really is a splendid creature."

"I knew you would agree once you saw her," said Arthur delightedly, "now I insist that you should come and take tea with us, and make a proper acquaintance."

"Does she then live in your house with you," asked Bookbinder frowning."

"Oh, I say, no!" stammered Arthur Banks, "I mean not in that fashion, she lodges with me but has her own rooms, you know."

"Well then," smiled Owen Bookbinder, "I shall be delighted to call, at the earliest convenience."

F

The egregious Horace Birket was quite naked but for a wreath of laurel leaves around his large tonsured head. He surveyed his hairless body, pot belly and infantile parts with some satisfaction, then strutted proudly to and fro before the glass.

"Caligula, was the greatest Roman of them all. Would you not say, Caliban?"

The servant looked up from folding his master's clothes and the white teeth flashed in his dark face.

"He surely must claim that distinction, sir."

"By Jupiter!" said the little poet excitedly, "I have it, we shall build a baths out at Snaresbrook. The finest marble, Caliban, and a forest of statues." He plumped into a large chair, where he bounced, clapping his hands, his short legs swinging, his eyes growing wilder.

Caliban grinned at Birket, and reached in his pocket for the phial.

"You must procure me boys, Caliban, small swimming eels of boys," he stuttered, "wriggling water-babies . . . nibbling gold-fish . . ." he choked.

Giggling, the dark servant poured a little of the draught into his master's constricted throat.

Downstairs in Arthur's studio and quite unaware of the scene being enacted above her head, Celandine was posed as the picture of propriety. As a bereaved widow she was severely encased in black bombazine, her pale face only just visible through the heavy veil dependent from her bonnet.

"Mr. Bookbinder has asked me to marry him," she declared, watching Arthur's face for any sign of the emotion she hoped might be expressed there. Not once in the time that she had lodged with the artist had he evidenced any reciprocation of the tender feelings she felt for him.

"Splendid, my dear," said Arthur putting down his brush and coming around the canvas. His handsome face was wreathed in smiles, noted Celandine dejectedly. She had only

accepted Owen Bookbinder's persistent attentions in the hope
of stirring some response from Arthur.

"I made no answer to him, however, until I had spoken
with you."

"That was very considerate of you, Celandine. I am of
course concerned for you, somewhat in the manner of a guard-
ian, there being none other to fill that position. The whole
affair however meets with my approval. Not that Bookbinder
need wait for that of course. He may now properly consider
himself engaged to you and publish the banns at once, for
silence gives consent."

"Oh Lord!" said Celandine, growing pale. "I said naught
for I knew not what to say."

"It is of no moment, my dear. You are well-matched, despite the disparity in years. Bookbinder has not wasted the
virility of manhood in his youth, and should last to a good old
age, he is of some estate and a more manly, kind and honest
soul I have never met."

In truth, thought Celandine, slowly recovering from the
shock of discovering that she was engaged, Owen was all the
things that Arthur said, even Maudie would have approved of
his position in life. He was a gentleman, but to the girl he
seemed such an old gentleman.

Arthur Banks turned towards the door at the sound of
giggles and laughter from the hall, displaying his Greek profile
in all its perfection.

"I shall of course give you away myself."

Celandine decided that it must only be his beauty that
infatuated her, for he was really very stupid indeed. What
of Dick Blackstone whom she had always imagined she would
marry? She had not seen him since she had taken up with
Arthur, but had more feeling for him despite his lack of fortune, than either men. He was neither old nor stupid.

Her thoughts were broken by the studio door bursting open,
and the monstrous spectacle of the naked Birket, carrying

a flaming torch he had made from the 'Observer' dipped in tallow, the laurel wreath tipped over his eyes nearly blinding him.

"Come Arthur, we must away to Snaresbrook Abbey," he screamed, "you'll come if I have to burn you out."

Celandine could hardly contain her amusement at the spectacle they must have presented; her own mournful appearance in widow's weeds, the poet's quivering white limbs as he stumbled about attempting to ignite the articles of furniture in the room, and Arthur's distressed face as he tried to restrain his friend, shouting:

"I say old fellow that's not really the thing. The girl's just got engaged you know." Far more concerned at the thought of Celandine being compromised than for the possibility of his curtains catching fire.

"Promise you'll come, or by God I'll ravage her before your eyes," screamed the little man, looking as fiercesome as a Tipsy Pudding. At this Celandine with tears of laughter running down her cheeks beneath the veil sobbed helplessly into her gloved hands.

"Look here," said Arthur, white-faced, misconstruing the girl's sobs, "this has gone far enough, you wretch."

"Then promise! promise!" yelped the little poet, leaping up and down, to the girl's further disconcertion.

"Very well, Birket, you have my word on it."

"Capital, Arthur, I'll not disturb your work any further." So saying, Horace Birket rushed through the french windows into the garden, bearing his flaming torch above him.

"He's a splendid fellow, really," apologized Arthur to Celandine, "and dooced clever, but sometimes not quite himself I fear." He stopped suddenly and his face set. "By Heavens, the neighbours," he said, and bolted from the studio after Birket.

Celandine threw back her head with relief and wiped her eyes. Her ribs were aching with constrained laughter.

"If it please *Khrishna*, Miss Spencer," murmured a deep voice next to her ear, "you shall enjoy *Ras lila* equally at Snaresbrook Abbey."

Celandine drew back from the musky proximity of Caliban, who had this alarming habit of appearing silently.

"If Mr. Banks should request me to accompany him to Snaresbrook, I shall certainly comply," replied Celandine stiffly. The huge dark fellow was dressed more like a Maharaj than a servant, in plain black breeches, that displayed calves quite as extensive as Thomas the footman, above shoes decorated with silver buckles. A large pearl stick-pin sat in the stock at his neck—brilliant white between the dark broadcloth tailcoat and his swarthy face. Around his head was a bejewelled, green silk turban. All-in-all a complete contrast to his puny master. The man and his strange words made her feel exceeding uncomfortable.

"Perhaps of more immediate concern, is the fact that your master is quite beside himself and is at present cavorting naked in the garden, where I am sure Mr. Banks would be grateful for your assistance."

"*Abou laaba* awaits impatiently for satisfaction at the *Ras Mandali*," grinned Caliban. Bowing formally to the girl, he turned and walked into the garden.

24

THE DEATH OF MODESTY

"The Pre-Raphaelite Brotherhood is dissolved and the Round Table quite broken up," said Rossetti savagely, "I'll not say another word on the matter and there's an end to it." He sat morosely, staring at the beautiful Elizabeth Siddal seated opposite him, seeming to derive some comfort from this exercise.

The heavy gloom that succeeded this pronouncement settled over Rossetti's house, at 14, Chatham Place, and mingled with the poisonous afternoon vapours drifting in from 'the big stink' that lapped oilily just outside the windows.

Not daring to break the stultifying silence, Celandine too, studied Rossetti's famous model, not without some envy. Miss Siddal suited admirably the atmosphere of the place. She gazed unseeingly out of the window, a slim ethereal figure, full of melancholy. Her crimped, unbound hair fell back from a broad forehead, and her hands rested calmly in her lap, so still, that in the miasma of the room, she might have been a painting.

Celandine sighed, never could she assume a pose so naturally, and those that she did achieve, she soon became impatient with.

Bookbinder did not believe that Rossetti was unduly vexed at the disbanding of the Brotherhood. In truth, now that Millais, a founder member and the most talented draughtsman of the P.R.B., had been elected to the Royal Academy and gone over to that arch enemy—the Pre-Raphaelites were virtually at an end. What hurt Gabriel, considered Bookbinder, was that Millais' painting, 'The Order of Release', had received such public acclaim that a police guard had been necessary to protect it. But Rossetti and Millais had never been on such excellent terms and Bookbinder was not prepared to have his visit overshadowed by Gabriel's affectation of depression.

"What of 'Found', Gabriel, have you completed it yet?"

"No, nor do I think I ever shall."

"A great pity. It will be a bold artist or penman, who first forces the delicate minded to look at the plight of the fallen woman. He has but to raise the curtain one inch higher than decorum allows and outraged society will be aghast at the man's audacity not to say indecency."

"Such an artist or penman, it seems, would lose both his value as a moralist and his livelihood at one and the same time," said Rossetti dryly. The social problem in the abstract did not interest him.

The maid came into the room : "It's Mr. William Miles, sir."

"So, I still have one patron that has not deserted me. Show him in, Mary."

As soon as Billy clapped eyes on Owen Bookbinder amongst the company, he recognized him, despite the beard and extra girth, as his old enemy the Chartist agitator, who had lost him his tommy-shop. He felt a small satisfaction at seeing the grey in Bookbinder's hair—his own head of hair was as thick and dark as it had been those many years ago.

"I believe we are already acquainted, Mr. Miles," said Bookbinder. I have followed your progress in the city with some interest."

That damned self-opinionated uprightness was still there, thought Billy, as the keen grey eyes examined him.

"I fear you had dropped rather out of sight, Bookbinder, and I lost touch with you. But at last that has been remedied." He saw that Bookbinder had no intention of revealing to the company the circumstances of their previous relationship— which could have been a considerable embarrassment if conveyed to his business acquaintances, who were unaware of his lowly origins. The fool was too high-minded to take such an unfair advantage, other no doubt, than to prevent his friends from investing in any of his companies. Nevertheless the man was a constant source of danger to him.

"May I present my fiancée, Miss Celandine Spencer?"

Now here was a beauty, considered Billy. How had Bookbinder snared such a creature?

"Enchanted!" They looked at each other for a moment and Billy could scarce believe what he saw in her eyes. How very strange. "Come, Gabriel," Billy turned away of a sudden, "you promised you would have something fresh to show me."

"Fresh indeed, some splendid canvases without a mark upon them," replied Gabriel. "You may take your fill of blank canvas."

"Not even a drawing?"

"Mere scrawls, I hardly had the mind for it. But come, who knows, they may be at least of some interest to Bookbinder."

Owen offered his arm to Celandine, but the girl sat as though in a daze. The yellow eyes of Billy Miles had brought back with a rush the recurrent nightmare of her childhood that she could never quite forget, draining her energy and taking away her will.

"Celandine, are you coming?" asked Bookbinder.

She trembled a moment and silently took Owen's arm.

"Are you not well?" he whispered. Celandine shook her head speechlessly, and they followed the two men into another room, where Rossetti had spread a folder of drawings out for them to examine.

"Ah! That is a study for 'Found' is it not?" said Bookbinder with satisfaction.

The drawing depicted Fanny Cornforth, posed as an unfortunate of the streets, discovered by her former lover.

"We have similar tastes, Bookbinder," said Miles slyly, "that is a picture I too covet, if it is ever done."*

"These are splendid drawings of Miss Siddal, Gabriel," said Owen without comment, turning to another pile.

"Laboured scraps, I fear," deprecated Rossetti, "these are better I think." They were soon in earnest conversation.

Celandine started as she felt Billy's hand on her upper arm.

"Does the drawing of that fallen creature offend you, Miss Spencer? You seem pale."

---

* This painting never was completed although Rossetti made many attempts at it.

"N-no, it is not that, Mr. Miles," she stammered, feeling quite faint at his proximity.

"Then I shall take you for some fresh air."

"N-no."

"Nonsense, my dear," he squeezed her arm painfully and led her to the door.

"With your permission, Bookbinder, Miss Spencer desires a little air. No, don't trouble yourself, Gabriel. I'll just take her on the balcony. Depending on the direction the wind has taken, Miss Spencer will either revive, or we shall both of us suffocate instantly. Come, my dear."

Billy Miles led Celandine firmly along the balcony that hung over the Thames, until they were out of sight of those in the house. Without any prior blandishments or attempt at preliminary endearments, he placed her against the wall of the house and loosened his straining clothes. The girl stared straight into those yellow eyes, her own pupils so enlarged that they almost engulfed the deep blue of the iris. She made no resistance as, lifting her crinoline and raising one of her legs, he was of a sudden into her.

Past his shoulder in shuddering glimpses, the smoke and swinging bell of the bumboat man, plying his drinks to the ships and barges, frozen oars high and jaw agape, either in awe at the sights of the river, or bemused by his 'purl' of piping beer, seasoned with gin and ginger. A gleaming shaft from the heavens engulfed the bumboat, transforming the purl-man to chivalry, sliding a sheen of gold over the waters— the colour of strong green tea—flecking into the black marble shadows, transmuting the very reeking vapours golden to veil the tippings of tan-pits, glue yards and sewers. A final unbearable burst of illumination : and her scream cut short by Billy's mouth as the afternoon died.

The wind stirred in the sudden darkness as they adjusted their clothes, picking its way amongst the reflected lights that crept across the oily swell—intent on driving them away. Billy wrote quickly on a scrap of paper which he rolled tightly and gave to the girl.

"Be there tomorrow, my dear. Keep this safe in your sleeve and bring it with you."

They walked back into the room. Owen Bookbinder broke off his conversation with Gabriel to smile a welcome at the girl.

"That brief spell of air has quite returned the colour to your cheeks, Celandine. Thank you for your kind attentions, Miles."

"No more than I could offer to such a charming member of the fair sex," murmured Billy Miles.

She lowered her head to conceal the renewed flush in her cheeks and the confused state of her emotions. She looked at her neatly-gloved hands, demurely clasped before her, and wondered why her wanton shame did not cry out of itself to the whole room.

Celandine twice walked past the entrance to the accommodation house. It presented quite a respectable front in one of the first streets of Mayfair, but she could not bolster herself sufficiently to cross the threshold.

She had determined not to obey Billy Miles' peremptory command, yet she was here. She was engaged to be married to another man, an honest, upright fellow who would never stoop to theft, as she had discovered Billy capable of, nor pursue the practice of debauching young girls.

Cart-ropes, she had sworn, would not bring her to this vile wretch, who had not yet offered her a tender or loving word, or the slightest indication of honourable intentions.

She walked hastily through the open door, and with a backward glance to the street, asked of the old woman there for Mr. William Miles.

The room was well enough furnished, with handsome red curtains drawn back from the windows, a large bed, Coburg chairs and sofas, wax lights, glass chandeliers and a cheval glass large enough to contain the reflection of the liveliest couple.

"Did you bring the note I gave you?" asked Billy at once.

"That is the only reason that could bring me here," blazed Celandine. She unrolled the paper with the address written upon it and turned it over to show Gabriel's sketch of Fanny Cornforth. "I had not thought that in addition to taking advantage of me, you would also make me an unwitting accomplice to your thievery. You have used me in the most vile way, sir, and I hope you are sufficiently a gentleman never to present yourself before me again, and to observe an honourable reticence on the manner in which you have so compromised me."

Tossing aside the drawing Billy Miles took the furious girl in his arms: "Convince yourself, if you will, that your main intention in coming here was to call me a blackguard, but my belief is, that a good stroking will soon set your temper to rights."

He took her to the bed with a gentleness and consideration she hardly expected. At first she would not let him lift her clothes.

"Pray draw the curtains," she murmured.

"You have already felt my member up you. There is no need of such mock modesty between us and I would see you in daylight."

Leaving her for a moment, he began to remove his clothes. She watched him breathlessly, her uncertain emotions changing from shame to desire and back again. When he was quite naked she saw evident proof of his desire for her in the stiffness of his male appurtenance. His body was thick but hard with a deal of black hair about it. He lay down beside her again.

"Take off some of your things, my dear, we shall be more comfortable."

His hands roved over her pouting belly and gently down her thighs, to find the cleft between them.

"You are wet, my dear, as eager and expectant as I."
Celandine could not bring herself to discard completely her
apparel, retaining her shift as a last vestige of modesty. Ardently
Billy played, until Celandine, with a gasp, pulled the shift
impatiently over her head. But the man was not ready to
consumate their love-making, until the last vestige of timidity
in the girl towards him, that might dampen their efforts, had
gone. Overcoming a reluctance implanted in her by education
and custom, he proceeded to kiss that part of her person not
generally thus saluted. Only when the sorely-taxed girl was
ready to plead for the solace she so required, in plain language
—did Billy consent to tail her in earnest. With long practised
strokes, thinking more of the girl's pleasure than his own, he
brought her to her climax.

Fulfilled and sleepy, Celandine lay with her eyes closed—
while Billy ordered some wine to be sent up—and would not
let remorse disturb her satisfaction. How strange that so many
things hidden from her, heretofore, were now so abundantly
clear. An education was indeed a splendid thing.

But her tutor was not yet satisfied that her education was
complete, there were still some familiarities they must practise
before he could be sure that all sham modesty had vanished
between them. Indeed it was some hours before he was entirely satisfied.

Complacently, Billy admired through half-closed eyes that
extraordinarily voluptuous arrangement of female flesh that
had at last blunted his desires. No longer pressed by physical
urgency, he lounged in the sweet rutty smell of her and could
appreciate the fluid grace of the girl's well-rounded form half
twisted away in the act of refilling their glasses—her hair
flowing palely golden the length of her body, darker, where
stray tendrils stuck tangled flatly to her damp skin. There was a
degree of satisfaction in watching her that an artist must feel,
he thought, as though she were his own creation—which in
her present mode of conduct she was. For there were many

women amongst his acquaintance, including some gay, who had never overcome their reluctance to disport themselves completely unclothed before a man. Whilst not wishing to deprecate the advantages of such a fair and willing pupil : he had to congratulate himself on the masterly superiority of his instruction. Billy almost felt quite fond of the girl.

"I could just stand a little wine, my dear," murmured Billy.

"Indeed, you are presumptuous, sir," said Celandine holding the glass away from him. "For it is not you who has stood so gallantly and fought so hard." So saying she took the glass to him, who by his obvious dejection, was the true casualty in their encounter. "Drink, sir," she ordered. Momentarily piqued, Billy was nevertheless amused at her inventiveness. Absently she passed Billy the other glass. "Why see how he nods his head already in approval. I shall content myself with the droppings from his sweet lips, for he does not appear to have an inordinate thirst."

Making herself comfortable, Celandine proceeded to suck up her wine in a manner scarcely acceptable in polite drinking circles. Before however she could quite convey the whole contents of the glass to herself, the instrument of conveyance had become too inflexible to complete the operation.

Billy's face contorted and the surface of his glass shivered dangerously, quite forgotten—as Celandine proceeded to demonstrate that he still had resources of vigour that he himself had been unaware of.

As the night shrunk; so inversely did Celandine's desire and perverse inclinations grow—nor would Billy give her best in this battle of love.

In truth, he thought with relief, as day broke, the taste of food seemed only to increase the appetite. Obediently the girl dressed when wearily he said they must leave and a conveyance was immediately ordered. Celandine clung radiantly to his arm as they went out together into the first light. Billy felt as though he was walking on a bed of feathers, six inches above the cobbles.

"It would be more discreet if we parted here," explained Billy, helping her into the cab.

"Oh, my love, I thought you were to accompany me."

"There will be other times, my dear."

"Tell me you care for me at least, before we part."

Billy laughed and kissed her gloved hand through the cab door.

"My dear," he whispered, "you have the first grand requisite of a courtezan, namely lewdness, and with that you may command any man's heart."

As the cab clopped her away home, Celandine, shocked and miserable, cried into her handkerchief. This was what the man had reduced her to. She must put him from her mind and have no more congress whatsoever with him even though the temptation might be ever so strong to come running when he beckoned.

25

THE DRESS LODGER

THE very handwriting spelled out the character of the man to Celandine, the strokes thick and strong, full of fire and unswervingly cruel. She placed Billy Miles' letter unopened with the other two in her box and ran down the stairs and out into the street, she was determined to put Billy right out of her mind, for she had come to appreciate Owen Bookbinder's admirable qualities and straightforward honesty.

Today was to be a holiday. Owen was leaving his printing works early and she was meeting him at Shadwell, where they would take a steamer down to Cremorne Gardens. She was wearing a new silk dress and mantle of a pale yellow that complimented the gold of her hair, which the shallow bonnet of Italian straw, worn far back on her head, set off to advantage. She had placed small yellow celandine inside the brim, and with the streamers flying from her bonnet and her parasol up against the spring sunshine, she was able to forget that evil force lurking within that could drive her to the depths of debauchery. Certainly the onlooker, seeing her setting off for the omnibus to meet her betrothed would have thought her as innocent as the morning.

"I swear you become more beautiful each day," said Bookbinder when they met, his voice husky with love, "there will not be another to compare to you in the whole gardens."

"Thank you, Owen, and should you see some lady more fair, I trust you to hold your silence, for I want nothing to spoil this day."

"Have no fear, there could be no other to my eyes."

Celandine held his arm tightly with happiness, secure in the knowledge that this was not just a lover's platitude, for she had observed the change in herself from the glass and from the manner in which tradesmen and passers-by regarded her.

"We shall take a cab at the first rank, this is not the parish in which those with decent clothes to their backs should loiter, even in daylight." They had walked a part of the way in the sun and were approaching the Ratcliff Highway, a notorious thieves' den, where the mere sight of a gentleman had been known to enrage the inhabitants.

It was here that had occurred, some forty years ago, a series of horrid and unparalleled murders. Two whole families had been done to death, down to the child in its cradle, horribly massacred with a carpenter's ripping chisel. Nor had the district changed overmuch since that time.

Celandine clutched at Owen's arm, her face pale and her guilt of a sudden returned.

"Owen, it is Maudie coming this way and she has already seen me."

Knowing little of Celandine's former mistress, only that she had left her employ unexpectedly, Owen was puzzled at the girl's consternation. But Maudie, even more gaily attired than Celandine remembered, ran to her friend with such obvious delight at the chance meeting, that tears of self-recrimination came to Celandine's eyes.

"I feared you would not wish to renew our acquaintance after the manner in which I left your service," she cried. Maudie kissed her tears away. "Silly goose, I knew that sooner or later Jem would become partial to you and 'as 'ow you'd away rather than stand for that hoary old wretch. I was that vexed that I taxed 'im with it and was cast out, bag and baggage, for me pains."

"Oh, Maudie."

"Well, I did let slip like, that the brat in me belly weren't his, which didn't make for no reconciliation. But 'oo's yer gentleman friend, dear?"

Celandine introduced them, Maudie obviously charmed by Owen's respectful gentility.

"I'd best tell you straight," said Maudie, "they've set a watcher on me, not I fink that he'd tackle a gentleman as powerful as you appear, Mr. Bookbinder. But I'd best not stay long, or he'll down me with a one'r in the back or side, at the first chance, not in the face mind, for fear of spoiling it."

"What are you talking about, Maudie? Who is this man who threatens you? You must not go yet. What of the baby? You have told me scarce anything of your fortunes. Owen, please persuade her to have some conversation."

"Oh, the baby, Celandine, I'd love you ter see 'im. 'Little Jem' I call's 'im. Well I know, but I was fond of the old fool you know. He wasn't a bad sort."

Bookbinder had frequented the low parts of London sufficiently in his social work to have a fair idea of the situation that Maudie found herself in, and recognized her as a dress lodger. It was not his way to make moral judgements, but rather to try and remove the conditions that created immorality. He had already spotted the watcher, a thickset indolent fellow, lounging against a wall not far away from them. There was a public house nearby that did not appear too disreputable. He had judged of Maudie's character that she was honest, but that her persecutors, if able to contrive a way of robbing them would be rather pleased than otherwise. Owen approached the watcher direct, much to the fellow's surprise, and gave him half a sovereign.

"That's to close your eyes for ten minutes you wretch, while I talk with the girl in that public house yonder."

The bully eyed Owen's bulk and the heavy cane he carried, not at all the wispy wand that most swells affected, and pocketed the money: "Ten minutes mind or she's a'for it." Bookbinder's knuckles whitened on the cane. He turned on his heel and took the frightened girls into the public house, past the throng of ragged men and half-naked boys with pots sent out for beer, for it was dinner time.

There was but one old trull, asleep behind her glass, in the parlour. Bookbinder sat them down there and ordered pale gin for Maudie and sherry cobblers for Celandine and himself.

"Gave me a turn did that harpie asleep there," said Maudie. "I thought it was Old Mother Mitchell. That's how it all started. I met her over a drink and she offered me board while the baby was born. Kindness itself she was. Till I got on me feet again. Then I found me box, clothes and money was all gorn. Spent on doctoring and nursing, she said. Fact was, I owed 'er money and if I wanted food for little Jem and clothes for me back, I'd best get on the streets and earn it. They brought me clothes and I signed a note saying Lord knows what. Now I 'as ter get out after men and bring 'er the money, and Bill out there sees I don't spend time in the public houses, work for anyone else, or try to skip orf. And all I does is get deeper in debt to 'er."

"If you were better acquainted with the law, Maudie," said Bookbinder, "you would know that this woman Mitchell can have no claim on you for money, board or clothes. Any consideration could only be an immoral one and therefore bad in law. I could take you away with me now, if you so desired."

"Please let Mr. Bookbinder help you," pleaded Celandine.

"What of little Jem? I couldn't part with 'im and they've got 'im tight."

"If it is more to your inclination, you could return to your child and I would come with a constable or two and bring you both away safely."

Maudie thought a little. "No, I wouldn't like no-one to get 'urt. I'll slip away when the time's right, though they do say no-one baulks the Cap'n and gets away with a whole skin."

"The Captain," breathed Celandine.

Maudie got to her feet. "Now I'd best be orf, or Bill will start getting ugly." She kissed Celandine and shook Owen's hand. "You did mean what you said, Mr. Bookbinder?"

"I shall be expecting to see you any time, my printing works is not far away."

"I know it, Mr. Bookbinder, and you'll see me just as soon as I'm able."

26

LOVE IN CREMORNE GARDENS

DISTRESSED as she was to find her friend so cruelly circumstanced, Celandine tried to present herself in a good humour for Owen's sake. He hardly knew Maudie, but had surely done all in his power to persuade her to forsake her wretched life.

The steamer was gay with young couples, families and children. Old and young were out to enjoy the excursion: drinking porter, lemonade, ginger beer, rice-milk, and all manner of cooling drinks; eating cakes, tarts, nuts, oranges and fruit or sucking penny pickwicks each according to their age, sex or proclivity. Then besieged at each halting place by purveyors of all manner of foodstuffs, from the penny-pieman in his Jenny Lind, wide-awake hat—to the seller of the more novel and aristocratic luxury of street-ices.

There was great interest and a rush to the side, causing the boat to keel dangerously over, when they passed one of the Citizen steamers, towing a balloon just inflated at the Vauxhall Gas Works, bound for the same destination as themselves. Clutching Owen's arm, Celandine desperately wanted to be a part of this jolly respectability, and fancied that she must truly be in love with him.

Bookbinder bought a ticket from the money-taker when they reached the ornate iron-work water gate of Cremorne and the lovers went into the gardens. They strolled past the well-kept grass plots and geranium beds, amongst the matrons in their bettermost clothes and their offspring—allowed at last to roll their hoops, which seemed to be all the rage with the children. Owen was silent, frowning until they reached the comparative privacy of the garden walks, then he blurted out:

"I should like to fix a date for our wedding, Celandine."

The girl squeezed his arm pressing it close to the side of her ample breast and glanced quickly at Owen, her eyes sparkling.

"Whenever you will, my love."

Why should this young and lovely girl so readily accept his proposals? wondered Bookbinder. Was he not a base wretch to take advantage of the unworldliness of a girl young enough to be his daughter?

"I must of course discover the whereabouts of your mother

and seek her consent before the matter can finally be arranged."

"You are so kind, Mr. Bookbinder. If only mother were
at our wedding, then indeed would my happiness be complete."

"Pray call me Owen, my dear."

"Forgive me, Owen, of course."

Bookbinder was painfully aware that his powers of oratory
were of little use to him with this young creature. Although
fully conversant with the ways of women of the lowest classes,
his work taking him much amongst them, that same labour
had removed him much from the society of gentle, respectable
women, in which class he placed Celandine. He was unskilled
in the words of lovemaking, and could not find the manner
to tell of his love and draw her close to him.

They watched the arrival of the balloon, in company it
seemed, with all those present in Cremorne Gardens at that
time. The gallant aëronaut, Lieutenant Gale, at last indicated
that he was comfortable in the balloon car and ready to
ascend, when the ropes were cast off and the aërostat rose
immediately to a great height, to immense cheering and encouragement from the crowd.

As a young man, Owen had been enjoined that all excitement was to be studiously avoided and that his conduct as a
gentleman should be stoical, never talking much unless soli-
cited, rather to follow conversation than to lead it. This advice
had proved a severe handicap to overcome later when he had
followed his calling as a radical orator.

He recalled further early teachings, that in discourse with
members of the opposite sex, for whom one felt affection,
one should never intimate in any way the silly things that
passed through one's mind, although with ladies, wonder,
astonishment, ecstasy and enthusiasm were necessary in order
to be believed. He understood, however, that one should avoid
treating them as children and that it was quite in order to

make observations on matters of a graver nature to an intelligent woman.

"This ascent has been undertaken for mere amusement," explained Bookbinder, "but those taken for scientific purposes have proved to be of immense interest. Air brought down from great heights for analysis has been found to have the same composition as that at the surface of the earth, although the temperature is always very much lower in the upper regions. A series of well-appointed scientific excursions are now planned to make observations with such instruments as: hygrometers, dry and wet bulb thermometers, aneroid and mercurial barometers and electrometers. Who knows what form of aerial locomotion this may lead to."

"How brave and handsome, Lieutenant Gale is," sighed Celandine.

How singularly useless had been all his early instruction on correct deportment, thought Owen.

They sat for a while beneath a tulip tree and listened to the scarlet-coated bandsmen rendering airs from the operas, then they had tea and water-ices in a small kiosk amongst the poplar trees, close by a tinkling fountain embellished with plaster cherubs.

As the afternoon progressed, Owen's stiff manner slowly dropped from him. He determined on a sprightly, amusing vein of conversation, not rampant witticisms requiring laughter which might prove fatiguing for Celandine, but allowing her to be grave without offence and to smile without pain. He both surprised himself and charmed the girl. At last the steamer hooting from the river, giving warning of impending departure, led their feet slowly back down the paths.

Reluctant to relinquish such a pleasurable afternoon so easily, Celandine broke away from Owen laughing, and ran, holding her voluminous skirts high, up a grassy incline to a small embowered temple. Aroused of a sudden at the sight of her shapely calves, Owen gave chase. He caught up with her in the tiny shelter and pulled her to him roughly in a flurry of rustling yellow silk. She could feel the pressure of his aroused pego against her stomach and a thrill of desire caught her. He pressed his mouth hard down on hers until the girl struggled for breath. Contritely Owen released her, aghast at his own impropriety. Celandine gazed at him, amazed at his fire, half-hoping he would ravish her and expunge all memories of Billy Miles from her eternally. She felt the hot blood suffuse her cheeks as though those grey eyes of his could read the immodest thoughts in her head. Fearfully, she lowered her eyes. Bookbinder observed the shocked, trembling girl and outraged maidenly modesty, remorsefully.

"I pray you can find it in your heart to forgive me," he said brokenly, leading her from the temple and down to where the steamer waited.

The steamer was well on its way westward when the fireworks broke the night sky in glittering display over Cremorne Gardens and the river. Lord Furlingham paid them scant attention as he paid off his hansom in the King's Road and walked through the fanciful gates of Cremorne. Slowly he paced the gas-lit paths. It was hardly the scene of debauchery that he had expected. Now that the penny steamers had departed, the gardens had filled with gentlemen of the middle and upper classes, some seven hundred of them. And three hundred or so demurely-silked Cyprians had arrived to receive their advances and accept any offer of refreshment. Not that any obvious signs of immorality were taking place. Couples danced to Borini's band of fifty on the raised monster platforms, waltzes and polkas being the favourites, while waiters plied others sitting around at tables with lemonade and sherry. By far the majority, however, were sauntering along the paths, around the platforms, treading and retreading the same ground. Each it seemed engaged in some grave and profound problem that only the breeze of the river could help solve, hardly aware of each other but for the barely-given recognition to some acquaintance who passed by. The female visitors walked in propriety, their eyes more often than not, cast down, making no attempt to solicit the attentions of the gentlemen. Only when they were approached did their immediate acceptance of any overtures cast any doubt on their respectability. But unless this moment of meeting was observed, who was to know, two seconds later that the couple walking the dim-lit paths were not of the highest respectability.

After a sojourn in one of the hundreds of accommodating arbours, the gentleman and lady were released once more to pursue their separate paths through the gardens.

Lord Furlingham sat at a table by himself, ordered a lemonade and took out his notebook.

Fine the men, he thought. Impose a fine on any man discovered in such vile practices. That would place a check on this social evil, and if the figures he had compiled during his investigations were only half true, would supply government with the richest source of revenue.

27

THE CLAW CHISEL MURDERS ON RATCLIFF HIGHWAY

BLACK MARIA had been doing a brisk trade. She was normally at this hour as full as a tuppenny omnibus. Celandine, the unwilling interrupter of this business was the sole occupant, swaying on one of the two wide benches in the grim interior, as the conveyance rattled through the streets.

The constable would say nothing other than Sergeant Blackstone must see her immediately. It must surely be of some import thought the girl, for Dick to drag her from her bed and subject her to the humiliation of being taken away behind bars.

The bodies lay exactly where they had been found that evening, on the floor of Owen Bookbinder's private office in the printing works at Shadwell. It was an even more soul-harrowing spectacle now in the harsh naked gas light. A great deal of blood polluted the premises, the place had floated in gore, black on the walls and the stained carpet, and on the muti-lated, chalk-white faces of the cadavers. Celandine, unwarned and untold of the heart-shocking news, entered the charnel house and giving one long scream of horror, fainted next to the corpses before Sergeant Dick Blackstone could reach her. But not before she had recognized the tortured faces, frozen in a horrible death, as those of her lover Owen Bookbinder and her friend Maudie.

White-faced, Dick revived the girl with brandy in the outer chamber where they had discovered the baby. He had thought to shock from the girl information that she might otherwise have been reluctant to confide in him, but had not intended to reduce her to such a state. At that moment his love for the girl was as strong as it had ever been, but though his heart ached in pity as her long wet lashes trembled over her dear brimming eyes, he had his duty to perform.

"Can you identify those dead persons that you saw, Celan-dine?"

"Oh, my poor dear friends, who could have done such a thing?"

"Do you make formal identification of the bodies as one Owen Bookbinder, printer, and Maudie Bates an unfortunate of the streets?"

"My poor, poor friends," choked Celandine.

Sergeant Blackstone got to his feet, "I fear we shall get little more from her tonight, constable. We shall take it as a positive identification."

"Yes, sir," said Plain Clothes Constable Hardy, phlegmatically, inwardly surprised that the matter should be allowed to rest there. Sergeant Blackstone was not renowned for his forbearance in these matters.

"The constable will take you home now, Miss Spencer. I should like to converse with you later when you are more composed."

Hardy helped the girl to her feet, when the baby began to cry.

"Little Jem," cried Celandine snatching the infant from the arms of the Woman Police Constable. Dick indicated that the girl should be allowed to hold the child. "What is to become of you now, Little Jem," crooned the girl.

The irony was, thought Dick, that the child would go to the workhouse where shortly its mother would be laid out.

When they had gone, Blackstone walked back to the murder room to examine the corpses once more. Bookbinder's head lay to one side, the back of the head frightfully battered. He had been a powerful man to take on and must have been surprised by a blow to the back of the head which had first shattered the skull. The fearful blows to his face could have been made later by a sharper cutting instrument. The girl had been slaughtered by the same sharp weapon. Something lay beneath the girl. Blackstone lifted her sufficiently to take out the object. It was a carpenter's ripping chisel, with blood and a quantity of hair adhering to it. Was some madman attempting to emulate the Ratcliff Highway murderer of 1811? If so, surmised Dick, the only reason the child had been spared was that Maudie Bates had left it asleep in a comfortable chair in the outer office. It had been the baby crying that eventually brought the nightwatchman on the scene some hours after its mother had been done to death. Yet Dick was puzzled. What madman would have been capable of opening the Chubbs patent locks fitted to Bookbinder's safe?

Taking the ripping chisel with him, Dick Blackstone closed the door on the two cadavers whose lives he would attempt to unravel: Maudie, who without thought for the future, had pleased so many men with her infectious gaiety and generosity, and Owen Bookbinder, whose life had flickered out with Chartism and seemingly as uselessly. Dick's investigation would not uncover the indefinable appeal the Chartist had made to the worker's imagination, the discontent with their lot he had sown and the self-respect he had put into the hearts of men. Bookbinder's victory was that of the vanquished.

"I wasn't aware that you had acquaintances in high places," snarled Superintendent Pearce from behind his desk.

"Sir?" said Sergeant Blackstone at attention.

"Lord Furlingham, d'yer know him?"

"Know *of* him, sir. Fifth Earl of Furlingham. Extremely moral and religious gentleman. Author of many papers on Social Improvement for the Lower Classes and head of more committees of that nature than I would care to name."

"Is that all?"

"Yes, sir. I've never had the acquaintance of the gentleman in person."

"You haven't forgotten to mention that your father, the Rev. Mr. Blackstone holds a living in Lower Furlingham?"

Blackstone frowned. "I hardly thought that was relevant, sir. I have been estranged from my father for some years now."

Pearce glared at him for a long moment. "Stand easy, Sergeant," he said at last, "or should I say, Inspector. I've just approved a recommendation for your promotion. I don't care for these meteoric rises in the force usually, but since we won't 'ave to pay your wages for a while, I suppose it's all right."

"Sir?"

"Furlingham wants to hire you, to seek out the murderer or murderers of this double killing. Commissioner says he seems more concerned about the safety of trollops on the street than he is for Chartists. But that's neither 'ere nor there. Now don't imagine you're off working on yer own. I want the same reports Furlingham gets. You'd 'ave been kept on the case without Furlingham's kind intervention. The difference is 'e's paying yer wages. I seem ter remember you didn't exactly make a hit with the late Duke of Wellington. Just remember sometimes you 'as to bend a little. Just a little mind. It could do you a lot of good or a lot of harm, this case. That's all, Inspector."

"Thank you, sir."

"Oh, Inspector."

"Sir?"

"Congratulations."

Inspector Blackstone pulled a hard-backed chair close to the bed where Celandine lay so palely, while Arthur Banks hovered nervously at the doorway.

"So far as I have observed in the matter, Inspector, you would be better occupied out hunting this ripping-chisel murderer than pestering Miss Spencer in her bereavement."

"Don't fret yourself, sir," said Dick cheerfully, "we are old friends, Celandine and I. May I beg you for a glass of porter to bring a little colour to her cheeks, and perhaps a sip for myself to keep her company."

"Well in that case . . . yes, of course . . . that ain't no trouble at all. I shall be but a moment."

"You never were so pale in the cornfield, Celandine Spencer."

"Nor you such an important person in your yellow waist-coat, Inspector Blackstone." They smiled at each other. Then seriously he said: "Were you very much in love with Book-binder, Celandine?"

The girl followed the impression her finger made drawing on the white sheet.

"I planned to marry him, Dick."

"I see." He paused, then. "My purpose is to bring his

assailant and that of your friend Maudie to justice, will you aid me in this?"

"It shall never bring them back I fear, but willingly I'll tell you all I know of the matter."

Dick wanted to know all the details she could remember of Maudie's friends, and there had been a considerable number of followers in the almost three years Celandine had been with Mr. Pickles.

"Why did you leave your position with Pickles, Celandine? I never did understand why you should run away without a word to anyone."

The heightened colour was very obvious on her pale cheeks. "Oh, I met Arthur Banks in the street."

"And just ran off with him?" Her colour deepened.

"Of course not, I thought I could better myself as an artist's model, and I did. I met Owen through Arthur." She sniffled into a small piece of cambric to cover her confusion.

Dick studied her thoughtfully.

"Do go on."

Celandine told of their chance meeting with Maudie the day of the excursion to Cremorne, and of how Owen had been expecting to hear from Maudie.

"And this is all you know?"

"Why yes, Dick."

"Have you ever heard of someone called the Captain?"

Arthur Banks made a welcome interruption arriving, followed by the maid, with the drinks.

"This is all very jolly, like a party, what? I say, Celandine you look dooced pale. What has this fellow said?"

"It's all right Arthur, I think I'm rather tired just now that's all. Yes, I had forgotten Maudie mentioned the Captain, I think he must have been Mother Mitchell's employer."

"And another of your acquaintances knew Bookbinder, I believe, Mr. William Miles, the financier."

The glass slipped from Celandine's trembling hand and

spilt on the floor. She began to understand why Dick Blackstone was so successful as a detective. His probing questions
would continue searching out the truth until her life would be
laid naked before him. She would have sworn that only she
knew of the enmity that had existed between Owen and Billy.
Yet Dick would certainly ferret it out. She would not help Dick
in this. Thief and lecher Billy might be, but never a murderer,
of that she was certain.

"I say old chap, can't you see the girl's in an awful state.
Old friend or no, I can't give countenance to this interrogation
any further."

Dick rose with a smile, and kissed Celandine's trembling
hand.

"I beg your pardon if I have over-taxed your strength,
my dear. May I return in a few days when you are stronger.
Mayhap other trivialities will come to your mind in the inter-
val. Although insignificant to you—such little peddling things
might well be the means of solving this case."

"Damn Paul Pry," said Arthur, after the Inspector had
gone, "when you are quite fit enough to be moved, I'll take
you down to Snaresbrook Abbey. Horace Birket's a strange
cove but we'll be shot at least of these beastly bloodhounds."

28

'BIG DICK' INVESTIGATES

DAY after day as the investigation proceeded, the carpenter's
ripping chisel lay at the back of Inspector Blackstone's desk in
Scotland Yard, a constant reminder of how slowly the matter
was proceeding. Each afternoon the sun came through the
window until the gory instrument glowed black red in a pool

of light. Statements arrived at the desk only to prove who hadn't perpetrated the crime. Bill the bully had the perfect alibi, being up before the magistrate's court on the day of the murder, accused of knocking a man's eye out in a fight. He was acquitted for insufficient evidence. Old Mother Mitchell who had been 'follower' that day to Maudie, had lost the girl and been unable to catch her on her ancient legs, and was the last to see Maudie alive. Reports coming in on the acquaintances of Maudie Bates and Owen Bookbinder and on the movements of habitual criminals in the Metropolis, were placed before the murder weapon, perused and filed. Slowly a description of a tall dark man emerged from witnesses near the scene of the crime; quickly there amassed a pile of terse memoranda from Superintendent Pearce; daily a fresh set of newspaper cuttings vilifying the force and clamouring for action were placed on the desk.

Three weeks from the day of the murder, Blackstone mused over the information he had digested. It was significant, he thought, that amongst this morass of detail, there was only one mention of the Captain, and that from a suspect interviewed in the nearby rookery.* An accomplice in an atrocious midnight murder, he had narrowly avoided the gallows by turning Queen's evidence. Well lushed on spirituous liquor, this villain had told the detectives to save their breath, that the Captain would no doubt look after his own. He had been silenced by his pals and would say no more. No one else it seemed had heard of the Captain. No one except Celandine. And what of William Miles, Esq? There seemed surprisingly little information relating to that gentleman. Superintendent Pearce's warning would need to be borne in mind, not to upset those in high places—Miles was a very powerful man. It was about time he paid another visit to Celandine, considered Blackstone.

The blood, caked on the handle of the ripping chisel, baking

* District inhabited by criminals.

in the afternoon sun, cracked a little and a flake fell to the top of the desk. Blackstone looked up thoughtfully from his work in the quiet room and took out his penknife. Carefully he scraped some of the blood from the handle. Beneath a further layer of dirt and grease lay the initials of the owner of this fearsome tool: the initials R. W.

At eight o'clock Arthur Banks went away in a cab for the Row. He rode his cob several times a week in the park with a few cronies. There was more to selling canvases, he had discovered, than merely daubing paint on them.

Dick Blackstone gave him a few moments to return for anything he had neglected to carry with him, then went across the street and rang the doorbell.

It was only by assuming a gruff manner and producing his warrant card that he gained admittance to Celandine's chambers. Frightened as the maid was, she was unwilling to leave him alone in the room.

"This is private police business," Dick sternly told her.

"It's perfectly all right, Jane," said Celandine sleepily, "Inspector Blackstone is an old and trusted friend."

"I wouldn't trust no peelers, notwithstanding they flashed ever so many cards. I shan't be far away, Miss," adding darkly, "you just 'as ter call if yer wants me."

"What is it, Dick," asked Celandine when the door had closed, "what brings you here at this hour?"

"Would you sooner I waited until Arthur Banks returned, and asked you to tell me before him, what you know of the Captain?"

The girl's hands covered her cheeks as the blood rushed to them.

"I told you all I know of the Captain."

Dick sat on the edge of the bed and furiously pulled her hands down. "You are not experienced enough to deceive me with a lie. Where did you meet this man?"

"I never have, Dick, believe me, I heard his voice one time."

"Where was this?"

"I knew not, it was when I first came to London, they took me to a house somewhere in the Borough."

"Well, we know his line of business. How long did you work for him."

"Oh, Dick, I was but thirteen and a virgin."

"You were at that time, you mean."

"I don't know what I'm saying, I'm half asleep, I mean I escaped from them."

"And what did the Captain say?"

"He said he wanted me taken over to the House," sobbed Celandine. "I never found where it was. He just called it the House."

Dick let her cry on his chest for a while.

"Tell me," said Dick quietly, "when did you first take up with William Miles?" He felt the girl stiffen in his arms and he knew that his guess was correct. Feeling the jealousy churning up within him, Dick seized her shoulders and held her at arm's length. "Was Miles so infatuated with you that he killed the man you were to marry. Is that what happened?"

"No!" screamed Celandine wildly. "It was but once and I've not seen Billy since."

"How many others were there, Celandine?" asked Dick tightly.

"No one else," sobbed the girl.

"So your little game of fox and goose with me over the years was just to save your virginity for this swell?"

"He was not the one . . ." started Celandine.

"You whore," whispered Dick, "I can believe not a word you say." Seizing the bedclothes, he pulled them from her. The girl pushed her shift down and watched him with fearful eyes.

"Please, Dick, I have always cared for you, more than any other. You must know that."

"In which case, you should not object to granting me the same favours the others have enjoyed." Fully clothed as he was Dick fell on the girl, his weight pinning her helplessly down as he kissed her face and bare shoulders. Somewhat of the panic she had felt so long ago in the barley field returned to Celandine, she turned her head this way and that to avoid his lips.

"Do you not normally kiss your lovers, whore?" asked Dick breathlessly. He forced her head to his and Celandine buried her small teeth in his lower lip.

"Slut!" he roared painfully, and hit her face hard with his open hand. The force of the blow from the powerful policeman knocked the senses from the girl for the moment. When she came to, Dick was cradling her in his arms, gently kissing her fluttering eyelids.

"Celandine, forgive me. I love you so, my dear, it made me wild with rage to think of your lovers."

"You were always my true love, Dick," she said, allowing his hands to rove beneath the shift. Was she just naturally gay, wondered Celandine as he caressed her. Despite his cruel treatment, she felt her affection returning with a rush. She shivered as his fingers brushed her taut nipples sending a thrill of desire through her.

"Dick, you are sending me mad," moaned Celandine.

Aroused as she was, the girl viewed his actions with some trepidation, when he stopped his love-play to attend to that unruly member bulging so formidably beneath his trousers.

Her childhood fears of Dick's prodigious size had not been misplaced, she observed with dismay when it stood released before her—but whether from love, self-abnegation or lechery, she determined to carry the business forward.

"Do be gentle, Dick," she murmured as he fell upon her. Yet, in truth, there was a strange, fierce delight in the agony she endured in accommodating that fearful guest—that stretched and rended her beyond the proper extent of her

G

parts. She welcomed each flesh-tearing thrust as though only in the mortification of her body could she be cleansed of her guilt.

Dick could not long sustain that sweet restriction and after but a few strokes was spending copiously, at which libation in her innermost secret being—Celandine answered with a shriek that might well have brought the servant running.

Labour as she would with the skills she had learned from Billy Miles, it seemed that the agonizing ecstasy was not to recommence—Dick's thoughts were already elsewhere.

"Tell me once more of how you came to London, Celandine, I would know every detail. There should be no secrets between us now."

Sighing, Celandine settled in close proximity to that over-sized article which she had sooner they favoured with their joint attention—and commenced her story. She told him of her early days in London and eventual debauchment—casting about in her mind meanwhile how best she might renew his interest in matters more pertinent to their situation. A glass of wine would scarce serve her on this occasion: she doubted that a tumbler would provide sufficient harbourage for the affair in hand.

The story, which Celandine in her innocence so readily un-folded, offered up intriguing opportunities to Dick's ambition.

He had taken the unusual course of sending to those same morning newspapers, that had so persecuted him for the last three weeks, a description of the murderer and of the weapon used, and this was already on the streets. The public acclaim should he nail the murderer would stand him in good stead with Superintendent Pearce, but perhaps uncovering the Captain, the vice-king of the Metropolis, might secure him influence in higher and more powerful quarters: Lord Furlingham, for example, and his pious friends.

When she had finished, he said: "Not a word will the underworld tell me of the Captain, but I have heard rumours of the House—an extravagant bordello visited by the highest in the land, where there is no lech or inhuman taste that is not catered for."

Celandine shuddered, "And the Captain would have put me there at such a tender age." Had she survived it, thought the girl bitterly, she might at least have acquired the cunning to renew Dick's desires. Those twin spheres she cradled were full and bursting enough if he would but turn his attention that way.

"Celandine, if I could insinuate a trusted agent into this establishment I should soon discover the identity of the Captain, for I am certain that it is he who instigated the murders, even should he not have executed them himself. Will you do this for me and revenge your friends?"

Celandine frowned. "I have said I would aid you all I could—but would this not place me in frightful danger if I should be discovered?"

"You need only to keep your ears and eyes open and leave the House when you have discovered who the Captain is."

"But why should they give me a position in such a place?" she asked puzzled. "How should they know that they could trust me? Unless you would have me go as a courtezan there." She laughed.

"Why what else," said Dick uncomfortably—remembering her skill of a short while ago. "It can be of little consequence to you, and with your talent and beauty, you would surely be accepted readily enough."

Celandine gazed with horror as—for a reason difficult to ascertain—the object of her earnest solicitations this long while, only now began to bestir itself. Pulling herself away she cried : "You fearful wretch. That you could take advantage of my love in such a manner—or believe that I am a harlot after I have told you the truth about myself."

"Dammit, Celandine, you are well enough practised at the

art and would appear to take considerable pleasure in it. Surely you have no scruples where you can both revenge the death of your friends and receive no mean financial reward for your efforts."

"It would have been better had I kept you at arm's length for eternity," said the girl brokenly. "Now go, for I never wish to see you again. If you do not go this instant I shall scream for Jane, show her the ravage you have wrought on me and put up such a story that would surely cut short your career."

Furious and red-faced, Inspector Blackstone adjusted and straightened his clothes, retrieved his crushed silk hat and left the room.

When Blackstone returned to the Police Office his ruffled feelings were considerably soothed to learn that a carpenter, Robert Weeks, was waiting to see him, claiming that the much publicized ripping chisel was one that had been stolen from his box, with several other tools, less than a month ago. In truth Inspector Blackstone doubted that the Captain had any connection with the murders other than as head of the organization that employed Maudie, but he could feel the assassin almost in his grasp, later he would return to the matter of the Captain—and to Celandine.

Dyson had supped at the 'Coal Hole' in the Strand and was well content with himself, seated in an omnibus, his feet warm in the straw. The cracksman's modest but well-cut clothes gave no indication of his true calling and he had been as acceptable taking oysters at the Judge and Jury Club as he was now, travelling by one of 'Wilson's Favourites' from Charing Cross to his lodgings in Shepherd's Bush. He sighed contentedly in the cabbage-like odour that the colza oil lamps gave off, and broke open his paper.

He had carried on pretty well in the bill-stealing way whilst in the States but had arrived back in the country in complete penury three short weeks ago—yet already he was on his feet again, and already he had set all London in a panic. It had been an ugly moment when the man and girl returned, ruminated Dyson, there'd been nothing for it but to burke* them. He was a big cove that Bookbinder and the mot's scream could have been heard in Bow Street. He'd as soon swing as shin scrape† or rot in the hulks.‡

The snacky§ trick with the ripping chisel had managed very well to put the peelers off the scent and put them looking out for a madman instead of a professional. The last he had read of the matter was a speculation in one of the newspapers that the wrong man had been hung forty-three years ago and that the murderer had returned to the scene of his crime. Dyson chuckled at the considerable discomfiture this must have caused a great number of venerable carpenters.

Dyson did not have to look far for fresh news of the investigation. On the front page of his paper was an illustration of that same ripping chisel showing the initials R. W. on the handle, and beneath was a passing fair description of Dyson himself. The door swung into the night, to let out a passenger, taking the lamp with it, plunging the interior of the omnibus into darkness and concealing the pallor that spread across Dyson's face.

The owner of the initials and one-time owner of the chisel, Robert Weeks, left the police office wishing he had never come forward. He had spent the day being closely questioned until he expected them to put on the darbies ‖—and lost a day's work into the bargain. Still he was better off than some, he comforted himself, carpenters answering to the description of Dyson, tall and dark, had been brought in by the police all over the country—mostly to protect them from the infuriated mobs. It was as well he was short and ginger himself. He rued

* Murder, usually by suffocation or strangulation.
† Work the treadmill at hard labour.
‡ Prison ships.
§ Clever, sharp.
‖ Handcuffs.

the day he let Dyson share his lodging and left his carpenter's box unlocked.

The private-clothes constables that followed Weeks back to his lodging in Shepherd's Bush were settling down to a long wait when Dyson appeared, hurrying along the pavement and went into the house after the carpenter. One constable stood guard whilst the other went back to the station. Their orders were to do nothing until Inspector Blackstone should arrive to take charge.

When the house was completely surrounded, and all exits properly sealed off, Dick Blackstone and a large body of constables marched up the stairs, broke down the door and poured into Weeks' room. Dyson was caught literally red-handed with the unfortunate carpenter's blood and brains still on his life-preserver.

29

HAPPINESS FOR A PENNY

LONG before the summer afternoon began to fade, the gardeners were out lighting the candles in the grounds of Snaresbrook Abbey. Within the seven miles of high walls surrounding the estate, there were a thousand holders, niches and clefts, encrusted with the droppings of long-dead candles, where fresh flames would sputter alone through the night. Clusters of baroque barley sugar candles reflecting in the lakes, forests of candelabra flickering in the follies, censorious black candles casting their tall shadows on the ruined chapel walls. Isolated flames in the dells, in the hollows, in amongst the ivied crumbling statues—springing from such a diversity of intricate wax stems, that some were too large for a man's arms to encompass while others were no thicker than his thumb.

And all but a few to be admired only by the hoot-owl and the wheeling bats.

The men engaged in this task were certainly entitled to be called gardeners, in that they dressed the gardens of Snaresbrook Abbey—but their husbandry of the soil differed considerably from that of gardeners on other estates. Their skill was to make the water lily bloom on the foul surface of a stagnant pool, preserve rotted fruit on diseased trees in perpetual putrefaction, and watch while canker spread, weeds strangled and maggots defaced the innocent petals.

Hidden in the cob-webbed wilderness of the rose garden, Arthur Banks and Celandine were at work. The artist's easel was set up with a white primed canvas, for his ambitious painting from A Midsummer Night's Dream: 'Titania waits on Bottom while the Woodland Ghosts look on'. Arthur had spent the morning making studies in his notebook and adjusting the rough design in charcoal on the canvas, and Celandine had been in turn: a frightened elf hiding in an acorn cup, a pale spirit floating through the trees and Bottom. Apart from the addition of an ass's head for the latter role, her costume required only the simple re-arrangement of a flower garland.

After her initial shyness on disrobing—she had never posed before in the open air—the familiar immodest desire to flaunt herself came over her: followed by increasing boredom as her limbs become stiff with inaction and Arthur, quite indifferent to her desirability, scratched away at his drawing in a world of his own.

Wearing the ass's head she found to be the most tedious. She felt that the kinship between her and Bottom, the fat weaver, was confined to that portion of her limbs that the costume left uncovered. It was unbearably hot in the mask and the view between the ass's jaws of the beautiful Arthur, with a yellow lock of hair tumbling over his handsome brow, was equally unbearable.

To Arthur's consternation, the ass's head with the garland

streaming from its neck hurtled through the air towards him
and bounced on the grass at his feet.

"Now you have done, Arthur Banks, whether you like it
or no. I'll not bear it a moment longer."

She was transformed from a fairy to a fury, thought Arthur,
rocking on his little stool, what a stunning picture if he could
but capture it : feet astride, hands on her splendid hips, breasts
heaving, eyes blazing, face flushed and the sun streaming
through her tangled mass of hair like burnished gold—
just so.

"Forgive me, my dear, I have become so caught up in my
labours, that it has made me indifferent to your comfort. Pray
rest a while."

Instantly her annoyance was gone. He was so unlike any
other man she had known, so gentle and so good, perhaps too
much so for a man. But at last he was looking at her like a man
looks at a woman, and she intended to hold his attention.

"I am all over as stiff as a board," she said plaintively,
arching her back and flexing her shoulders so that her breasts
nodded and pouted at the sky in a manner so bold that she
was sure it would arouse him.

There, thought Arthur, she had moved and the moment was
gone. 'The Furies' was a subject he must think on. He bent
to see if the ass's head had been damaged in the fall.

Celandine would have rammed the mask over his silly head
if the crash of bodies through the undergrowth beyond the
brake and the sound of Horace Birket's high-pitched voice
had not reminded her of her modesty. She barely had time to
pull on her robe, adjust her bonnet and button her gloves—
a hand being a part of her body not lightly displayed to a
member of the opposite sex—when the little man danced into
sight, leaping and capering amongst the kingcups and poppies
in the plain garb of a monk. It was hard to see in this insignificant creature the master of Snaresbrook Abbey. He was followed by the sly Caliban resplendently dressed as a caliph in

wide silk trousers caught up at the ankle, silver belt, bare chest and turban. Then came eight well-matched footmen in the same habit as their master, carrying ladders, Japanese lanterns and all manner of provisions for a banquet. There were no women servants at Snaresbrook Abbey, even the cleaning, the little required to make the dining-room and bedrooms habitable, was attended to by men. Caliban cleaned out his own pantry, where the flat cakes of opium rested, covered in leaves and capsules of rumex.

"Blot out the very sun, Caliban," screamed the poet, "I cannot wait for the awful mystery of night. No! Hold! We will savour it more deliciously creeping slowly down. Ah! Sweet Arthur, what unmentionable depravities we shall enjoy tonight. Together we shall plunge into such shameful evils, such infamous obscenities, such indecent . . ." he choked on the spate of words that were tumbling over themselves and staggered to one of the intricately carved black chairs that the footmen were putting out. His eyes bulged with excitement and he seemed about to have a fit until Caliban soothed him by pouring a draught from a tall glass into his mouth. Slowly he calmed, breathing heavily.

Celandine shivered as though the sun had truly been blotted out. What had seemed childish nonsense in London could not so easily be dismissed in the musty decaying gardens of Snaresbrook Abbey where the black-robed servants moved silently at their tasks. She pulled her thin robe more tightly about her. The pelisse-robe she wore was of gauze sylphide, alternate stripes of transparent gauze and marshmallow ribbon, brocaded with bouquets of flowers looking curiously deflated without the stiffening of petticoats beneath it. It was fastened by a black silk ribbon that passed under the wide mantlet collar, tied in a bow at the neck and dropped down to the ground concealing the edge to edge front of the robe.

The footmen, either from excellent discipline or their natural proclivities, spared not a glance for her naked limbs that could

G*

be glimpsed through the material. Most of the time the little poet seemed unaware of her existence, only Caliban's dark eyes lingered over her. But Horace Birket had not overlooked her allegorical value for the evening revels. Revitalized from the draught he leapt to the girl and took her hand, the wild fringe of hair around his tonsured head on level with her bosom.

"Nor should our shameful ceremonies be complete, sweet lady, without your virginal presence, as chaste Diana."

Celandine curtsied down to the large white face, anxious to appear to treat lightly his sinful words and conceal the dread she had of the forthcoming celebrations. Did she not too, belong to this cosmopolitan world of the arts?

"Thank you, sir, I should be honoured."

"On the contrary, my dear, you shall be dishonoured, diabolically, as a seemly sacrifice to the midsummer night."

"Fear not," laughed Arthur, "Birket's tongue runs on a pace, faster than his intent to follow."

Celandine's laughter, she felt, was a little hollow as she allowed herself to be led to the table that the footmen had set up. It was laden with the most exotic victuals, which Arthur and Celandine could scarce recognize. One dish consisted of an ugly scaly fish as a centrepiece, with a baby octopus in its open mouth, the tentacles writhing amongst the poisonous-looking scales—whilst live eels in a bed of ice slithered around it.

Another was of a skull lying amongst a red spicy-looking sauce, with a long-handled spoon protruding from the greenish jelly filling the open cranium.

The girl was relieved to see that only goblets of red Venetian glass had been set before them, she had quite lost her appetite.

"Only Caliban knows the secret of this elixir. He'll not even share it with his master. But certainly there is laudanum in it. Eh! Caliban? A little tincture of opium and the ground black shells of a certain beetle, eh?"

The master and his servant nodded and laughed at each other.

"For I caught him unawares in his pantry in the preparation, and he could not quite conceal all the evidence of it."

Caliban giggled and his white teeth flashed as he set a porcelain bowl in the centre of the table between them.

"Howsomever, the black devil knows what he's at."

A worried look crossed Arthur Banks' face.

"I'd as soon have a glass of port, if you don't mind, Birket."

"Come, dear fellow, let me prevail upon you to try the elixir before you dismiss it too lightly. There's no poison in it I do assure you, other than the poison to be found in the small amount of alcohol it contains, considerably less than if you were to choose a glass of port."

Arthur smiled at his little friend's enthusiasm.

"Very well, Birket, let's sample this devilish brew."

Despite her misgivings, Celandine followed suit and raised the goblet to her lips. It tasted a very heavy sweet wine.

While they drank, Caliban affixed three flexible pipes to the porcelain bowl and arranged one before each of them. Next he took a small portion, about the size of a pea, from a jar of black viscous paste, placed it on the end of a spoon-headed needle, and warmed it over a lamp.

"I'll warrant the elixir is to my liking, but what tricks are you up to now?" asked Arthur.

"Have you tried opium-smoking?"

"Is that what you purpose, you'll not have me smoking opium like some damn Chinee."

"Pray don't take offence, my good fellow, but you are truly a child when it comes to the deeper mysteries of life. Opium is one of the most civilizing habits. Unlike wine which disorders a man's brain, clouds his judgement and affects his reasoning—opium introduces order, legislation and harmony of thought."

"Even should this be so, what of the unpleasant after effects and the debilitating results if you should contract it as a habit?"

"The connoisseur suffers no torpor or depression afterwards, but awakes reinforced with a clear head. One can obtain happiness for a mere penny with some modest phial of tincture of opium from a chemist. But the true connoisseur will buy the best Turkey opium at eight guineas the pound and boil away all impurities—this is where poisoning can occur and produce ill-effect if the raw opium is not cleansed, moreover, there is no reason for the habit to be deleterious to the health if it is properly controlled. The medical profession in their ignorance—for they never prescribe opium in the doses and frequency of which I am concerned—misrepresent grossly the action of the most common drug in medical practice. They even doubt the phenomena of the dreams and visions which can be so valuable to the artist. With the correct dosage, time and space are enlarged or contracted offering such a rare insight that a man could never gain unaided."

"By all that's holy," exclaimed Arthur, excitedly, "I'll do it. What of you, Celandine?"

"I fear I have a poor head for such things. Nor do I think it would be quite nice for a woman to attempt to understand such visions as you speak of," she answered modestly. In truth she was very content with the effect that the draught was producing on her and would not change it.

"Just so," murmured Arthur absently, as he watched Caliban perforate the opium pellet with the needle and bring it to the flame of the lamp. Birket took his pipe.

"Inhale the smoke slowly, in several inspirations," he instructed, "try to fill the lungs with smoke and hold it there, then exhale through the nose."

Caliban recharged Celandine's goblet with more of the elixir as the sickening smell of the burning opium drifted across the rose garden, then he returned to his task of preparing fresh quantities for the smokers.

30

THE BEASTLY PRACTICES AT
SNARESBROOK ABBEY

WHEN the sun balanced like a red penny on the distant hills, the food was still untouched and in fact had amplified as the robed footmen continued to bring more victuals. Celandine watched the flushed faces of the men in the animated discussion that had engaged them for the last two hours. Was it the effect of the opiate, she thought to herself, that made her seem able to follow their jobation* so effortlessly? Surely a woman's comprehension could never be the equal of a man's intellect; beggar the thought that it could be superior. She didn't wish to set herself up against them but in truth they talked the most unmitigated nonsense.

"The guests!" screamed Birket, breaking off the conversation as the music of pipes started up. "Sweet harbingers of the night."

From where the long row of laden tables stretched down the rose garden into the evening mist, appeared the great Pan himself, a little capering old man playing the pipes, quite naked but for the filthy white beard stretching down between his knees. He danced towards them, with a white ass following on, that was almost obscured by the group of dwarfs that sat him and tumbled around, their stunted bodies adorned with garlands, tiny wire wings, pixie boots, and elves' caps in pathetic caricature of fairyland. Then came the evilest bunch of mendicants and cripples that Caliban could gather from the surrounding neighbourhood. Dressed for the occasion in the rich jewels and robes of the Athenian court they fell upon the food more like starving wolves.

* Tedious talk.

Celandine wrinkled her nose, 'Sweet harbingers of the night', she repeated to herself. The sun suddenly slipped over the edge of the world and the cleverly designed flimsy paper lanterns strung in the trees and bushes, took on a new dimension as the flaring eyes and mouths of demons and horrendous spirits lit the revels with flickering ghastly coloured light.

"Stunning, stunning, oh simply stunning, Birket," shouted Arthur, his over-stimulated imagination seeing apparitions even more fantastic than were present in the scene before him.

Birket was trembling like a leaf, his eyes bright and wild looking.

"Indeed the edges of the night are assuming a delightfully decadent taint, but later, dear fellow, when the Prince of Darkness is at full strength, when the lost souls and evil spirits we can feel amongst us now, themselves hide for fear : why, then I have a treat for you."

"Titania," said a falsetto voice and a stumpy manikin climbed clumsily to the table between them. The wreath of flowers was askew on his big head, and despite the tiny sword hanging from the garlands around his middle, getting between his legs, he achieved a bow to Celandine.

". . . your Oberon waits, come let us dance with fairy grace."

Birket was so delighted with this doubtful couplet, that he broke into a paroxysm of coughing, beating the table impotently in appreciation.

"Yes, yes, you must dance with the fellow, Celandine," chortled a flushed Arthur.

Celandine smiled uncertainly, she felt strangly light-headed. With the spirit of the charade she said, "I would be delighted, my Lord, but I fear there would not be room for the two of us."

Birket recovered his voice, "Put the tables together we shall have a play."

To the chagrin of the voracious courtiers, the nearest tables were stripped to make a stage. Half-eaten meat, fish, fruit and dishes of sauces tumbled in the grass where the starved beggars immediately followed.

Leaping to the stage, Pan twisted and cavorted, playing the pipes the while, his beard swinging between his lean shanks, while Celandine was helped and half-carried up to her suitor by the grotesque fairies.

Feeling light as thistledown, her spirits soaring, Celandine turned gracefully around on the improvised stage. The full skirt of gauze sylphide billowed out amongst her tiny companions as they rocked the tables, leaping grimly from one short leg to another in their awkward dance. But it wasn't fast enough for the manikins.

"Faster, faster!" screamed one, seizing a fold of the delicate material and swinging out, his feet leaving the boards. The others followed suit and at the first tear the dance became a grim game to rip the pelisse-robe from Celandine's back.

When Celandine was reduced to the black bow around her neck with its long tails flowing down her middle, Birket stared with astonishment to see the fine golden hair curling around the black silk. He had never observed any such representation in the Royal Academy.

Distracted by the moon breaking above the trees, Birket climbed unsteadily to the seat of his chair to bathe in its light.

"A sonnet," he cried, "a sonnet to the night."

The ever watchful Caliban made a signal, and from the still shadows six footmen moved out to stand behind their master's chair.

Horace Birket's eyes glazed, he had passed over into the drug-induced fever of his mind. The servants caught him as he fell backwards into their arms. Gently, slowly, as though he were a coffin, they carried Horace Birket back into the Abbey.

"Arthur!" called Celandine, "come join the dance."

"You will dance with ME!" snarled her tiny Lord Oberon, drawing his sword. Celandine flew up to sit on the shoulder of the tallest demon in the garden. From here she could see all the lights of fairyland twinkling below her. Was that Caliban standing unmoving in the shadows, his dark eyes glinting? But not a sight of Arthur. Only her lover waiting neglected and alone munching the grass.

When she returned to the stage, Oberon was cursing, and beating her with his sword. No wonder she had transferred her affections. He was very harsh and it crushed her so. She would be with her true love. Celandine fluttered across and settled on his deliciously furry back, but was not alone with him for long. In next to no time her naughty family were upon her again, drenching her in wine from flagons as large as themselves, filling her sweet mouth with grapes from their own until the juice ran down her chin, putting a chocolate-bracca biscuit where each faithful tongue could take its turn: nibbling, suckling, teasing, showing their affection in a hundred curious ways, that would have been quite indelicate in other than fairies.

At last exhausted with their play, Celandine gently detached the tiny brood and fell across her lover's back, whispering into his silky ear. The fairy band threw long garlands of flowers over their queen and drew them beneath the ass's belly. Over and under, more and more, until the lovers were at last alone together, hidden in a bower of flowers. But the ear that Celandine whispered to, stiffened, and stamping his hooves, the ass's bray sounded through the wood.

"Such a sweet voice, my dear," murmured Celandine, "pray sing again." Then through the flowers she saw the cause of his alarum. They were ringed about with the Athenian courtiers, replete from their banquet and anxious for a post-prandial course from the fairy queen. It wasn't in her way to give her love to more than one mortal at a time.

Despite the brave defence of the elfin train, the richly-clad courtiers would have taken her, but snorting furiously, her gallant mount broke through the cordon and thundered into the woods followed by a fusillade of bottles and crutches. Celandine had fallen from his back at the outset and swung cradled beneath her lover, her cheek against his heaving chest.

"The most intelligent of mortals," she soothed him, stroking his sweating flank, "as wise as you are beautiful."

Full of her love, Celandine rode ecstatically deeper into her dreams.

31

A REVELATION OF FUSTIGATION

WHEN they cut her from the sensual contentment of her soft floreal womb, the night was carved in cold black rock about her. The tall hooded monks growing from the stone of the chapel floor were as still as death itself, yet it was their granite hands that had drawn her reluctantly into the alien world. She ran beseechingly from one sculpted figure to another, an ethereal vapour about her from the sanguine fructifications condensing on her moist skin; but there was no sign of life in the deep shadows beneath their hooded cowls. Time had frozen around her, moving so slowly that it had chiselled the yellow flames from the rows of black candles. Yet when they placed her on the marble altar she could not discern their movement.

The moon had abdicated, sliding icily from the sky, leaving Celandine in pale emulation, spread whitely on the marble. They covered her nakedness with a stone crucifix, heavy with encrusted gems, so cold that it burned her hot skin.

She lay, feeling the stone drawing the vital living warmth from her, reducing her by infinite degrees to its own inanimate state.

A sensation of warmth awoke Celandine to the presence of the mighty god Pan. He stood, fiery black, his great horned head towering into the sky; melting the iced marble with his cloven foot as he climbed to the altar. The cross on her breast stood only between her and the prince of darkness, and it was as nothing when she stared affrighted into his sulphur-yellow eyes. In a shaft of exquisite agony, there was sudden illumination. It was as though a veil had been drawn lightly over the world before, and being suddenly removed, showed everything in its true clarity.

I was two years old and carrying out the task that I loved best, namely, black-leading Mrs. Brooker's fireplace. It wasn't for love of Mrs. Brooker, who Mamma said was a pauper just like ourselves, that I took such care in blacking the ornamental cast-iron flowers—I thought the fireplace was the most beautiful thing in the whole workhouse.

"Oh, Liza," I said, "shall we have a pretty room like this one day?"

Eliza Screece was my friend, although she was a grown woman of thirteen with a bosom like Mamma's. But unlike Mamma, she never troubled to wash herself too frequent. Her face, as now, was normally smudged with dirt and one could scarce tell, that when clean, her hair was bright as corn in the field.

Liza sat back from the carpet she had been sweeping and took a long look through the open door before she answered.

"First off, Celandine Spencer, it ain't such a special room, and second I reckons as 'ow you'd earn it gallows 'ard to get it the way Mrs. Brooker does. Less of course you're partial to whey-faced toads."

I could not help but shiver as I tried to grasp her meaning.

"You mean Mr. Miles."

"None else."

"*Are they such friends then, Liza?*"

She shifted uncomfortably on her haunches. Liza had been punished, I knew, some weeks ago and it still caused her some discomfort. But for what she had been punished and in what manner, I could not discover.

"*Ain't you the little innocent, lovey. I don't know 'ow yer Ma keeps you that way, an' I don't know as I 'olds with it. But I'll not go against 'er. You'll 'ave to ask 'er that question.*"

Then, unbelievably, came the sound I waited on all day, that never came till well after sunset. The shuffle of dragging feet of the women and Mamma returning from the fields. Something was awry, it was but the middle of the morning and there were the raised voices of both men and women. I looked fearfully at Liza.

"*Folks say them Chartists are causing trouble at the mill. It won't never do no good but to break a few heads and rest us from the fields a while.*"

Running to the tiny window, I could see across the cobbles to the poor-house gates.

"*There's soldiers with long knives, Liza, and men with sticks, shouting. They're trying to come in with the women but the soldiers won't let them.*"

"*Them Chartists would find precious little bread were they to get in,*" said Liza.

Then I saw one of the soldiers raise his musket butt to a woman and the crowd moaned all together like an animal. Who was that tall slim figure that fell through the gates with a bloodied head?

"*Mamma! Mamma!*" *I screamed.*

Forgetting Eliza, the black lead I still held in my hand, and all, I flew from the room, down the stairs to search amongst the ragged women straggling into the great flagged hall. I found her at last, her high cheekbones paler than usual, standing, as was her wont, a little apart from the others. Thankfully it was

*not she who I had seen struck down. She was by far the pret-
tiest woman there, despite the streaks of grey in her hair and
wasted appearance—the latter defects in her looks she owed to
me, I thought with a sob. Liza had told me how Mamma had
deprived herself of her small rations that my limbs would grow
up straight, and crouched sleepless over me for two years, to
keep off the rats that scampered freely in our crowded sleeping
quarters. There were children here without toes or noses to
show that their mothers had been less considerate. With a
rush of gratitude and love, I ran to her and buried my face
in her skirts.*

*"There, there, sweet Celandine, I am here and all is well."
she sighed and dried my eyes with her hand that was hard
from the work in the fields.*

*As I quietened I could hear that the women around us
had also stilled. An extra chill seemed to creep into the icy
hall and a faint smell that I had not known before that frightened me.*

*I looked round to find that the paupers had moved silently
from one end of the hall leaving an empty space before the
stone steps, at the top of which stood the master, Mr. Miles:
a great fleshy man straining the seams of his frock coat, his
clean-shaven jowl as blue as his tall beaver hat. Behind him in
the shadows was Mrs. Brooker, the gold—that Liza had sworn
to take from her head one day—flashing dimly amongst her
black teeth.*

*With less aversion for their company than the pauper
women felt, a large black cockroach came from a crack in the
steps beneath them, and crawled upwards, uncertain perhaps
in the gloom if it was yet time for his nightly foray.*

*Prior to the yearly visit of the inspector, we children had
been put to the task of making traps: which consisted of a
paste-board cover well-suspended by two pins over a vessel
of water and treacle. But the women very soon removed the
trapped creatures and ate the treacle, and the army of cock-*

roaches continued to grow until it was not unusual to see them in daylight.

"Miss Spencer," whispered Mr. Miles, in soft sibilants that hissed to every corner of the still hall.

I clung quickly to Mamma, but gently she pushed me behind her skirts.

"Aye, sir," said Mamma.

"Come forward, Miss Spencer."

As Mr. Miles brought forward the birch he carried, the faint smell I had detected before increased, over-riding the normal sour unwashed stench of the women. I thought it must be the smell of fear itself. The birch was truly a fearsome thing, the handle being made from a broom-handle, so thick, that his fingers only just met around it.

I clung even more desperately to Mamma, but she pushed me roughly amongst the tattered skirts of the other women, and with a composure that she did not feel, for I had felt her trembling, stepped forward.

"Not 'er," screamed Mrs. Brooker, pushing a furious face past the weighty figure of Mr. Miles, "it was 'er damned brat."

I squirmed deeper amongst the women. What had I done to vex Mrs. Brooker so.

"I'll answer for aught the child's done."

"You may yet, Madame," whispered the master, "but show the child direct."

A damp moment of silence hung over the hall. In the space afforded between the women's dresses, I could see the large boots of Mr. Miles and the stone steps beneath them. The cockroach was far braver than I, who for fear, could not have moved had I wanted. I stared fascinated as the black insect completed his laborious climb to the next step, paused for a moment rubbing his feelers above his head, as though in self congratulation, and advanced with wonderful courage towards those formidable boots.

There was a sharp intake of many breaths as the birch suddenly whistled through the air and the master roared:

"You defy me? Burn my body! There may be reds outside but I'll not countenance rebellious rabble in here. Show her to me I say!"

Of a sudden unsympathetic hands were pushing me forward, galvanized I supposed by a fear for their own skins. Faces above me that I thought I knew well, hardened against me, despite my pleading, and I fell at the foot of the steps still unbelieving that the women could treat me so cruelly. I looked around for Mamma, but she was struggling in the hands of the women, with her friend Francis Roberts choking her to silence.

"Be still," she hissed, "or we shall all of us suffer."

I could not bear to look at the cruel faces of Mr. Miles or Mrs. Brooker, instead I watched the only thing that stood between us: the cockroach—still climbing. He reached another step and was giving his customary self-satisfied dance, when the master's descending boot narrowly missed him. He scuttered quickly aside—but too late to avoid Mrs. Brooker's vindictive shoe.

I screamed in order not to hear the crunch of its shell and looked up in horror at the awful face above me. I had never seen the master so close before. His eyes were like an animal, flat and yellow, draining away any thought I had of fleeing.

"Take her garment and spread her," he commanded.

A long drawn-out sigh came from the women. Too late I felt their sympathy, perhaps they could not believe that Mr. Miles would beat me with that huge birch that stood taller than I, for whatever crime I had committed.

Before Mrs. Brooker could move, Eliza Screece, grey of face, pushed past her, the black lead in her hand.

"Leave 'er be, you've no call to touch 'er. I spilled the black lead on your lousy carpet."

I knew she was lying. It came back to me now. I had thrown the black lead aside in my haste. Mamma was suddenly by my side and pulling me back amongst the women and I was too frightened to say anything.

"It might pay you to do the civil to Master Miles," said Mrs. Brooker slyly. "Less you enjoy the taste of his birch so dearly."

"Go to blazes you whore-hog!" shouted Liza. The master's huge hand fell on the collar of her shift and lifted her from the ground. Liza fought desperately her curses muffled as the shift covered her head. Mrs. Brooker joined in the struggle, only to retire winded by a kick from one of Liza's plump exposed legs. A final wriggle and the girl was free, leaving her garment in Master Miles' hand. I could not bear to see my friend naked before everyone and the tears ran silently down my face, and still I said nothing.

Liza's courage had left her with her shift.

"You'll not beat me Master Miles," she pleaded, "for such a trifle."

She looked around forlornly for support. Mamma would have gone to Liza but once again Francis Roberts stayed her, and after a glance at me, Mamma bit her lip and did not move. There was a curious look on the women's faces and they were moving closer in now.

"God in heaven knows! she always was a stuck-up jade," someone muttered.

"Aye, an' there's flesh a plenty on her to stand a good birching," answered another. Their eyes were bright and they were wetting their lips. Shakily Liza backed away, the goose pimples forming on her grimy skin. Mr. Miles followed slowly, regarding Liza so intently, that she half-tried to cover the tiny nipples on her big trembling breasts.

I could stand it no more.

"I did it! I did it! I did it!"

"Quiet the brat," whispered Mr. Miles without taking his

eyes from Liza's quivering flesh. He was not to be dissuaded now. "You'll not wheedle out of this slattern. There's a lesson here in obedience and proper respect for parish goods, and the whole company will be the better for the teaching of it. Put her on the plank I say."

Mrs. Brooker was still winded from the kick in the middle. "Bring her to the table," she snarled.

But Francis Roberts turned away. Cursing, Mrs. Brooker roused herself to run forward and seize Liza's hair. Poor Liza was no match for the heavy woman and was soon spread across the long table, held firmly at the wrists by Mrs. Brooker. The Master carefully removed his frock coat and rolled up his sleeves and Mamma placed the hand that had been on my mouth over my eyes. But she could not shut from me the sound of the birch rushing through the air, or the awful thwack as it met Liza's flesh, nor such a blood-curdling scream as I had never heard that chilled to the bone. It seemed to awaken Liza's spirit and she cursed Mrs. Brooker for a whore and the Master for fornication until the next stroke cut her breath away. Then she accused Mr. Miles of taking vengeance because she resisted his advances. The next stroke fell and Liza put her tongue to the vilest and most obscene words she could find. I felt something drop on to my hair, then again and again, it was Mamma's tears. The flogging settled into a slow awful rhythm and a quivering rattle started up, as though from a convulsive movement of the girl on the table. Interpersed with her terrible cries Liza began to plead for mercy—that she would do all that the master asked of her if he would but stop. Still the beating continued. Gradually the force of my unfortunate friend's screams died into a sob until she was whimpering like a tiny baby and the thwack of the birch had an awful wet sound to it. At last there was only those pitiful whimpers.

"Go to your quarters," whispered Mr. Miles.

Mamma released me, and half-blinded with tears, pushed me

towards the door. I managed to divide myself from her in the press and hid just inside the doorway watching the flushed and occasionally tear-strewn faces of the women filing out—until the four of us were left in the hall. Mr. Miles set aside the broken birch, spattering the flags with tiny red droplets and Mrs. Brooker released Liza's wrists. My friend made no move: but she was still alive.

A shuddering movement ran through her as the Master placed his hand on the raw flesh at the back of her legs and ran it up and over the raised welts on her wet buttocks, so that the blood ran through his hairy fingers like a second thin red hand. He reached for the buckle of his belt and I screamed but no sound came at all. I watched from the shadow of the doorway and screamed silently the while. When Mamma came to take me away, he must have heard something for he turned and the last I saw was those searching animal yellow eyes, that should have seen those things done to me: not to Liza that I loved.*

The beggars, in a drunken pile, stripped of their rich robes and jewels, were bumping along at the bottom of an open wagon far from the estate; and a troupe of dwarfs waited, shivering with their boxes at the railway station, consoling themselves with the thought of the sovereigns weighting their pockets : when Celandine awoke.

The thin yellow edge of day was lifting up the night and Celandine, cold and naked, lay on the altar. Her head spun and her tongue was dry. Which of the night's events had

---

* The New Poor Law of 1834 discontinued all outdoor relief for able-bodied paupers—forcing them to the workhouse. Conditions were made as unfavourable as possible with the separation of the sexes and harsh workhouse tests. Much brutality and corruption of officials went on in some workhouses under this system. In 1840 charges were placed before the Rochester Magistrates regarding the flagellation of little girls just turned the age of two. Francis Roberts made a further statement turning on the flogging of Eliza Screece of thirteen years by the Master, Mr. Miles.

taken place and which had been imagining? This was real, in truth, the nausea and her cold aching limbs, and the imprint of the stone cross that had not yet faded from her body. The beating of Eliza Screece—that had not been just a dream, but was an uncovered memory. Had she not let down her friend Maudie in the same fashion by refusing to help unmask the Captain? Those staring yellow eyes in her nightmares, had come from the past. Was this the power that Billy Miles had over her? Must she always be atoning for her guilt? So that any man, at his whim, could reduce her to a wretched compliant vessel?

"Celandine!" The girl recognized the shadowy form of Arthur Banks picking his way through the ruined chapel towards her. "Such a dream I had whilst sleeping beyond the walls." Arthur noticed that Celandine was shivering and taking off his cloak, absently placed it around her shoulders. "What are you at, you'll catch the devil of a cold." Celandine trusted that was all she would contract.

"Such a dream," continued Arthur, "to be sure it would make a stunning painting. I dreamt that you were a knight as pure and chaste as Sir Percival seeking the Holy Grail," Celandine got carefully down from the altar with a grimace of pain, and wrapped the cloak about her, "doing vigil all night over your armour and weapons in the chapel, whilst I, your faithful *escuyer* slept beyond the walls. . . ." Celandine tried a few steps and found that she could walk—but painfully. "I saw your saintly face, the clear beautiful line of your profile against the moonlight, your hair tumbling over the chain armour, hands raised in prayer. I shall call the painting: 'The Lady Knight in Vigil'."

Celandine viewed the prospect of clanking around the studio at Millbank without enthusiasm feeling that a suit of chain armour would add little to her personal comfort. Arthur dropped to his knees before her: "Whither goest thou, O purest of the pure?"

"To the most expensive whore-house in London," answered Celandine, and limped away, leaving Arthur open-mouthed, still on his knees.

Breathlessly, Arthur caught up with the girl outside the chapel—when with a furious rattle, a coach loomed out of the morning mist and pulled to before them. Caliban, a flash of teeth against the dark sky, laughed down at them from high up on the box. Birket's head popped out from the carriage window.

"Quickly. Inside! Time is short." Arthur bundled the reluctant Celandine into the coach and they were off. Caliban whipped up the frantic horses until the equipage thundered along the half-light of the estate roads at a suicidal twelve miles an hour. Intent on preserving their seats in the rocking interior—the passengers had little spare breath to ask where they were bound. At last the flying horses left the road and the wheels hushed and slowed in the grass, until they rolled to a halt at the bottom of a lush hollow. Celandine stumbled with relief from the carriage, viewing Birket's clear eye and vibrant vitality with disfavour as he pranced amongst the dew. From the corner of her eye she saw Caliban drop to the grass. He brushed against her, as if by accident.

"I beg your pardon, Madame." He bowed and whispered "When an *Ashwa* makes the acquaintance of a *Mreusi*, then indeed is *Krishna* to be praised." He bowed, smiling, and moved away from the puzzled girl.

"What's all the dashed hurry, Birket," said Arthur Banks.

"Apollo will not wait," said Birket, rubbing his hands together gleefully. "At the first breath of his steeds shall the fiery hoof of man burst upon us. Mark you well the edge of the estate, Arthur."

Puzzled, the artist observed the rapidly lightening scene. They stood at the bottom of a valley, with wooded slopes rising on either side, and beyond, the distant hills still dark from the night, with the lighter-coloured fields patchworked at their base, following the shape of the good soil. Before them stretched the rippling grass at the bottom of the valley coming to a sudden halt when it met the high wall surrounding the estate, effectively cutting off their view of the country beyond.

As Birket had promised opaquely, when the tip of the sun flared over the top of the wall, a series of explosions rocked across the valley and the wall was obscured in rolling wreaths of smoke, billowing lazily upwards to the shafts that the sun had as suddenly shot across the sky. Arthur had never beheld such a sight. The smoke hung like a great red and gold curtain across the valley, shot with purples and mauves in the shadows of its under belly, and beyond, the orange disc of the sun rose inexorably, turning to gold as the curtain slowly cleared.

A final attack from the morning wind, that had sprung up, and the curtain parted as though drawn on strings. For a moment the watchers were blinded by the brilliance of light and then they made out that the wall had vanished and beyond was a scene of teeming activity. At the extreme end of the valley puffs of smoke appeared from a tiny locomotive as it started towards them, and the chug of its engine came to their ears. Through a cutting it came where the chalk was still being cleared. Hundreds of minute figures, like spiders on silken threads, flew up the steep slopes with their barrows or down again backwards. Each man attached by a rope from his belt to a horse beyond the escarpment, dangerously guiding his laden barrow up narrow planks, with a possible death awaiting every moment, should he slip or his horse stumble.

Was 'Puffing Billy' amongst those labourers, wondered Celandine.

Onwards came the train until it stood panting where the rails ended at the ruined wall, and the spectators by the coach could smell the smoke from the reeking funnel-pipe of the engine.

Before they had fully stopped, gangs of navigators spilled from the trucks and began clearing the ground before them—

laying rails into the estate, down the valley that Birket had sold to the railways.

"It has been estimated," said Arthur Banks, "that if the English navigator had expended his energies differently than on the railways, he could have built a pyramid one third as large again as the Great Pyramid of Egypt, with one fifteenth of the men involved in that venture and in a quarter of the time that it took them."

He looked around to find the grinning face of Caliban his only audience. Birket lay flat on his back, his feet kicking, overcome with excitement and Celandine was half-way down the slope to the railway line.

"Fetch our baggage you grinning idiot and bring it to me," he shouted, running after the girl.

32

BIG GOES AND LITTLE GOES

CELANDINE, a large hooded cloak about her, pushed through the throng in the Haymarket. Past the policeman, bidding the unfortunate, who wouldn't fee him, to move on, past the night vendors of this and that, under the cab wheels and between the horses legs, up to the entrance of the handsomest casino in London.

She favoured one of the ragged boys, who rushed to open the door for her, with sixpence and swept through the foyer, having no need of buying a tin check for her entrance— unaccompanied women always being singularly welcome at the establishment and admitted free.

As she walked in the promenade, railed off for respectable families to listen to the music and see the pantomime on the stage, the gas lights from the splendid chandeliers strung across the saloon dimmed and a chemical light-coloured flame radiated the place. A huge many-faceted glass ball turned in the ceiling sending points of light quivering over the throng of some three thousand—a large number of whom were rushing to the floor to join in the abandon of the shadow dance.

Paying a shilling to enter the enclosure, Celandine joined the company of the handsome women dressed in costly silks and satins, and gentlemen whose dress betokened them as members of respectable society—who had no fear of the gentle reproach from any of their womenfolk for their presence in such a place, since no respectable woman was to be found this side of the barrier. She passed falsely curled and painted women bestowing their blandishments for drink, without any disguise, on spoony young swells, and every description of 'respectable' gentleman lounging on the red sofas provided, from the gentleman in trade from Brighton, complaining loudly that he felt a cup too low; to the pale melancholy little lordling, who young as he was, had already bought a regiment.

Unhesitatingly, Celandine made for the canteen, a subterranean bar beneath the stage, and suddenly the glitter from the countless bars on the ground floor and those on the shilling and sixpenny galleries above—which only the lowest of the low frequented—had vanished and the fine music from the sixty piece band was hushed.

The canteen was shadowy, lit only from the glittering bar, presided over by two barmen in red velvet waistcoats, serving out champagne, Mosselle and oysters to the resting ballet girls and their companions.

Celandine slipped past a chalked and painted ballet girl of about fifteen, her head resting drunkenly on the shoulder of an elderly gentleman, and went to a curtained door in the darkest corner of the place. Here she showed a card to an enormous attendant, before she was allowed to proceed further, down a

long corridor hung with rich, red and gold tapestry, and lit
by handsome candelabra. Celandine threw back the hood of
her cloak and slipped on a black silk mask that covered her
eyes. Thus disguised, she continued along the tunnel, which
burrowed some hundreds of yards under the ground, until she
arrived at an ornate reception room. She was ushered straightway along corridors and up deeply carpeted stairs, and at last,
conducted to a luxuriously appointed octagonal chamber. The
woman who waited for her, was reflected a thousand times in
a most uncommon fashion, by the glass that lined the walls.
Celandine recognized her despite the mask that she too had
affected, by the wart on the side of her mouth. It was Miss
Grigg—enticer and bawd, to the House, the most extravagant
bordello in the Metropolis.

"Welcome, my dear," she greeted Celandine, taking both
her hands, "Angel, I believe is your name." She studied that
part of the girl's glowing face which was uncovered. "Yes,
indeed, they told me you were quite delightful. Pray show me
the rest of your charms."

The girl shrugged off the cloak, so that it fell from her
shoulders. She was dressed for the 'Bal Masque', as a vestal
virgin, wearing a simple diaphanous robe, quite open at the
sides, and a single band of pearls around her forehead holding
back the golden glory of her hair that tumbled in curls down
her back.

"Quite exquisite my dear, I must fetch the Captain, who
has expressed a desire to meet you just as soon as you arrived."

Steady herself as she would, Celandine could not stay her
limbs from trembling, as Miss Grigg returned with the tall
masked gentleman.

"Capital," said the Captain, his expert eye addressing itself
to the splendid form visible through the material of her gown.
"If your skills are but half the equal to your beauty, I can
put you in the way of making a fortune. You do have some
experience I believe, my dear."

"Why yes indeed, sir, and I am very willing to learn more of my craft."

"Capital," said the Captain, putting his arm around the girl, "seldom have we had offered to us such a likely recruit. Not, I believe since young Lady B. approached us, Miss Grigg. But then she was an oddity and would accept no financial reward, until chlorine eventually claimed her for the mad house and then the grave, so beware of such excesses, my dear. I much prefer a sound fiscal arrangement." The Captain sensed the girl's anxiety as he pulled a slim golden chain that extinguished the gas lamps.

"Have no fear, my dear, no harm shall come to you. It is to our interest to make you very happy here. I should just like to initiate you into a few of our mysteries and perhaps discover where your interests lie. This room itself has only been penetrated by the first in our establishment and is both difficult and exceding expensive for those outside to gain admittance. Prime Ministers of England, ministers of state of foreign powers and indeed royalty are amongst the privileged few who have paid dearly for what you are about to witness."

Slowly as her eyes became adjusted to the dim light, Celandine perceived that she was able to see through each glass set in the walls, to further rooms beyond. The Captain led her to the first mirror to begin the tour of his establishment.

"There you see the plump and merry arsed Thurlow, a natural lech if ever there was one, who thoroughly enjoys her work as you no doubt observe." Celandine was grateful for the half light which covered the embarrassment which she would have otherwise shown.

"Beyond this second glass you see two young ladies taking their ease, who are renowned for their representations, which they enter into with such enthusiasm that a client could never perceive that it is pounds, shillings and pence which is their motivation."

The girls were so beautiful and the rooms so sumptuously

fitted, that Celandine could hardly believe that this was not some Eastern harem, rather than a bordello in the heart of London.

"Mr. Arkwright!" breathed Celandine at the next glass, unable to contain her surprise.

"So you know the gentleman," laughed the Captain, "to have contented Mr. Arkwright is as good as a certificate of character. He has already blewed one fortune with us and is half-way through his wife's I believe now. But such gentlemen seem always to have another legacy falling to them from distant members of their family. He is a fine example, as you perceive, of how untrue is the theory that self indulgence long pursued, leads to early death or self destruction, for Arkwright goes from strength to strength."

Celandine moved rather quickly from the uncomfortable memories that the energetic Mr. Arkwright aroused.

"I had not realized that work of this nature required scholastic attainment," said Celandine innocently, for the next chamber was done out as a schoolroom with desks, a blackboard, and a teacher's desk on which a variety of canes were amassed.

"I can see your own education is not yet complete, my dear," chided Miss Grigg. "Let me explain that it is many gentlemen's peculiar lech, that they should be treated as children and severely chastised for being naughty. The 'teacher' is bedizened according to their caprice in a fashion hardly met in any of our great schools. Though many products of those schools have squeezed themselves into those little desks and paid extraordinary fees for that discomfort."

"This might well be to your taste, my dear," said the Captain, peering into the next chamber. Miss Grigg and Celandine joined him at the glass.

"Why surely that is. . . ."

"Quite, my dear."

"And also Mr. . . ."

H

"We never mention names of such notables, my dear, even amongst ourselves. Most of the cabinet are here tonight for the 'Bal Masque'. I do hope that they do not unduly fatigue themselves before that event. The wines tinctured with medicaments calculated to create an amorous frenzy and the application of saffron and ginger, are not always efficacious with the advance of years. But see! There is Fisher, the fine, tall dark-haired girl, and there . . . ah, she is lost from view . . . was the well-fledged Palmer, from whose tufted honours many a noble lord has stolen a sprig."

As the Captain pointed out the various fair incumbents of his establishment, whom Celandine found difficulty in identifying amongst the extraordinary mêlée, she reflected how soon with familiarity, such scenes ceased to shock one's senses.

The sixth chamber however, Celandine found both shocking and pathetic. There had at least been a certain irresponsible gaiety about most of the other chambers, but here the supply of torture instruments filled her with dread. There were: extensive supplies of birch, kept green and pliant in water; cat-o'-nine-tails; leather straps like coaching traces; battledoors with inch nails run through, to currycomb the toughest hide rendered callous by years of flagellation; holly bushes, furze bushes; the prickly evergreen called butcher's bush and fresh green nettles to restore the dead to life.

Miss Grigg detected the girl's consternation. "Have no fear that we shall press you to this line of business, my dear. Some of the young ladies will submit themselves to an extent, for the true glutton we provide women to take as much punishment as the gentleman can afford."

"This chamber is seldom out of use, my dear," added the Captain. "There would seem to be such public interest in the matter of chastisement, that one could name it as the predominant vice of society. The matter has been debated in the columns of 'Notes and Queries', and lengthy correspondence carried out in many domestic periodicals. Tracts on the treatment of inmates at Bridewell are always sure of a good sale. My extensive studies into the phenomena, force me into the belief that society is frustrated by the unnatural bonds placed upon it, and wishes to expiate the guilt that it is forced to feel."

Celandine remembered the flogging of poor Liza, and the manner in which she had nursed her guilt over it for so many years. She considered there was some truth in his words.

"The curious thing is, that I have come across few women who enjoy receiving the application of the rod, rather more do they enjoy applying it. However, such is the demand that we are equipped here to: birch, whip, fustigate, scourge, needle-prick, half-hang, holly-brush, furze-brush, stinging nettle, curry-comb, phlebotomize and torture till their bellies are full of it, or their pockets empty."

"And what of the final room?" asked Celandine. "There can be naught else you have to offer, in the way of lecherous amusement."

"This, my dear," said the Captain, conducting her to the glass, "is a machine constructed to the design of Miss Grigg. It is the last resort of wearied old profligates, and has proved a great popularity."

Celandine shuddered at the extraordinary scene, and could not conceive of the condition of those taking part in it.

"I have observed with interest your reactions to the various lecheries you have witnessed, my dear. Would I be truthful if I suggested that the fifth tableau excited you more than any other?"

How he could have arrived at this assumption, unless it was through the presence of his hand judging the palpitations of her heart, Celandine could not imagine. In truth, the spectacle had brought about a certain answering excitement in her breast.

"Why yes indeed, sir," she answered boldly, "that is much more to my taste, than the business of doctoring the jaded."

"Capital, just as I thought. Then take my arm. They should be ready in the salon to commence the 'Bal Masque', and it is always my custom to 'first take the floor', as it were, with a new arrival, before festivities begin in earnest."

"Oh Lor', I hadn't thought, I mean, I understood this evening was but for me to view the establishment and for you to decide on my suitability."

"Precisely, my dear."

"I had not thought to work."

"To one of your avowed temperament, Angel, I had thought to view it more as a pleasurable pursuit."

"Why, yes, of course," said Celandine placing a shaking arm in his.

Miss Grigg folded the girl's cape thoughtfully, as the couple left for the salon.

Billy Miles glowered at Celandine over his glass of champagne, as she stepped on to the cleared space between the revellers. Her disguise could not conceal her identity from one who had once had so close an acquaintance with that splendid body.

As the evening progressed, Billy did not join in the agreeable diversions provided by the establishment, as was his wont. The *Tableaux Vivants* in which the artistes dispensed with the normal flesh-coloured garments, could not attract his attention. He sat at the bar, his yellow eyes burning through the slits of his mask devouring every move Celandine made. Thus it was that only he, of the assembled company, observed that when at last the exhausted girl was allowed to rest on one of the sofas, two footmen appeared suddenly, wrapped her in a cloak and hurried her protesting from the place.

Through the night the coach rocked, with the frightened Celandine the sole occupant, bounced like a shuttlecock in the interior. Then to the smooth run of the turnpike in the moonlight, and the thunder of the horses' hooves an even drumming that lulled her into sleep, only to be brought violently awake as they careened around a corner and pursued rough country once more. There was a halt, flashing bullseye lights, the creak of harness and men's voices. The footman came down from his post to sit opposite the girl, stolidly ignoring her. When the horses were changed she was left alone once more to endure the bucketing journey.

Some hours later, the coach turned in through massive wrought-iron gates and the wheels slowed, crunching over a well-kept gravel drive.

There were no lights in the Great House. Celandine allowed herself to be taken up the stone steps and through the imposing doors. Dust sheets lay over the furniture she passed as she was conducted by lantern up the great curved stairs. The footman pulled the covers from a huge four-poster and retired from the room. Celandine crawled gratefully between the covers and slept.

Dismounting at the crested gates, Billy and Joe Salt led their horses up the drive.

"So your precious Lord Furlingham combines a pious aspect with running the flesh-pots of the metropolis."

" 'E was always good to me and Polly, for all that," growled Joe Salt.

"I'm sure," laughed Billy taking a swig from the brandy flask that had sustained him on the ride from London. "No doubt he was the first to enjoy her favours, for someone had stroked her regular before I arrived."

Joe Salt dropped the reins and swung a furious blow at Billy Miles, catching him on the side of the head, and sending him flying between the horses' legs. The animals reared, their hooves clattering around him and galloped off into the night as Billy rolled clear.

"You've baited me once too often, Mr. Miles. Now you're for it."

"You're past it you old fool," hissed Billy climbing to his feet, "I'll welcome the chance to teach you a lesson." Of a sudden he lowered his head and butted the huge man with tremendous force in that hard middle, but Joe's knee came up smashing his nose and splitting his lips. Billy staggered for a moment, his head feeling as though it was coming apart "That's for Polly," gasped the old man, "and that's for me," he said, smashing a fist as large as a ham and hard as granite into Billy's ribs.

"Sweet Jesus," spat out Billy through his own blood, with dawning comprehension, "It was you that was tailing her." He got to his knees—when Joe Salt's boot came flying to catch him under the chin.

33

MASTER STROKE

THE first pale light permeating the room awoke Celandine with a start. She could hear the murmur of men's voices reminding her of the doubtful circumstances of her forced abduction. Throwing the cloak about her—she had lost both mask and costume the evening before—Celandine quietly opened the bedroom door.

With some relief, she recognized Dick's voice coming clearly from below. She crept out along the carpeted landing, to crouch below the balustrade, like a child eavesdropping on its parents. There, below, sat the Captain, unmasked at last and confronted by Inspector Dick Blackstone—as melodramatic a scene as ever she had witnessed at the 'Vic'.

But something was at odds surely. Both men held balloon glasses of brandy. Nor did the Captain appear particularly disconcerted by the confrontation—to the contrary.

"Don't put such a despondent face on it, inspector. Your masterly detection shall not go unrewarded, and I shall determine that your talents if not publicly acknowledged, shall at least be recognized in more useful quarters.

"But let not selfish consideration of the perilous situation in which you would place yourself, alone determine whether you should attempt to bring the matter to court. Consider the condition in which you place England. With half the ruling class on trial as lechers, the lower classes would seize on it to throw over virtue completely—or worse to stage a revolution as in France. Rest assured, one stone cannot be uncovered, without all being exposed : royalty would be implicated, peers of the realm, government, the church itself—as landlords of the House, profiting hugely from the immoral earnings of the bordello—would not escape unscathed."

"My duty is to carry the matter forward to my superiors."

Furlingham swirled the brandy in his glass and smiled gently.

"In truth, Blackstone, we both know you would not be here if you had any such intention. No, you would be a fool if you were not content with what you have already achieved. You have seen Dyson, the murderer who set all London shaking in their beds, hanged and carried on a board in a cart dressed in his best suit of clothes. Carried past the scene of his crime as an awful warning and buried in a common grave with a stake through his heart. Your name is on all London's lips as the detective who took the murderer.

"I judge your ambition took a different turn when you sent the girl to seek out the Captain and informed me of your plan."

Celandine's throat constricted as she heard of Dick's betrayal, she waited, half hoping for a refutal, but all Dick said was :

"What of Celandine ?"

'That's of little moment to you, inspector. Of larger mutual concern is your decision regarding the present investigation."

Dick Blackstone climbed to his feet, the fruits of victory curiously bitter in his mouth.

"You have convinced me, Lord Furlingham, that the most satisfactory conclusion, would be to officially close this case."

"Capital, Blackstone, we'll shake on that, a decision you'll not live to regret."

"Thank you, my lord, and now I'll bid you good morning."

"Good day, inspector."

The door closed and the sound of Dick's carriage dwindled into the distance. Celandine dried her eyes, furious that she should feel such emotion at the departure of her treacherous sweetheart.

Always she had been a pawn in others' hands—to seduce, keep, abandon and then use indiscriminately—and none had been true to her. Mayhap she should take a hand in controlling her own destiny. This Lord Furlingham was but a man and Lord knows, men had many weaknesses. Whatever his reason for bringing her here, she might well turn it to her own advantage.

The sun was up, pouring long rays through the stained glass clerestory windows into the Gothick hall. Pricking pointed arch and rib vaulting into stark relief, and transforming the grey cobwebs hanging from shield and escutcheon into silvered tattered banners.

"Lord Furlingham."

The peer held a hand against the coloured dancing sunbeams and looked up to the hooded figure that stood half-way up the curve of the stairs.

"Who is that there?"

The girl threw back the hood and her hair burst out like molten gold, flooding around that angelic face, bathed in the unearthly light.

"Celandine," uttered Furlingham, his heart beginning to pound.

"Now that you know that I am a police spy," said the girl, descending slowly, "I wondered what plans my Lord had for me."

She stopped a few steps above the man and shook out her hair, allowing the cloak to slip off one softly rounded shoulder, and exposing the rich curve of her breast.

"None but the gentlest, my child." Furlingham gravely assured her. He lifted one hand to help her down the remaining steps. Celandine did not move, but gazed at him levelly.

"First I must warn you that having no such avowed temperament as I at first declared, my price is considerably higher than your early expectations."

"Oh, you wicked child to attempt such a bargain," said the handsome, outraged woman at the door. "God's punishment would indeed follow swiftly upon such illegal connection. Lord Furlingham is certainly your father or step-brother, one or the other, either which relationship would make you a party to the detestable crime of incest. You infamous creature, have you sunk so low?"

"Mother, you . . . here. . . ." said Celandine, stunned, retreating from the furious figure in black.

As her mother raised her hand she was returned to the daily scoldings of her childhood; to their tiny cottage and the silently sympathetic Tom; to the sly, watchful priest, the Rev. Mr. Blackstone; to the days when Dick Blackstone was her only friend. Celandine caught her mother's hand at the wrist before the blow could fall.

"Mother, I am no longer a child. Nor if I am come to such a pass are you without blame. Did you not send me away and then desert me?" Then with gradual comprehension, Celandine said: "And is your connection with Furlingham such a pious one? How could he be so related to me?"

"Ladies," interrupted Furlingham with a faint smile, "whilst I cannot but feel an intimate of the family, such reconciliation as might be effected would best be pursued without my presence. Might I venture the hope that it can be resolved in harmony, in which case I would be pleased to welcome you, Celandine, to my establishment." He bowed to the girl who hastily pulled the cloak more modestly about her. "I will send in hot chocolate, ladies."

When the Earl had gone, Lucy said: "I should not blame you for that wicked self indulgence in your nature, which neither I nor God could root out from you, for I know from whence it came. Do I not fight every day to help that dear pious man, Lord Furlingham to resist the very same evil."

"Come, Mother, speak plain," said Celandine impatiently.

"I had never thought to tell you of our shame, child, but it seems I must to prevent even worse befalling. When I was your age, Celandine, I was deeply in love with my cousin Will. I worshipped the man second only to God, and we were to be joined together under Him when Will's ship returned. One night your grandfather let the old Earl and his son in upon me whilst I slept. It was an ancient custom that the depraved old earl persisted in—to claim conjugal rights on lasses about to wed. I left the parish before you were born and when I returned, with you, let it be known that I had married Will my sweetheart, and that he was lost at sea, which indeed he was. Poor sweet Will. God at least spared him the shame I have lived with."

"How can you then consort with such a wicked man as Furlingham, mother, even should he be my father?"

"God works in strange ways, Celandine. He was young, unformed and much under the influence of his father. I truly believe that it was remorse for this single act which has led him so surely in the paths of righteousness." Celandine held her breath with disbelief as her mother continued : "He that truly repenteth so shall he also enter into the Kingdom of Heaven. To move amongst the evil in our midst and destroy it, as Furlingham does, that is the true test, and yet to remain untouched by sin."

Is she not aware, marvelled Celandine, that Furlingham was proprietor of a very going concern in just such a commodity. Of a sudden she felt very old and wise, and she held her peace. For where would her mother be, without a Christian struggle to engage in? And where else could she battle more valiantly against absolute evil and the wicked one?

"If only you could know of the unfortunates he has saved. Did he not save you from that terrible place, the House?"

"Indeed, Mamma, he did," lied Celandine.

"Do not look so shamefaced. Now we must stay together. Furlingham will be delighted I know to have you with us."

"Of course," said Furlingham returning and taking Lucy's arm. "We shall have very jolly times."

Celandine could well imagine the jolly times he envisaged. The footman brought forward the chocolate for the ladies, and soda and brandy for Furlingham. Then he bent to his master and whispered long in his ear. Furlingham frowned.

"Is it bad news?" asked Lucy.

"Rather unexpected, shall we say. This fellow William Miles followed you from town last night, Celandine. When I told him to take himself off and call at a respectable hour, he became most offensive. Owned to a grudge for me, and how he was my equal and could send out or call in millions. Chap seemed to have been in a fight all bloodied and well lushed-up. Told him a gentleman never showed his drink and bade the grooms confine him in the stables to cool his heels to the morrow. Robert took him some bread and bacon this morning and received a pitchfork through his thigh for his trouble. Seems the servants beat him rather badly I fear."

"Oh, I pray he is not too severely injured."

"So do I, my dear, head grooms are dev'lish hard to find."

"No, no, my lord, it is Mr. William Miles who is my concern. You had no business to lock him up. May I go to him please?"

"Really, my dear, he is new money you know."

"Where may I find him?"

"Why, he is being returned to London by closed carriage, I prefer his absence to his company."

"Then I shall acompany him. There is unfinished business I must attend to with Mr. William Miles," she said grimly, "and his present condition presents a suitable occasion. Goodbye, Mamma."

"Must you truly go with this Miles, can you not stay a few days?"

"It is better I should go Mamma. Good-bye." She kissed Lucy. Furlingham took her hand. "You know where to find me, should you ever need me. You will always be made welcome."

"Thank you so much, my Lord," curtsied Celandine sarcastically, "Now I must fly."

"You will write to me of your whereabouts?"

"Of course, Mamma," cried Celandine as she sped through the great door. "Good-bye."

"Come, my dear," said Furlingham, "I fear our daughter is lacking in that humble spirit of self denial required to place herself in His Hands and do His Will, to face evil, as you have done, to grapple with it and cast it out. We must help her to that true state of Grace reached only in His service; to struggle as I have struggled to wrest that worldly and fleshly devil from within—and never have I had such sore need of your aid as now."

"Oh, Charlie," said Lucy, rushing joyously to his arms, prepared once more to sacrifice herself in the Lord's Name, "I live only to serve Him."

Only let me not be guilty of the sin of pride in my work, she prayed, for there was such fulfilment and ecstatic fervour in the act of serving Him, that on occasion, it was as though God's Blessing had truly descended upon her.

The girl laughed softly to herself as the coach rocked over a bump and Billy Miles swore fulsomely. There was a perverse humour she discovered in observing the arrogant financier so reduced and laid low. He lay painfully along one seat, his apparel ripped and bloodied, his limbs bandaged and swathed in plaster.

Painfully he turned his head to her : "You'd not laugh, Miss," he gritted, "had I the use of but one arm."

Celandine fashioned a derisive kiss with her lips, and vouchsafed no reply. How fiercely his eyes raged, or the little there was to be seen of them behind the swellings. No longer could they command her against her will, if they ever had been able. Just at that moment, she could almost understand what it must be, to be a man.

"What are you smiling at, you jade?"

There, there, Billy boy, she thought to herself, it will profit you not at all to rage after that manner. She doubted he had bargained for such treatment when he came after her.

Furiously Billy peered up at Celandine as she leant over him. She loosed her hair and it tumbled down around his head, a shining curtain that suddenly veiled the interior of the coach from them, and forced him to look to her face. There was a strangeness about the girl, that made him uneasy about her intentions. Celandine held his eyes as she began to loosen his clothing. Her cloak had fallen open and Billy sensed below his fascinated gaze, the easy, rhythmic swing of her naked breasts, whilst her fingers moved lightly down his body. With an agonized quickening, Billy was gratified to learn that he was not quite a ruined man. Howsomever, Billy could not entirely stifle a scream of pain when Celandine lowered herself, her cloak settling around them. Yet his good hand pulled down her head fiercely, forcing her lips against his broken mouth. For Billy had no intention of being raped by any woman.

AUTHOR'S NOTE

The incidents in this pastiche have been suggested by actual events in the nineteenth century. Where possible I have used texts from writers contemporary to the times. The possibilities of such a gathering, other than in this context defy the imagination—they include :

William Acton
Henry Spencer Ashbee
Thomas Beames
Mrs. L. Burke
William Cobbett
Disraeli
Thomas De Quincey
Frederick Engels
D. Morier Evans
James Ewing
James Greenwood
F. B. Head

Charles Kingsley
Henry Mayhew
J. L. Milton
Hannah More
Shaykh Nefzawi
Newman
Renton Nicholson
Robert Owen
E. & F. N. Spon
William Makepeace Thackeray
Anthony Trollope
Walter

"There's a flower that shall be mine,
'Tis the little Celandine." Wordsworth.

Newspapers and periodicals consulted at the British Museum Libraries and Westminster Reference Library :

The Era 1850
The Gentleman's Magazine
The Illustrated London News

The Observer
Paul Pry 1841
Paul Pry 1850

The Illustrated Police News   *The Times*
The Northern Star   *The Town* 1841–2
Notes and Queries

Selected modern sources:

British Railways Board and British Transport Commission
Science Museum and Victoria and Albert Museum

Douglas G. Browne   *The Rise of Scotland Yard*
Terry Coleman   *The Railway Navvies*
C. Willett Cunnington   *Handbook of English*
& Phillis Cunnington   *Costume in the*
                              Nineteenth Century
C. Hamilton Ellis   *The London, Brighton &*
                              South Coast Railway
William Gaunt   *The Aesthetic Adventure*
                           The Pre-Raphaelite Tragedy
R. B. Martin   *Enter Rumour*
F. C. Mather   *Public Order in the Age*
                              of the Chartists
E. S. Turner   *What the Butler Saw*
Aylmer Vallance   *Very Private Enterprise*

                                                   R.R.